RESTAURANT

A NOVEL

Stanford Pritchard

SPRINGSIDE BOOKS
MIDDLEBURY, VERMONT
NEW YORK, NEW YORK

To the memory of my parents
Mary Kyle Pritchard
Aaron Hunter Pritchard

and

For Elona Lanigan
with love

RESTAURANT

ONE

IF YOU CATCH HIM at an unguarded moment, say at the end of a long evening when his employees have worked hard and made him money, and he feels that some reward in the form of personal conversation is in order, or in Claggett's Drug Store, perhaps, in the dead of winter when the tourists have long since fled and, together with the wisdom of the ages and sundry profundities of small-town life, certain secrets may be safely exchanged over coffee at the lunch counter, Dutch Dugan will wink, smile knowingly, and tell you that there are two kinds of restaurants: "successes, and *learning experiences*."

If you are one of the bundle of nerves for whom a chair, a stiff drink, and silence represent a vision of heaven— that is, if you are one of Dutch's employees gathered around at the end of a successful evening to share his pleasure in the work you have done—you will laugh heartily and rely on a numb feeling of camaraderie to make him think that his happiness is, of all the things in the world at this moment, paramount, and hope that his good humor advances to the point where he orders champagne, or buys everyone a drink, or actually gives something away. On the other hand, if you are one of the sages whiling away the time at Claggett's, you will wince, and hope he doesn't go on to the old saw about "location, location, location." Such breezy cynicism would sadden you, and besides, location is something everyone in town takes pride in, something that makes Sun Town think of itself (as practically all small towns do) as unique.

The last town out on the sinuous peninsula known as Land's End, Sun Town occupies the spit of land where Scavenger Bay meets the ocean, sits clinging to the tip of the bay on its front, and crouching behind the swamps, dunes, and marshes that protect it from the ocean on its rear. The peninsula itself is entered by crossing Scavenger Bridge. Until recently, this was an iron swing bridge that was as popular with fishermen as with motorists, a bridge that made cars go slowly and tires sound flat, a bridge that was of the elements: hot on hot days, cold on cold, as fishy as the surrounding water. Not long ago, however, the old iron bridge was replaced by a sweeping cement structure of dizzying height and grade, so that now the traveler can zoom out to Land's End without slowing down, and hardly knowing he is crossing a river. For the old-timers of Port Kimball and Bucks Bottom and Sun Town, however—and the other towns that cling to Land's End like barnacles—"The Bridge" still marks the dividing line between their way of life and what they imagine is that of the rest of the world. Rocking on their front porches or musing over coffee or cocoa at Claggett's, the old folks will talk about how long it's been since they've been "over the bridge," and discuss "getting a Visa and going over the bridge" as if it were to a strange and foreign country. Besides those who claim never to have been over the "new bridge" at all, there are some who keep up the pretense, year after year, of not even knowing it had been built. Along with the natural beauty of its beaches, its coves and broad bay, it is this sense of isolation, of separation from the mainland, that gives Land's End, and especially Sun Town, its distinctive character.

Unfortunately, it is this aura of being remote and off the beaten track that in recent years has drawn tourists and vacationers to Sun Town by the car- and busload, in the process clogging the peninsula's main highway from June through August and raising a smoky haze of exhaust to vie with the sunsets. This flood of visitors has strained the town's water and sewage systems to their breaking points, sent property taxes through the roof, made the town a mecca for weirdos and drifters, created an almost schizophrenic split between winter somnolence and summer carnival, and given the town the reputation—whether it is meant sarcastically or with defiant pride—as "the last resort."

At the very center of it all, at the corner of Bay Street and Railroad Square, sits a famous landmark, a restaurant known far beyond the confines of the town, Dutch's Dockside. Years ago, when fishing was done under sail (before the town was discovered by tourists, fishing had been its main industry), the waterfront had been lined with sail lofts, places where canvas was patched and stored, and it is one of these ancient buildings that the Dockside now occupies. Not that the restaurant is any longer adjacent to a dock: with the increasing popularity of the town as a vacation spot, and consequent overdevelopment of the waterfront (the expansion of the marina, the opening of new shops along Bay Street, in Railroad Square, in Smuggler's Alley), it became necessary to create a new parking lot. Because there was no other direction in which to expand, a monstrous asphalt shelf was pushed out into the bay next to Dutch's property; now, where the old piers and packing sheds used to stand, there is space for upwards of two hundred cars. Children on roller skates circling the forlorn parking meters during that part of the year when the motorized tide has receded, or pounding puddles with dirt bikes (or otherwise looking for trouble to get into), are often heard referring to "Dutch's Curbside," or "Dutch's Backside," and as prices on the menu have risen to keep pace with (some would say, set an example for) inflation, dining at the restaurant has come to be known among the local wits and wags as "going dutch."

Given the location of the town, it is only natural that the Dockside should be outfitted with marine artifacts and nautical gear. Although Dutch has not gone so far as to drape the place with fishnets and cork floats, or to label the rest rooms "Buoys" and "Gulls," there are a fair number of marine objects in evidence: portholes and lobster buoys, harpoons and grappling hooks, shiny mahogany pilot wheels. In the foyer there is the compulsory mounted marlin, leaping out of the water in classic photogenic fashion and landing conveniently on the wall; beneath it a handsome display of the fare the restaurant specializes in: a fat bass or bluefish flanked by lobsters and lined with mussels, scallops, and oysters, all of it riding a bed of ice and dotted with parsley. It is a fact of life that at least once a summer the lobsters will be stolen, and Dutch, when he has room for it in his schedule of obsessions, makes a practice of reminding his already overburdened hostesses, Karen Willis and Kathy Shively, to keep an eye on them.

The most hoary and venerable nautical paraphernalia, however, adorn the lounge. The bar itself has been fashioned

from the remains of an ancient fishing dory, so that the arms
and elbows of the faithful rest upon what were once actual
gunnels. Felix Johansson, the bartender, the coxswain and chief
cheerleader for some years now, confronts his customers from
behind the remains of a boat that was probably last seaworthy
when his parents were children, and among the moments he
dreads most are those when a patron stands back from the bar
—as they do ten or twelve times a summer—appraises the
thing thoughtfully, slaps the gunnels, and says:

"I think with a little work we can get this thing back in
the water! Needs a little paint here and there, maybe a bit of
caulking. But hell yes! I think there's plenty of life in her! How
much are you askin' for her?"

It is this skeleton of a boat, along with the surrounding
nautical gear—the port and starboard running lights, the dusty
diving helmet, the lacquered painting of a pirate with the man-
datory eye patch staring at the treasure chest filled with manda-
tory doubloons, the muted light and vague sense of desperation
that characterizes the place by the height of the season—tourists looking for connections, locals looking for peace and quiet,
everyone looking for *something*, if only a seat at the bar—that
has led to the place's being affectionately christened, "The Lifeboat Lounge."

Dutch has had thoughts, over the years, about sprucing
up the Lifeboat Lounge. The one-eyed pirate, especially, has
often him given him pause for thought as he has stood kibitzing
with visitors, or hastening from chore to chore. Presented to
him years ago by his ex-wife, the portrait has been propped
on the shelf behind the brandies since the day the restaurant

opened. And that explains why it remains there, and why Dutch has done so little to refurbish the old part of the restaurant: It has become comfortable and familiar; precisely by virtue of being left alone and untouched it has attained a kind of landmark status. If there is one thing Dutch has learned in his years in business, it is *if it ain't broke don't fix it.* He could order new chairs from one of the fancy catalogues and have a patron compare them to the fancier chairs in a restaurant up the street, or he could salvage the old squeakers from the high school bandpractice room and have people think how charming and unpretentious it all was. He could install expensive lamps and hard wiring, and run the risk that someone would open a restaurant nearby with fixtures more stylish, or he could insert lightbulbs in old colanders and cheese graters and be celebrated for his refusal to go along with changing fads and fashions. On the other hand, there is nothing slovenly or slipshod about the restaurant's décor. Especially in the additions he has made to the original structure, which have quadrupled its size over the years and given him office and storage space upstairs, Dutch has aimed at a quality he thinks of as *informal formality*, a blend of elegance and simplicity. In the Chart Room, for example, there are polished brass railings and nautical brightwork, custom teak finishings, serene paintings on seacoast themes, and more than a few hanging plants.

Finally, there is a patio on the side of the restaurant where, during his early years in business, Dutch experimented with serving food. An incident that occurred there—or this being Sun Town, is said to have occurred there—established from the start his reputation as a person not to be trifled with.

Dutch had a temper in those days, and had not yet weathered the trials and tribulations which, over the years, have mellowed him considerably. It happened—or is said to have happened— on a warm, moonlit night in July. A group of people who had had to endure a long wait for tables were now exacting retri bution by refusing to get up and leave. The hour had passed when Dutch could legally serve alcohol, but there was nothing in the bright, full moon or soft, warm air to encourage ac- knowledgment of that fact; indeed, the lingering diners acted as if they were in a public garden or at someone's private party, and free to stay as long as they liked. Dutch instructed his staff to collect all the checks and remove all the glasses, and even- tually began supplying the precise language by which the crowd should be encouraged to depart. From the patio, meanwhile, he could hear the groaning and teasing, the cheerful remonstra- tions of the carefree crowd. Having had a few drinks himself, he finally reached his boiling point. He yanked the coxswain's megaphone off its hook in the Lifeboat Lounge, marched out onto the patio, took up a position at the center of the crowd, and announced:

"Ladies and gentlemen, it is my duty as the proprietor of this restaurant to inform you that the plants and flowers on this patio are watered by an automatic sprinkler system. I should further inform you that this sprinkler system is sched- uled to go on in exactly two minutes."

Marching out in a self-righteous huff, he crept around to the house next door—where he knew there to be a garden hose—and, squatting down behind the stockade fence that separated the two properties, began sending a fine spray over the top.

Does this mean Donald ("Dutch") Dugan is a hypocrite, a tyrant, an evil person? No. But in the three-ring circus that is a popular restaurant in a crowded resort town—in the combustion chamber of temperament and personality that this pleasure machine becomes as it heats up—one false step, one spark or added injection of fuel, can sometimes have disastrous consequences. The system is kept cooled by, and operates at the mercy of, certain pressure valves, and these valves are not infallible. Although Dutch still has occasional bursts of temper —which he defends on the grounds that they produce a smoother operation and better quality of product—his manner nowadays is more that of an earnest hardware salesman than a tyrannical boss. His hairline is receding, and his characteristic expression is that of a man more preoccupied with book-keeping matters than culinary ones, that of a decent, practical man who might keep nails and screws and hardware in little jars above a basement workbench.

Right now, however, Dutch is not wearing his characteristic expression. He is asleep, and having a nightmare. He's reliving the night when the cesspool beneath the patio backed up. Customers waiting for tables are asking the hostesses why they can't sit outside. *Tell 'em the flagstones are being repaired!* he screams. Suddenly it is a year later, and people are sniffing the air, winking, and asking, *Flagstones still being repaired?* On the parking-lot side of the restaurant, instead of miniature windows with antique mullions, there is now a giant picture window; as a truck passes by it fills with the words, WIZARD OF OOZE CESS-

POOL SERVICE. Furious, Dutch storms into the kitchen to confer with his chef. He finds Dave Lindholm staring into a huge pot of spaghetti. Dave is immersed in work and too busy to talk to him, doesn't hear him shouting, see him waving his arms. Instead, he reaches into the cauldron *with kitty-litter tongs* and pulls out a few strands, and holds them up and inspects them. Nearby, Lenny Knudsen, his *sous-chef*, is extracting some lumps from a gravy; he glances around absentmindedly, and *pulls a fly swatter off the wall*, and pours the gravy through. Dutch is frantic, he must do something to restore order. He bangs out of the kitchen—narrowly avoiding a collision with a busboy—and sees Kelly Furness *handing out antacid tablets* to the people she's serving. Next it's the fire alarm. Dutch rushes to the clanging bell, realizes he does not know how to stop it; his leg twitches, his whole body shudders, he gargles and rolls over restlessly—

And wakes up.

The phone. *The damn phone is ringing.*

He lunges for it. "Yeah?" he shouts.

"Mornin', Dutch." (The voice is insinuating, ingratiating.) "How ya doin', pal? This is Tony, remember me? We talked a coupla times last summer. I'm the guy who wants to help you with your restaurant business."

"Who the hell *is* this!" Dutch shouts, glancing at the clock on his bedside table. "*Who'd* you say you were?"

"Aw Dutch, you know who it is, you know perfectly well who it is. Now, I'm gonna be down in your quaint little fishing village in a coupla days, and I think there are a few things we should talk about. You see, Dutch, I got a service that no one else can provide—"

With all his might, Dutch slams the phone down.

Friday, May 15. Nine-thirty in the morning. In less than eight hours, the curtain is due to go up. Dutch rubs his eyes and massages his forehead. He hears one of his Dobermans scratching behind its collar. He leans over to his bedside table, picks up a pen and note pad, and writes: "More parsley. Get stemware out of storage. Call Frank." He pulls the pages back and reviews the scrawls of previous days, crossing out a few things he has taken care of or for which there will not be enough time. Reflecting on the ominous call, he decides that if the matter has waited this long, it can *continue* to wait.

He goes downstairs, makes a pot of coffee, and lets the dogs out. Soon he is outside in the bright sunlight, loading restaurant equipment into the back of his van, then hurrying through town: first to the lumberyard to consult with Shep King about a skylight that never came in, then to the post office to check his mailbox, then to the bank to iron out the new credit card procedure. With all his years in business, it is still a mystery to him why he will be fussing with details right up until the minute the opening-night crowd walks through the front door. This year it's the Hobart dishwashing machine, and Frank Manuski—after underestimating the time it would take to fix it—has the thing apart, and pieces spread out on the floor. When Dutch arrives at the restaurant around two o'clock, Frank is still acting like—like time and the tide or any other elemental force—he will not be rushed. His assistant, meanwhile, is scrabbling around in the crawl space beneath the kitchen, fiddling with the wiring. But Dutch also has the new credit card procedure to think about. He reminds himself to talk to Debbie

Fensen, and some of the others, to make sure they understand it. *These people tell you how good they are, and how much experience they've had, then comes one of those nights when the place is a madhouse, and they can't take it. They start making mistakes, screwing up.* Even as he goes about his chores, Dutch talks to himself; even as he exchanges friendly or obligatory remarks with those around him, he visualizes the crowd that will begin arriving at five o'clock for complimentary cocktails and hors d'oeuvres. *Oh, here's Kathy. Good. Knows almost as much about this restaurant as I do. Sometimes I think she knows too much. Faithful employee, though. Probably wouldn't steal a bread stick if someone wrapped it for her. Wonder when she'll ask for a raise. Oh-oh, one of the loudspeakers isn't working. Well, I don't know about such things! Get someone else to fix it! But where is the band going to plug in if Frank doesn't get the wiring reconnected? Better go see how Leonardo Da Vinci is doing. No, no, don't let me disturb you, I wouldn't want to interfere. Hell, this is just a restaurant, we really don't need a dishwasher. We can just wipe the dishes off on the seat of our pants, and put 'em back in service. Hmmm. Dave's burger-flippers seem to have things under control, though maybe I ought to sample a dish or something, just to let 'em know who's boss. But this kid with the murderous expression, opening oysters: they sure didn't teach him how to do that in graduate school. Wonder if he'll last the summer. Better ask someone to clear the cartons out of the passageway. Have to be able to get in and out of the walk-in. Hope Felix remembers what I told him about not too much vodka in the punch; everybody tends to get carried away at these things. Yeah, sure, they aren't having to pay for it. The phone. Phone for me? The piano? Has the piano been tuned? Of course it's been tuned! Jesus, I have a hundred and twenty-five, a hundred and fifty people coming for cocktails, seventy-five, a hundred dinners to serve after that, and the goddamn piano player wants to know if I've had the piano tuned. I shoulda told him I let Bart Perry use it for a mooring for his boat, all winter, but we got it out of the water and it's drying out just fine. Better go have a look in the Chart Room and see how things are coming along. If you don't ride herd on these people, they'll set the vacuum cleaner down right where they're standing, and fall asleep. Jesus, father and his twenty children. Now what was I doing, and what was it I told Frank I'd see about? Oh yeah, the lightbulb in the Exit sign. The lightbulb in the Exit sign needs replacing.*

By the time five o'clock rolls around, Dutch has for so long run from duty to duty, chore to chore—all the while wondering why he isn't beyond all this—that he is not aware, at first, that people are drifting in his front door. But suddenly it dawns on him that the person he is talking to is not someone asking him for advice but someone who wants to congratulate him, and that an increasingly buoyant tide of humanity is coursing through the door. It slowly sinks in that his help have arrived and set up, the floors and fixtures and counter tops have been cleaned, the punch and hors d'oeuvres have been set out, and Frank Manuski and his assistant have solved their problems. Dutch smiles without realizing he is smiling, his adrenalin kicks in, and the Other Dutch begins to surface, the Dutch of expansive gestures and limitless friendships, the Dutch who is the genial host, the friend of man, the *paterfamilias*, the *bon vivant*, the wizard and king, the celebrity and maestro. The band is playing in the background, food and drinks are going out, and all around him people who live practically next door to one another are shaking hands and kissing, talking as though they haven't seen one another in years. Here is Kerry Critchfield and Barbara Hussey, and Gloria What's-her-name and Denise Lefevre—looking heavier than ever—and now Lee Castleton is presenting him with a bouquet of flowers sent over by one of the other restaurants. Raising his voice above the babble, he asks Mrs. Haycraft about Officer Donaldson, and listens to Wally Terhune's account of how he got, or almost got, his boat in the water. He wants to have a few words with Bill Macklin of the Macklin Real Estate Agency, but gets caught up in a conversation with Kitty Solomon of the town's Planning Board. He sees Ellen Kastner—with whom he came close to having an affair during the winter—standing in a corner, and turns so that she will be outside his sightline. Still the pageant swells, broadens, expands. Here is Vodka Man, living proof that the smell of alcohol has carried as far as the Beach Variety Store, and Justabout Dunne, and Grubby Eddy, looking downcast and ill-at-ease, and Hi-Beams, and Roger the Lodger, and the two women from the health food store. Here is Liz Whizz and Monumental Man and Rejeck, and over in the Lifeboat Lounge, Jeanne Strick and the selectman Jack Pettigill—who generates a pocket of interest until Jim Kiernan, the Town Manager, arrives; everyone feels like he has secrets to hide until Big Jim, too, is swallowed up in the noise and confusion. Still the tide of humanity pours in, distributing itself in clusters, eddies, and pools. Here are Sylvia Meeks and Spacey Stacy, and Lying Larry and Stretch—still on crutches—and Fishbox, and Moose Kenley from the crafts shop, and dozens of other people he hasn't seen all winter, but who are quick to protest they have been in town all along. Even the sun becomes a welcome guest, filling the room with light that grows more golden as it descends. The town is home free now, the sun seems to say, and summer is on its way; the long hibernation is over, and like spring flowers or the peepers on the back shore, people may emerge from their hidden lairs and hiding places. For this moment, the annual Dockside opening, marks the beginning of a time of expansiveness and freedom; it is the turning point, the crossover from the quiet, self-contained town of locals and year-rounders eking out and making do to the noisy, exuberant town of tourists and washashores spending money and living it up. In the background, the band takes off on a light, bouncy tune and people begin to dance. Others return to the punch and hors d'oeuvres tables, or head into the lounge for stiffer fare; with all the talk and food, the liquor and excitement, no one wants the party to end. The sun is inexorably setting, however, and people are beginning to notice what they would have preferred not to notice, that the cheese wheels are down to their wax coverings, that the ham and turkey have been reduced to bone and gristle, that the shrimp and oysters have been consumed, that the dips have thinned to smears on the insides of bowls, that the tide, the happy tide of humanity, is beginning to flow in the direction opposite that from which it came.

By seven o'clock Dutch's thoughts are returning to business, the glorious balloon of affability and friendliness shrinking noticeably as he orchestrates the removal of glasses and food. There is a moment of awkwardness and indecision, as when a tide turns, those who have reservations for dinner trying to ignore the commotion, those who don't trying to exit gracefully. The band takes a break and until someone remembers to turn on the background music, the predominant sound is that of furniture being bumped and scraped about.

Eventually the restaurant has been returned to order, places at tables have been set and candles lit, and the thread of pleasure, having unwound to its end in one direction, begins to rewind in the other; the mood of excitement returns, and for the lucky ones the party goes on. For some, however, the serious drinkers and compulsive talkers, the momentum was never lost, the intermission never noticed; as they seat themselves, these merrymakers become more and more vociferous. With this and the inevitable kinks of opening night, the rest of the evening goes forward like a runaway roller-coaster. Several hours of drinking have made everyone hungry, but now all the dinner orders are going into the kitchen at once. The waiters and waitresses, the cooks and busboys, Felix the bartender, Karen Willis and Kathy Shively—Dutch himself, who alternately flits from table to table disseminating charm, and storms through the kitchen dispensing rage and frustration—do their best to keep up with the onslaught, to smooth rumpled nerves and rectify the delays and oversights, but opening-night confusion has destroyed the normal rhythms of the restaurant, and the atmosphere of pandemonium that prevails from the start of dinner crystallizes in endless bumps and snags as the evening wears on, and hangs in the air with a disquieting echo after the last patron has departed.

For the Dockside staff, it has been an exhausting day; it has been a celebration, but none of the workers feels celebratory, none of them has energy left with which to care. It is definitely not one of those days when Dutch is going to come forward with personal or institutional largesse. Like exhausted gladiators, the waiters and waitresses slump into chairs near the kitchen, kick off their shoes, light cigarettes, and try to reconcile themselves to the fact that the new season, in Sun Town, has begun. In the Chart Room the band is packing up; otherwise the battlefield is quiet and deserted.

Suddenly there is a shriek of breaking glass, a noisy banging and thudding. With a mixture of horror and resignation, all turn to see a man trying to disengage himself from what has apparently become a deadly trap, a table and a chair.

"*Christ*," says one of the waiters. "Is *he* still here?"

At last the man extricates himself from the vicious torture machine in which someone, with devilish intent, has placed him, and gets to his feet. He sets his sights on the exit, but loses his bearings and heads into the Chart Room.

"Let him go," says one of the waitresses. "He can't get out that way. Serves him right."

But there is some premeditation in his behavior, after all; as inebriated as he is, he is still a man with a purpose. Weaving across the Chart Room, ricocheting from table to table as he goes, he approaches the bandstand. The musicians pointedly turn their backs to him, and begin helping the drummer with his drums: all except for the piano player, that is, who comes to the edge of the stand.

"Uh, I was in here last summer," the man says, staring glassy-eyed at the scene.

He stops to allow the importance of this fact to sink in, and to identify the next boxcar in his ponderous train of thought. Eventually:

"And you were *playin'* somethin'."

Again he pauses, his face contorted with perplexity.

The band members glance at one another. Will he begin to hum the tune?

No. Instead, he rocks back and forth on his feet, sways gently, rocks a little more, and finally says:

"Do you remember what it *was*?"

Even the lowly musicians know that the zaniness, the craziness, the borderline madness of a season in Sun Town has begun.

TWO

IF IT'S THE SEASON WHY CAN'T WE SHOOT THEM?

As she dresses for work, Kathy Shively thinks with amusement of the bumper sticker she has seen recently. Her apartment in the rear of the Sunrise Apartments on High Street is ethereally quiet, and the sound her bureau drawer makes when she tugs on it is loud and jarring, the violation of a mood that seems communally ordained. She pauses and eases the drawer out quietly. In the muted light she studies its contents, and decides on a tank top that will complement the print skirt she has chosen; then she quietly eases the drawer shut. Tiptoeing over to a full-length mirror, she is suddenly seized by a feeling of complete isolation, finds herself wondering where everybody has gone, why the town, the apartment—the air itself— seems so devoid of weight and pressure. Have the tourists already packed their bags and left? Pleased by the thought that the town has temporarily emptied itself out and that modesty is therefore unnecessary, she goes to the screen door that opens onto the back yard and, clad only in a half-slip and bra, leans against the door jamb.

The smell of lilacs is all-pervasive, their sweetness all-encompassing. Somewhere a dog barks, but because all sounds seem distant and dreamy, she cannot tell from which direction. She imagines the waterfront, the broad, muddy flats, the silky stillness of the water beyond them, the soundless, ghostlike movements of people working on the wharves. From Mrs. Lacavalla's kitchen, next door, there emerges the clatter of pots and pans, a commotion that is not the least offensive but full of purpose, an interior coziness that makes her smile again; it is as if the entire world were a cozy kitchen in a little seacoast town at supper time. Feeling like a voyeur, she stands there, watches and listens. Mrs. Roderick's cat, from up the street, wanders into the yard exuding nonchalance and self-absorption—as if it were not perfectly aware of the robins perched on the storage shed near the lilacs; businesslike, the robins remove themselves to a flowering shad tree several yards over. Gazing down the yards of High Street, Kathy contemplates the lobster buoys that cling to Bob Harlan's fence like gumdrops, or roosters' wattles. Are they functional, she wonders, or merely ornamental? Nearby are some crumbling lobster pots and a pile of float poles capped with orange balls and reflectors; by association, her eye jumps to a whirligig one house down. Perched on their narrow platform, two wooden workmen in orange jackets stand motionless, awaiting a wind that will set them to chopping wood. But their workday is over, for the wind is off on other errands. Several yards beyond them is the Canada goose which, on stormy days, flaps frantically and goes nowhere, the wind whipping it to a frenzy of motion while an iron pole keeps it firmly rooted to its spot. Oh, the yards of Sun Town are filled with such things, Kathy knows: birdhouses on poles, little chapels with ornate steeples and scalloped eaves, multiple-family units for purple martins; pinwheels constructed from tin cans and the frames of bicycle wheels; religious icons in upturned bathtubs; flowers spilling from decaying dories and brightly painted tractor tires.

Kathy focuses on the cat again. With regal composure it is taking inventory of the domains it has inherited. High above the roof, a great white seagull materializes, circling, floating aimlessly. Kathy studies the cat, gazes up at the seagull; each somehow betrays its awareness of the other. Now, as quiet, secret, and intimate as the window from which it comes, there is the smell of cooking from Mrs. Lacavalla's kitchen.

At the Dockside Restaurant, what amounts to a shakedown cruise to acclimate the crew to its ship—it is the first of the summer's rites of passage—has been completed, and now the staff are gearing up for their first encounter with out-and-out battle, Memorial Day Weekend. There are certain recognizable hurdles that the town must cross, every summer, and after the excitement associated with the various shop and restaurant openings, Memorial Day Weekend is the next. As have the other restaurateurs in town, Dutch Dugan has been nervous and fidgety for two weeks, for the fickle nature of tourism makes it impossible for him to know in advance what kind of season he will have. He has kept a watchful eye on the price of gasoline, he has driven down the peninsula to get a sense of the number of cars in motel parking lots, he has probed every reassurance that the town has not gone out of fashion, that the town has not lost its cachet, that the tourists are, indeed, coming. In addition, he has spent many evenings poring over his books from preceding years. His books have the importance to Dutch that scripture has to a biblical scholar, celestial charts to an astrologer, a packet of love letters to an aging Don Juan; he has consulted them endlessly for inspirations he has had, strategies he has employed in his quest of the Holy Grail, profitability. It is his books, rather than outward appearances (which Dutch knows can be deceiving), that are the real measure of the restaurant's performance. More than that, they are his comfort and consolation, the testament to his marriage and record of his devotion, the work of art that transcends the mundane business of ordering food, and hiring people to cook and serve it. Patrons may come and go, supplies may dwindle, dishes break, and brass tarnish, but his books are proof to Dutch that he is somehow above it all, that he and only he is the mastermind and kingpin. In a world of physical things and bodily functions, they represent, in a sense, his soul.

Kathy nudges the screen door open, and holds it there with her toe. The spring day is almost over, but not quite, summer is almost under way, but not quite; it is as though time itself were trying to tack, but had not yet caught its new wind; there is a moment of quiet, of drifting, doldrums but without any sense of frustration. Kathy crosses her arms, watches and waits; she has become the hunter in a landscape whose only quarry is the slightest change of color, the barest hint of movement. The collage of chimneys and dormers, gables and skylights, that she looks down on seems almost cubist in inspiration, at one moment fragile and gaunt and the next, cozy and cheerfully self-contained. The antennas that dot the houses and cottages, and the telephone poles that line the streets, render the town as spindly and prickly as cactus; where, beyond Bay Street, she can see the spars and masts of the fishing fleet, the effect is corroborated. Antennas. . . . Symbols of a world far different from that into which the town was born, they nevertheless complement the town's spare angularity; it is as though the rods, reels, and grappling hooks once used by fishermen to haul fish up out of the sea had been moved to the tops of houses, and were now pulling signals down out of the sky. *Talk to us from the outside*, they seem to say, *we are here, we are listening.* But what of the marine antennas, the CB antennas, the antennas of the police station, the gas and oil companies? *We wish to be left alone, to talk only to ourselves. We wish to conduct our lives as we always have, to keep our homes and families intact and free from outside influence.* Is the town listening only to itself, Kathy muses, or is it eagerly awaiting news from the outside world? Is the prickly carapace designed to fend the world off, and keep intruders away, or is it the most efficient way of welcoming the world in? In this, as in all things, the town is of two minds, she reasons. As it is a town of locals and tourists, natives and washashores, gays and straights, it is a town of sea and land, a border town, a town situated on an edge. And the people who, though not born here, choose to live here? They, too, are fringe people, artists often, dropouts sometimes: border personalities, people who need the sense of an edge to corroborate the reality of their lives.

The bell above Town Hall chimes five o'clock, leaving long silences between each strike; Kathy is reminded that she must quit daydreaming and get ready for work. But she does not. Not yet. She continues to contemplate the town below her, to bask in the still, soft air, the sweet, lilac-scented air of the late-spring afternoon.

Dutch is pleased that the shakedown cruise has gone well this year, and that his staff are settling into their roles. What the Dubnow kid's problem was, therefore, is a mystery to him. If you don't want to be a busboy, if you think you really ought to be a star of stage and screen—or President of the United States, for that matter—fine, you should go out and devote yourself to becoming those things. But if you're hired as a busboy and someone asks you to clear a table, you shouldn't be so busy with your *Bates System of Eye Care Exercises* that you can't get up off your duff and go do it. Just what every restaurant needs, someone standing behind a ficus tree and rolling his eyes to the ceiling, squinching them open and shut as though there were sand in them. And what happens when the kid finally gets himself motivated to do what he's supposed to do? *He talks to everybody.* He asks the diners where they're from and how they're enjoying their vacations, he acts like it's a private party or a floor show—and he the garrulous host—he tries to jolly people through their meals. The waitresses practically have to drag him off the floor and sit him down, and explain that it is not the business of the busboy to jolly the customers through their meals, *that the food and its presentation will take care of themselves*; he must stop talking, he must *just stop talking.* Then, the other night, he goes too far and pushes Dave over the edge. Dave storms out from behind the steam table, chases him out onto the floor, grabs him by the neck, drags him into the kitchen and knocks the bejesus out of him—*slap, slam, bang, pots falling, mops going down*. Dubnow escapes out the door, and Dave chases him again and pulls him back in—*wham, ka-pow*—stuff going down all over the place. Finally he makes it to the front of the restaurant and keeps on going, never to be seen again. No doubt he'll be filing for unemployment soon. Or worse, spreading his charm, his infinite charm, in another restaurant. Well, you can have attitude and work in a restaurant, and you can be a moron and work in a restaurant. But you can't have attitude *and* be a moron, and work in a restaurant.

The final tone from the clock tower fades, and the town is returned to silence. Kathy thinks of all the times she has listened to the tolling of the hours, and what a consolation it is. There is a reassuring regularity and constancy to it, she reasons; though the hours change and life moves on, the sound of the bell never varies its rhythm but remains always composed and unhurried. She stares absentmindedly at the terrace of rooftops beneath her, and thinks of other sounds the town has in common. The fire siren on the water tower: harsh and abrasive, activated every day at noon as a test—and dividing the day squarely in two—it is a reminder to those whose lives are losing time, an exhortation to those whose attention is flagging. The fog horns that mark the channels out to sea: faithful sentinels on a stormy night, they create a feeling of coziness even as they *haunt* the town; they are a warning from the outside, a warning from the dark, all-encompassing mystery, the unknown, the incomprehensible. The edge again. Kathy contemplates the mottle and clutter of a town that looks to the water for life even as it clings to the sides of hills for security, and thinks, *Perhaps that is where coziness comes from, from comfort achieved in the midst of surrounding danger. Like a fire on a hearth, while outside the wind howls, snow rages. . . .*

Then there is Roy Oberholzer: what a piece of work *he* is. For all his swagger, Roy doesn't quite get it. Roy is still trying to be nice to his customers, which only gets him in trouble. A waiter has to be pleasant and nice, all right, but in an efficient, businesslike way. Otherwise people will sit and talk, and keep the table from turning over. It's the old *flip flop.* Dutch extends his hand, flips it over and back, and rehearses the lecture he has prepared for Roy Oberholzer. *Flip:* the party is seated by one of the hostesses. The waiter must appear, take drink orders, return and take dinner orders, then begin moving the meal along—appetizers, salad, main course, dessert, coffee—until *Flop:* the party has finished, they have their check, and the busboy can prepare the table for the next seating. *Flip:* in. *Flop:* out. So what if people tease me by saying, *Good evening, can I get you something from the bar? And I'll bring your dessert and coffee.* Or, *Here are your appetizers, and I know you're going to want these doggie bags.* When there are people waiting to be seated, it's only good business to seat them as quickly as possible. But oh, there's that other problem. *Nobody's replaced the bulb in the Exit sign. Got to get that thing fixed. Violates fire codes. Is it time to institute a fixed service charge for parties of eight or more?*

Reluctantly, Kathy lets the screen door swing shut. Although she can no longer procrastinate, the stillness of the air continues to define her movements, to lend a soft, dreamy quality to her preparations. When she returns to her bedroom, it seems to her that the clock on her bureau is ticking very slowly. After pulling her chosen top over her head and smoothing it out around her waist, she takes a flowery cotton skirt from its hanger in the closet, and steps into it. It feels like many minutes pass before she has gotten the two adjusted to one another, the skirt adjusted to her hips, the buttons buttoned, and many minutes before she has found a pair of stockings and selected a pair of earrings. With her head tilted to one side as she installs the first earring, her eye falls on the clock. A momentary curiosity whether its hands have frozen gives way to the realization they have not; she is being given the gift of time. *Time inside, time outside, time of private rooms, time of public space*: it is the universal ritual of preparing to enter the theater of the world. She tilts her head to the other side, and catches herself in the mirror. She knows she will soon go into the bathroom and, standing beneath the bright light, apply her makeup. With each refinement of her costume, she will become less alone and less solitary; with each addition to her disguise, her solitude will yield to the demands of public function. She will return to the bedroom a final time, put on her shoes, then, in the muted light, stand before the mirror and brush back a few strands of hair that have already strayed. As she studies herself with an eye to seeing what others will see, her thoughts and personality will slowly adjust to *being* what others see. She will place her hairbrush and cosmetics in her handbag, dig out her house keys and, being careful not to let the door slam, let herself out of the apartment. She will tiptoe down the walk and pull the latch on the gate, and in this, too, she will feel it appropriate not to make any more noise than necessary.

As she hastens down High Street, however, she will be surprised to discover that the gift of time has not been rescinded, that her daydreams are still partly intact. At the foot of the hill she will turn right onto Cross Street, and as she passes the third house down, the stately old mansion with the mansard roof, she will pause and peer over the hedge. There will be a load of bright white wash on the line—bed sheets and pillow cases hanging in perfect stillness—and nearby, outside the house's shadow, a small carpenter's stool. Actually, there will be no wash and no stool today, but she will place them there in her imagination so as to relive the pleasure of the story that Sadie Winslow once told her. Sitting on the little rough-hewn stool, she will imagine Jeremiah Winslow—the grandfather Sadie had known as a child—and she will have the old man frail and white-haired, just as Sadie described him, his knotty hands clutching the gnarled stick he held between his legs. As she peers over the hedge, she will hear the wind come up, just as Sadie described it, and see the sheets on the line begin to ruffle and snap; she will imagine Sadie hiding in the hedge at the corner of the yard. Then she, too, will watch the old captain begin to rock back and forth on his stool, in his senility thinking the sound of the wind-whipped wash has called him back to sea.

"Pull in the sheet, there!" he will shout, to laundry that is flapping on a clothesline. "She's luffing there, boys, pull her in! That's it! The jib, too! Now look to the mainsail! That's it, pull her up taut! Oh, we've got a wind now! We'll make some headway now!"

Jeremiah Winslow had gone to sea at seventeen, and by Sadie's account had spent more of his life there than in the house he built for his family on Cross Street. After his death—so Miss Winslow said—the family had rummaged through his sea chest, and at the bottom, beneath some oilskins, tobacco tins, and bits of scrimshaw, come upon the thing he must have put their first: a scrap of paper on which was written, in now-faded letters, "Port, left. Starboard, right."

Was Sadie telling the truth? Or was it only a story she made up to tease a washashore?

As Kathy hastens down the hill, the flowers on her cotton print skirt dance with their models along the fences and in the gardens that she passes. Smiling at the thought that the town is full of secrets, brimming with stories, bursting with folklore and legend, she turns back for a final look.

But there is no breeze stirring, no wind to rustle them, and the sheets are perfectly still.

THREE

"Oh, nurse. . . !"

From Table 2 in Station 3 comes the signal to Lee Castleton that her services are desired. Lee does not take offense at the manner in which the summons is issued; she has worked in Sun Town long enough to know that no behavior can be considered so outrageous that one could say with certainty, *that* will never happen. And while experience has shown that a deuce or a triple can be managed (the server can work on the principle, divide and conquer), it has also shown that in parties of five or six or more, the temptations to infantilism are sometimes irresistible. Lee has spent more time than she would like to remember playing mother to a tableful of mischievous children, and is not surprised that the dependency level, here, has reached the point of:

"Oh, nurse. . . !"

Unfortunately, the big-mouth with the bald head who is the ringleader of this little circus-of-six is acting as if he's gotten off one of the world's great laugh lines, a howler of truly magnificent proportions; as Lee approaches her charges they disintegrate into helpless mirth, a squinty, red-faced intensity interrupted only by over-the-shoulder glances at other tables for confirmation of, *aren't we bad?*

Then Lee remembers. Her father, too, was bald. And her father left her mother, and ran off with a younger woman.

She flashes on the night she was working a convention

of tuna fishermen down at the Shoreline Hotel in Port Kimball. The waitresses were distributing dinners from metal carts, one pushing the cart while another served. The task of feeding seventy-five hungry fishermen more or less at the same time required that the routine be kept intact, with each course going out in order so that as one was finished, they could retrieve the empty plates and start the next. It happened that one of her charges, an enormous man with a bald head—offered an appetizer—declined it. Fifteen minutes later, however, he changed his mind.

"I'm sorry, sir," she had explained. "We have seventy-five dinners to get out, and I can't stop to go in the kitchen for an appetizer. I asked you before. . . ."

"Well, I don't care!" the man snapped. "I've decided I want a shrimp cocktail, after all. You can leave my lobster right here, but I'm not going to touch it until I've had my shrimp cocktail."

What to do? Run the length of the dining room and find a shrimp cocktail—and break the routine—or leave the Glorious Buddha with a lobster growing cold and fantasizing about shrimp cocktail? In the best compromise she could come up with, she had worked along with the rest of the girls, then when she was again near the kitchen, dashed in to find a shrimp cocktail. Feeling very competent, she had raced across the dining room and placed it in Mr. Pink-Bowling-Ball's alley.

"What!" the man screamed at her. "Why do you bring this to me now? Can't you see I've started my lobster? Why on earth would I want a shrimp cocktail after I've started my lobster?"

"I did the best I *could*," Lee explained. "I *told* you we had to serve the courses in order, and because you didn't take an appetizer earlier, you'd have to wait until I could go get one."

"But look! What good is it to me now? I've started my lobster, my cole slaw, my corn on the cob—all of it! Take this thing away!"

The glistening head swung back to the table. The worldly-wise tuna fisherman to whom it belonged was clearly not going to have anything more to do with her.

Her father's abandonment of the family had coincided with the failure of his consulting business, and while his new young wife had plenty of money, Lee and her mother were forced to take jobs. Now as she looked on in horror, and from a distance, her hand reached out and slapped—pinged—the man on the back of the head. It was not a *man* she meant to strike, only a bald head. But it was a man who flinched, and a man who, shaken and cowed, turned and looked up at her with a plea for clemency, forgiveness.

After that, things could not have gone more smoothly. Every time she reached Mr. Pink-Baby-Bottom, she would smile and say, "Are you ready for your dessert now, sir?" and "Can I bring you more coffee, sir?" and he would reply, "Oh yes, please, that would be wonderful. Thank you so much." They had acted more and more chummy toward one another, syrupy almost—practically outdid one another with courtesy— until at the end of the evening she was wondering if he were going to ask for her name and address, suggest that they become pen pals.

"Did you call?" Lee inquires, when the amusement at Table 2, Station 3 has subsided.

"Yes, we'd like some more coffee," says Mr. Shiny-Top. "And you can bring us our check. Oh, and I wonder if it would be possible to get something, uh, gift-wrapped."

"You mean you want it . . . put in a doggie bag?" Lee says, without expression. "I can do that."

The man reaches to the center of the table and picks up a plate of clam shells.

Lee stares at him incredulously.

"You want your clam shells gift . . . uh, put in a doggie bag?" she says.

"Please."

Dutifully, Lee takes the plate. As she hurries away from the table she can hear a new geyser of mirth erupting, a burst of appreciation commensurate with what Jumbo the Elephant gets when he stands on his head under the Big Top. *I should have asked a busboy to do it*, she thinks. *A dozen clam shells. What are they gonna do, take clam shells halfway across the country to scatter in someone's driveway?* She thinks again of that evening at the Shoreline Hotel. *That man doesn't know how lucky he was.*

But Lee has other things on her mind, and the weird request temporarily gets sidelined by them. She owes a bread basket to Table 1, and now someone at Table 4 is asking for ice water; she kicks herself for having forgotten to tell a busboy to bring both. Her number on the call board is illuminated, and that will almost certainly be the mussels for Table 5; she reminds herself to bring a bowl for the discarded shells, and a Wet Nap. Now the two old biddies at Table 3 are calling to her again. What a pain they've been—and a pair of five-percent tippers if there ever was one. The lady on the left started by ordering a bottle of wine and drinking half of it, then deciding it was not to her liking and demanding a replacement. Lee had demurred, they had argued politely, and finally the woman had resorted to histrionics:

"Listen, honey. I knew Dutch Dugan when he was still in knee pants. You go ask him." So she had to go look for Dutch in the kitchen, and in the lounge, and eventually found him upstairs in his office. Grudgingly he had come downstairs. "Yeah, go ahead," he said, eyeing the woman to whom Lee pointed, "give her another bottle. She's an old friend of the family. She went over the bridge years ago and became—or should I say, almost became—a great actress." So Lee had poured out a sample from the new bottle, and reached for the bottle it was replacing.

"No, honey," the woman said. "You can leave that. You can leave that *right there.*"

Now as she stands before the women, Lee realizes that both bottles are empty, and with predictable results. Speaking in tones Desdemona might have used to reach the last row of the house, the Great Actress rehearses the triumphs and vicissitudes of her career, and slowly builds to a climax whose import is that she would like her steak wrapped to take home.

Relieved to see the women prying themselves from the table, Lee removes the plate and, being careful not to let anyone else get her attention, heads for the kitchen. "Behind you, behind you, behind you!" barks Roy Oberholzer, as they file through the swinging door. Lee is tempted to say, *Hold your freekin' horses. I'm just as busy as you are, and besides, when Kathy and Karen ask us to fill out the Specials cards, how come you and the other guys always manage to duck out of it?* Oblivious, Roy almost tramples her as he hurries past.

The kitchen is in pandemonium, as hot, noisy, and intense as the engine room of a small destroyer. Lee takes two doggie bags from the pile, asks a busboy to fill them, and goes to the bread locker where Polly Schreiber is at work. The two trade a few words of quick-fix therapy, then fly off again, Lee to the soft drink dispenser, then to the pick-up counter for her mussels.

"I got a surf and turf!" Dave Lindholm calls, over the noise and confusion. "I got chicken bosom! Let's get with it, people! I got chicken goin' hungry!"

But now Lee must deal with Mr. Shiny-Pate and his Gang of Merry Pranksters. She pulls her checks out of her apron, tallies up their bill, grabs a tip tray off the pile (*this had better not be a practical joke*), and heads out to the floor. She makes her deliveries (the aging actress has decided she would like a third bottle of wine, but her friend talks her out of it), and begins steeling herself for the encounter at Table 2.

The group is still awash in joviality, and as she approaches them Lee senses a new element of excitement in the general festiveness. Mr. Lost-His-Hair motions her around to his side of the table, takes the doggie bag from her, and whispers:

"We're social workers. We work with children in the inner city, the ghetto really. Most of these kids have never even been to the beach, much less seen a clam. We'll take these shells home with us; we like to play a game where we put unfamiliar objects in a bag, and ask the kids to reach in and try to guess what they're feeling. It improves their sense of touch, as well as their body awareness, therefore their sense of themselves. I hope you won't mind if we've been a bit silly."

He presses a very generous tip into Lee's hand, and she thanks him profusely.

He shoos her away.

From across the room, she hears strains of "Summertime," and stops and glances at the piano player. "Summertime" is Lee's favorite song, and one of the things she likes about Ed Shakey is that he will play it any chance he gets—two or three times a night if she asks him to. She waves to him in acknowledgment, and he lifts one hand from the keyboard and motions to her. She puts her tray on her shoulder and, ignoring her tables, makes her way across the room.

"Would you get me a *drink*?" Ed says. He wears a crazed expression, as if the piano had collapsed on his legs and pinned him, and he needed something to ease the pain until an ambulance could arrive.

"Sure," Lee replies. "What do you want?"

"Scotch on the rocks," Ed says. "No, forget the rocks. Just Scotch. And make it a double. Put it in a coffee cup. Please."

"Consider it done."

For the Dockside pianist, it is neither the best of times nor the worst of times but a night on the job which, in its quotient of the bizarre and unusual, is all too typical. Ed's first encounter with the anonymous public occurred when a frizzy-haired child had been allowed to get up from his table and wander over to the piano. Ed has learned that whenever there are children who must be shielded from boredom while their parents go about their adult pleasures, the world will look upon a person trapped behind a piano—and paid for the single task of getting music out of it—as being ideally suited to a second one too, that of babysitting. This little moppet had the routine down pat, seemed skilled at getting even more for his money than his parents might have imagined. He had turned up at the piano with a smile so innocent that for a moment even the veteran of a thousand and one nights had been fooled. The child pretended to be fascinated by what he was doing, but in fact the business of playing the piano had about as much interest for him as a whack on the seat of his pants. *I'm just a little boy!* his expression said, *I don't know what I'm doing!* Smiling up at Ed, he had begun jabbing the keys at the end of the keyboard. "Keep your mitts off," Ed said, under his breath, "this isn't a goddamn petting zoo." Then, hoping that he and the child might come to some understanding before the situation deteriorated: "Don't do that, okay?" He was playing "God Bless the Child," and a number of diners glanced at him knowingly. Again, Little Angel Face pressed some keys (*is this how you do it? you just push these flat things down and make noise?*), and Ed swatted his hand away. "Don't do that, I said!" he said. Now the game became more interesting. Smiling at him mischievously, the child raised his hand six or eight inches above the keys, pointed his forefinger straight down, and began slowly lowering it. Closer and closer it came—and again Ed swatted it away. But the hand was lifted again on its imaginary crane, and began descending toward its ivory target; Ed began to feel like he was trapped in a plot of Edgar Allan Poe's devising. The drama of torture and dissuasion went on for a few more rounds—the child smiling gleefully and relishing Ed's petrified gaze—but in the end the hand was quicker than the eye. Slapped only slightly harder than before, the child broke out in a howl, raised his finger as proof that the keyboard cover had been slammed down on it, and in a flurry of tears scampered back to his table.

Ed lowered his head and concentrated on his playing. When he eventually dared to look up, people were casting sidelong glances at him, as if he were dangerous and they had known it all along.

Where is Lee? he thinks. *Where is Lee with my Cup of Coffee?*

Not long after the encounter with Dennis the Menace, a diner had come up to the piano and requested a tune that Ed didn't know. On the breezy assumption that every musician who plays in public knows every tune ever written, he sauntered back to his table. From this point on, Ed felt that *someone out there* was listening to every note he played, waiting through each tune to see if the next would be his, growing disappointed when it wasn't and spreading his disappointment to those around him. *Four hundred tunes I could have played for you,* Ed thought, *things you would have liked, things you would have enjoyed. But no. You had to choose that one.* His entire repertoire seemed as nothing compared to the one tune he didn't know.

As his party was leaving, the man had returned to the piano.

"Thanks for playing my song!" he said cheerfully. "I just

love that song!" With a flourish he had stuffed a five-dollar bill in Ed's tip glass.

Lee appears with the promised cup of coffee and lingers by the piano, watching Ed play. He is doing a bouncy version of "You Took Advantage of Me." When he gets to a point where he can do so, he looks up. "No, I am *not* playing this for you," he says, smiling. He means to say something more, but finding it necessary to concentrate, returns his eyes to the keyboard. He plays a two-handed run that ripples all the way up the piano, and looks up again. "It's all done with smoke and mirrors," he says. The presence of the drink and, more than that, Lee's attention, have cheered him. He brings the tune to a conclusion, slides smoothly into a ballad that he can do with eyes closed, and wondering whether it would be appropriate to ask her out, looks up.

She is no longer at his side, but halfway across the restaurant. Feeling lonely again, he slips into "What Are You Doing the Rest of Your Life?," then picks up the beat and plays "Ain't Misbehavin'."

At the end of the tune, he has a long pull on his Cup of Coffee.

They expect a musician to do what he's doing while simultaneously carrying on a conversation, but how many people can read, swim, or operate a power saw while carrying on a conversation? After the patron who left him the tip for the tune he never played, there had been the man who approached him while he was doing "Sweet Georgia Brown." The man didn't show the least interest in what he was playing, or if he had any, wasn't going to let it distract him.

Putting his foot up on the bench and leaning forward like a trainer whispering in a boxer's ear, he mumbled:

"I wonder if you, uh, know dis tune. I don't exactly, uh, remember da name of it, but maybe you'd be familia' wid it."

And because he couldn't remember the name of the tune, he began to scat-sing it!

"Ya-boo *be*-deep? Ya-boo *be*-deep? Dubah-dubah-dubah, ya-boo *be*-deep?"

Ed leaned to his side to try to make sense of the sounds.

"Du*wee*-du*wee* ba-*doo* bop! Yabala doo *be*-deep? Du*wee*-du*wee* ba-*doo* bop! Yabala doo *be*-deep?"

Ed had a hectic melodic line in his ears, but the working-class voice was now breathing garlic at him from two inches away. The sounds he was hearing were getting mixed up with the sounds he was making; his left hand was darting back and forth like a locomotive piston.

"Yabala boo-bee *doo*-bop! Yabala boo-bee *doo*-bop! Doo-bee *wam*pa, doo-bee *wam*pa, bah . . . bah!"

And still the *non sequiturs* flowed in! The man might as well have been talking to a player piano! Ed couldn't remember the name of the tune he was playing, he had to do something, anything, to get this insistent *zzzzz*—this persistent mosquito—out of his ears. He raised his right hand to swat it—or something—flubbed a couple of beats, finally unable to control his own voice in the surrounding noise and confusion blurted:

"Hey pal, go soak your head! Get the hell off my stand!"

The man stared at him, put his foot down, and shuffled

back to his table. His demeanor suggested that he had only been trying to do a guy a favor, and look what he got for it.

Ed has another sip of his drink, places the coffee cup in its saucer, and sets them on the piano. Though he has been trying to ease up on the sauce, lately, the drink and his encounter with Lee Castleton are making him feel like a human being again. He looks out across the room, and a woman on his right smiles at him. He makes a mental list of tunes he will play next, and begins with "Willow Weep for Me." The alcohol has made him mellow, and he plays with real feeling. He would like to go around again on "Willow," but sticks to his plan and moves on to "Sugar," eventually closes the set with "Sweet Lorraine." There is a burst of applause from the smiling woman, and a few others, and now a large man with a toothpick in his mouth approaches the piano. The toothpick is being decimated, pulverized.

"Let me read you something," he says, stepping up onto the stand and throwing his weight against the piano. He removes a book from his jacket pocket, takes the toothpick out of his mouth, and after looking for somewhere to put it, places it on the saucer next to Ed's coffee cup.

"Actually, I'm on break," Ed remonstrates.

Not hearing, the man thumbs through his book and opens it: "This'll only take a sec. Listen to this. 'Music is notoriously the consolation of an oppressed and frightened people. It is the one art in which one can be safely sincere in dangerous times.'"

He looks down at Ed—who stands up. But the man moves so as to block his escape.

"I'll read it again. 'Music is notoriously the consolation of an *oppressed and frightened people. . . .*' "

It's the last straw. Ed somehow slips around the man, and makes his way across the room to the Lifeboat Lounge.

It is dark in the lounge, and he is relieved to be among kindred spirits, people who, if need be, will come to his defense. He would rather have wandered up Bay Street and put some distance between himself and the restaurant, but just now the need for shelter is a higher priority. Spotting a vacant stool at the end of the bar, he heads for it; as he does so a number of people greet him.

"You sound great!" one says. "Don't worry, we've been listening!"

Ed thanks him and moves on. By the time he has hiked himself up on the stool, Felix has placed a Scotch on the bar.

"Happy Memorial Day!" Felix says, slipping a coaster under the drink. "How's it going?"

"You wouldn't *believe*," Ed answers. "Whew, what a night it's been." Though he doesn't like his tone of desperation, Ed very much wants to tell Felix—to tell someone—what kind of night he's having. "Listen to this, you won't believe this. I just had a guy come up to the stand with a book in his hand. I mean, this guy comes up and says he has something he wants to *read* to me."

Felix gets a distracted look, and raises his hand as if to say he's sorry, but he must put Ed on hold; he goes to the other end of the bar, where waitresses are waiting with drink orders. Ed takes a sip of his drink and tells his story in his mind, then tells it to himself again so that he will have it polished when Felix returns.

But Felix does not return. The dinner crowd is thinning but the drinking crowd is materializing, and for the moment he is responsible to the needs of both. He moves smoothly up and down the bar, serving and collecting, serving and kibitzing, always moving but never wasting motion. Next to the pick-up stand sits Mike Cavaliere, the charter boat captain. Mike has had a difficult weekend because none of his parties caught many fish, and though he never intended to stay so long, he has been sitting in the Lifeboat Lounge since early evening. Next to him is Doug Brindle, a young writer who has come to town to write what he supposes will be the Great American Novel. The plot he is currently working with follows the fortunes of a large southern family from the early days of slavery to the plantation's recent conversion to a museum. He doesn't quite know how to get started on this ambitious scheme, however, so spends his time seeking guidance from the man on his right, Flipper McDougal. Flipper has indeed written a book, *The Middle-Aged Man and the Sea*, but that was many years ago. He has plans for new work, and is constantly making notes on napkins and scraps of paper that he keeps in his pocket, but more than his work it is the aura he exudes that keeps Doug Brindle at his side. Flipper is serenely oblivious to the world's opinions of him—or of anything or anybody else. He wears lederhosen during the summer despite his vein-lined legs, and sports himself in thrift shop clothes year-round. To Doug, Flipper is the voice of experience, a man who has seen and done much, and come through it all unscathed; Doug hangs on his every word, finds significance even in the way he lights his pipe, and hopes one day to have such self-composure. To Doug and Flipper's right are some vacationers, the women sitting, the men standing, telling jokes and laughing. On the stool he usually occupies, Grubby Eddy sits in brooding silence, oblivious to everything going on around him. His eyes drift from the television to his drink, and back again. Farther along is Jack Freund, the sidewalk portrait artist from Smuggler's Alley. Jack has just come from work, and has his eyes fixed on the bottles across the bar in a dazed, thousand-yard stare. Finally—bumping into Ed Shakey as they shift and squirm—a young man and woman are so physically entwined that they appear intent on consummating their passion right there on the spot.

As Ed nudges his stool out of harm's way, he notices that Grubby Eddy, as usual, is staring at the television. A chubby, taciturn man with intense, piercing eyes, a smoldering integrity leads him to shower scorn on what he sees even as a need for self-punishment keeps him watching. *Goddamn horse opera*, he thinks, staring at the manicured cowboys he sees on the screen. *The furniture, the clothes, the horses. They're all too clean.* He stares down into his drink and bristles with anger. *They've had their hair done, for chrissake!* He talks to himself for a while, then resumes his endless cycle of capitulations, and looks up. *Oh sure. It's a hot summer day and they've just romped through miles of sagebrush and cactus. Now they're going to walk into a bar and order shots of whiskey.* The student of human folly pursues his investigation, finding more and more reasons why it is an insult to his intelligence, and again takes consolation in his drink; when he looks up, a newscaster is reporting a fire. What he perceives as the announcer's hypocrisy infuriates him. *Oh goody, a fire. They're really rubbing their hands over this one, they can hardly contain themselves. Nothing like a good fire with plenty of smoke and flame to make a newsman feel important. Coming up at eleven, News of Fresh Disasters.* He averts his eyes long enough to order another drink; when they wander up to the screen again, he sees an ad for deodorant. He studies the images as though doing sociological research, and an hour later is distressed to find that he can still remember the brand name.

Ed Shakey glances at his watch, then down the bar again, and his heart jumps. Saying "Excuse me, excuse me, please!" Lee Castleton is elbowing her way through the crowd. The drinks he has had have softened Ed's opinion of himself, and now his feelings about Lee are congealing into something he finds very pleasing, romantic attraction. He tries to catch her eye, but she is caught up in Felix's explanation of which drink is which. Disappointed, he drains his glass, rolls the ice around, and drains it again. Trying to keep his eyes off the smooching lovers next to him, he slides off the stool. He has only one more set to play, and is thankful it will not have to be a long one.

The rest of the evening goes without surprises. It is Memorial Day so there are plenty of stragglers, plenty of loud talk and laughter in the bar, but there are no surprises. In the kitchen, the weary crew gets out the last meal and shuts down the ovens and broilers. Kathy Shively comes in, and over the noise of pots and pans being piled by the dishwasher, Dave calls to her:

"How many'd we do tonight?"

"About two hundred and fifty, I think!" she calls back. "I don't have the final figure yet!"

Dave glances at Lenny Knudsen, and they exchange the weary smiles of generals who, deep in a bunker, have received news that the battle they have been orchestrating has ended in victory. As immersed in their element as butchers or coal miners, each is covered with smears and stains; even after they have removed their aprons, the smells of fish and garlic remain as pungent reminders of their trade.

"Hey, we cook the old-fashioned way!" Dave calls, as he uses his wadded-up apron to wipe a spill off the steam table.

"Yeah, we use a *manual* can opener!"

Dave dutifully bends over the grill, and begins working his soapstone on it.

Ed, meanwhile, finishes the evening with a soulful rendition of "Show Me the Way to Go Home," his knees wedged beneath the piano to help him keep his balance. Hoping that Lee will pry herself loose from the table where the waiters and waitresses are having their nightly post-mortem, he wanders into the lounge. *Should I offer to walk her home?* he thinks. Dutch is much in evidence now, and clearly pleased with the night's performance. He stands with his arms around a couple at the end of the bar, and they shine in the limelight of his attention. Dutch at his most gregarious is capable of making each of his acquaintances feel that he or she has a special place in his affections, and the restaurant being as popular as it is, there are few who don't enjoy being seen in his company. Conversation in this charged atmosphere tends to be more ceremonial than substantive, however, and neither of his listeners is willing to tell Dutch that his opinions about sailboat prices and performance are completely out of line. After a while, Ed gets up and goes to the men's room; when he returns, Lee Castleton is nowhere to be seen. Feeling vaguely estranged from the younger workers around him, he goes to the table where she had been sitting.

"Uh, did Lee go?"

"Yeah. Left about two minutes ago," says one of the girls.

Ed contemplates the fact, decides it's a blessing in disguise, and places a tip on the bar. Except for Felix, who waves from within the crowd, no one notices his departure.

Even in the change of shoes she has brought for her walk home, Lee's feet hurt and her calves ache. She is overjoyed to be out of there. Although she has made good money over the holiday weekend, it's been a struggle; now the peacefulness of the summer night surprises her. Slowly it sinks in. *It's over, I'm off work. There's no need to hurry.* Her shoulders relax and her pace slows. But her mind continues to race, to fill with orders, snip-pets of conversation, things to see about, check on, do. She takes a route that leads her away from the traffic on Bay Street, and turns up Puritan, and across on Quesnel. Her pace slows further; it's as if her shoes were weighted, or she were stuck on a treadmill. Eventually she lets herself into her cottage behind Mrs. Bernardi's, but even while she reads a magazine, her mind continues its hyperactivity. Slowly the relentless train of images slows down; now, however, the work of the evening begins playing itself back like a movie. In her movie, she hears herself taking the request for dessert from the man in the tennis sweater, then—with equal clarity—sees herself going in the kitchen and forgetting about it. She studies another scene, and remembers that she never gave the folks at Table 1 their salads. The images continue to play themselves back in excruciating detail (the accidents and oversights for some reason appearing with greater frequency than the moments of competence and efficiency), and it is not until she has brushed her teeth and gotten into bed that she has finally put them to rest.

Still there is something wrong with one of the scenes. Something preys on her mind, and will not let go. It's as if she were a detective studying the scene of a crime, and there were one detail out of place, the crucial clue—if she could only identify it.

As she pulls the covers up, it finally comes to her. She lies there for a moment and stares at the lightbulb in the floor lamp next to her. As she reaches up under the shade to pull the chain, the last thing she thinks is:

Steak for the children of the ghetto, clam shells for two tight-fisted old biddies. Perhaps there's some justice in this world, after all.

FOUR

Lee is lost in dreams when, about four A.M, a discreet and modest noise penetrates the sleepy somnolence of the town. The noise does not interrupt the stillness so much as sneak in under it, perhaps (for those still awake) making the silence for the first time noticeable. It is a sound that is as unobtrusive as the drone of a refrigerator, at once purposeful and hollow, furtive and premeditated, deeply suggestive and all but lost on the night air. Nor, for all the activity associated with it, is it much louder where it originates. A person standing on the town wharf at this hour would find himself joined by men plodding along, ghostlike, on the creaky boards. They would appear in twos and threes, carrying lunch boxes or sea bags, talking quietly and shoring themselves up for the coming work.

The draggers and scallopers of the town's fishing fleet will be tied at the pier four or five abreast, and the men will pick their way through the nets and rigging from one to the other, thankful when the tide has kept them touching one another. Because the boats that are the first to leave were probably the first to tie up the previous day, the crew that gets the earliest start will often have to extract its vessel from the ranks alongside. The captain will free his boat and, bringing it around, use its bow to nudge the remaining boats back into place. Then he will come alongside the outermost boat, and after they have retied the lines and scrambled through the rigging, his crew will clamber aboard. The deck lights that were used to facilitate this work will now be extinguished, and the movement of the boat will be apparent only in its mast light and red and green running lights. Muffled by water and watery air, the boat's engine will echo across the harbor, and seem to linger even after it has rounded Kinriddy Point. Now another engine will spring to life, and the air will again be laced with the smell of diesel fuel. The process of disentanglement will be repeated, and the quiet drone of motors will continue until all the boats, and all the men who are going fishing this day, have departed.

By sunrise, the draggers will be approaching the areas where their captains think the fishing will be best. The captain will rarely deign to tell his crew where he is headed, the choice being entirely his, but the most fertile spots for the Sun Town fleet have traditionally been the Whalen Banks to the northeast and areas off the Hensche Islands to the south, and an experienced crewman (even one who has been lucky enough to garner a little sleep on the way out) will usually be able to tell from the wind and water, and the position of the sun, where the boat is headed. The captain, meanwhile, will be studying his fathometer and gathering information on everything from the depth of the water and the character of the ocean bottom to the presence of fish, and even the *type* of fish. When he is satisfied he has found what he is looking for, he will order his men to "set the twine," either from a drum on the boat's stern or a sprawling gallisframe on its side. Held open by heavy wooden doors and metal floats, the net will be dragged along the bottom of the sea like a huge funnel, or cone. In the first tow of the morning there will be little for the crew to do but sleep; once the net has been hauled back, however, the doors raised on the gallisframe and the net hoisted up on deck, the romance of fishing will reduce to the story of muscle and sweat. The "purse string" at the bottom of the net will be pulled, and if the captain's instincts were correct, a bulging cargo of writhing fish will pour out onto the deck. After the string has been retied and the net inspected for tears and set out again, the crew will stand ankle-deep in this iridescent pile and sort the fish by species and size, bending over for hours at a time like field workers and tossing the fish into the partitioned "kits" into which the deck has been divided. Rocks and debris will have to be picked out and thrown overboard, along with undesirable "trash fish" and any of the sea's unpredictable yield of eels, seaweed, sea worms, skates, squid, and sand sharks that can't be blown through the scuppers with the deck hose.

Now there will be more work for backs and hands. The fish in the kits must be hosed down, and the most desirable species dressed by hand; then they must be gathered up and placed in wire baskets and carried—on a deck that is in constant motion, and often slippery—to the hold. While someone down below lines wooden crates with ice, the wire baskets will be lowered on a winch and emptied into them. As soon as the crates have been restacked and the hatch cover replaced, the captain will probably lean out the door of the wheelhouse and tell the winch man to get ready to haul back again—and the process will be repeated. There may or may not have been time for a "mug-up" in the fo'c'sle.

Standing alongside the wharf, a Sun Town dragger is a rugged, cumbersome-looking vessel supporting a mess of rusty-orange gear and painted-orange rigging. As soon as it leaves the dock, however, it seems quickly to diminish in size, and as it heads out across the harbor it becomes less imposing still. But once out on the high seas and surrounded by nothing but rolling water, it will seem to have shrunk in size to a toy, to be so unfairly matched against the element in which it moves as to be an object of commiseration and sympathy. At once heroic and forlorn, valiant and vulnerable, made to seem plodding and inelegant even by the kite's-tail of seagulls that hover over it effortlessly, the boat will plow the rolling meadows hour after hour, its harvest always hidden and unpredictable: a tiny tractor in an endless meadow, a bump on the ocean. On this fragile platform, in an environment that is always wet, usually slippery, and often cold, using machinery that is as sharp and crude as bodies are soft and pliable, men will drag a sometimes profitable, more often meager living out of the sea. Hands lose their fine tuning doing this work, and when employed at it long enough, become thick and meaty; there is more than one person around the waterfront who wears an eye patch or a windbreaker with a sleeve pinned up, or who favors a leg as he walks.

Still, Jody McGuire knew from the day he set foot in town that he wanted to go fishing. He had hitchhiked to get there, and his last ride, with Father John Mahady of St. Peter's Catholic Church, had featured a helpful introduction to the town.

"It's really two towns," he said, "a winter town and a summer town. It's a town with a lot of pride and a lot of personality, a town that indulges every variety of personal behavior. (Sometimes I think it indulges *too* great a variety of personal behavior.) I'm afraid that in Sun Town, as in life everywhere nowadays, I suppose, people bounce off one another, fail to make connections. Therefore I believe it's important to establish a church home, a place where you can find community, and put down roots. There's so much *sand* surrounding Sun Town, if you see my meaning. But if you put down spiritual roots, you can greet each day with a smile, and say about life what I say about the weather in Sun Town: 'When it's good it's good, and when it's bad it's good.'"

Thanking Father Mahady and climbing out of the car with his suitcase, guitar, and over-the-shoulder sleeping bag, Jody headed down Bay Street on foot. When he reached the center of town, he noticed some shops with curious names, such as Russell of Spring, Juan in a Million, The Quick Brown Fax. He inspected the menu posted in front of the Dockside Restaurant, then, already drawn to the water, trudged out to the end of the town pier. And it was then, after being in town less than an hour, that the vague yearning for adventure that had prompted him to leave home, stick out his thumb, and take to the road blossomed into the more romantic fantasy of allying himself with other men, hitching himself to a more risky adventure, and taking to the sea.

The road from fantasy to reality was not an easy one. First he had to find a place to live, and a job. For a while he washed dishes at the Cannonball Café across from Town Hall, then he lugged tarpaper and shingles for some dope-smoking men who were known around town as "the reefer roofers." And he hung out in the bars where the fishermen hung out— the Whale's Tale, the Mermaid, the Alibi—where he often received very humbling advice. " If your ancestors didn't come over on the Mayflower, you probably won't make it in this town," one fisherman told him. "You don't really belong here until you've sold everything you own and moved away twice," said another. "On the other hand, if you hang around for twenty years, you may get introduced." And what was most humbling of all: "You aren't big enough to get a site on a boat."

Still, Jody McGuire knew he wanted to go fishing. When he stood on the wharves or peered into the shadows of the packing plants, he knew. When he talked to the day-trippers in their rubber boots and layers of shirts, he knew. When he carried a roll of roofing felt up a ladder and gazed all the way down Kinriddy Point to the ocean, he knew.

But it was not physical strength that got him a site, and it certainly wasn't his curiosity or enthusiasm. Jody possessed one talent which, when it became known to those around him, took over his case and did his arguing for him. He was standing at a pinball machine in the Alibi, one afternoon, watching some fishermen do battle with the forces of electronic ingenuity, when the man who was playing turned to his friends and said:

"I'd sure like to be sinkin' my teeth into a steak, right now. Or some spare ribs, or some decent spaghetti. Six-Pack may be a good fisherman, but he can't cook worth shit."

"Well, you can always go out to the Sundowner," one of his friends suggested.

"No no, I mean without having to pay an arm and a leg for it," said the first, looking back at the machine.

"Oh, I do a great T-Bone!" Jody interrupted. "And spare ribs, chicken, pasta—anything!"

So what do they care? he thought, embarrassed for breaking into the conversation.

Another fisherman stepped up to the machine and inserted his money, and began teasing and coaxing the ball around the board. After it had slipped down between the flippers, he stood back and studied his score. After exchanging positions, the first fisherman contemplated the score, rubbed his hands together, cupped and blew into them, and pulled the shooter back.

"You do, huh?"

He glanced at Jody, and let the shooter go. The ball shot up the alley. The fisherman began talking to it, pleading with it, cursing it, but for a certain member of the group all his muscular exertions and verbal gyrations were not enough to drown out the words: "You do, huh?"

When the ball dribbled down the hole at the bottom of the board, the fisherman looked up.

"Yeah, I do," said Jody. "In fact, I can cook just about anything, and well. I cooked during summer vacations, and considered going to culinary school and becoming a chef."

The player turned back to the machine and resumed playing. He pulled the shooter and again the ball careened up the alley, arced across the top of the board, and began bouncing off the rubber ropes, apparently deciding which gate it would pass through. Just when it was about to drop through a slot on the left, the player nudged the machine and it bobbed across the board and fell through a gate on the right. There was a murmur of approval, and now as the ball began ricocheting off the machine's stubby fire hydrants, the excitement turned to quiet, respectful concentration. While the player shook and rattled the machine, the ball tumbled to the left, hit the ropes like a disoriented wrestler, and was slung back across the board until it dropped in a hole; it rested there, then was kicked out and began hitting the ropes again. When it fell lazily toward the flippers, the player caught it with one flipper and passed it over to the other and slapped it back up to the region of the fire hydrants—where it bounced around some more in a delirious frenzy. In his ability to save the ball from oblivion, the player seemed to get an entire extra play out of it. Having at last managed to score an extra ball, and having grasped the shooter, he glanced at Jody:

"J'ever do any cooking on a boat?"

"No, but I guess if I can cook on—"

The release slapped shut, the ball catapulted up the alley, and the fisherman leaned forward again. The machine began ringing and thumping, lighting up and going dark. The player shook it and slapped it with his wrists, then bent forward as though following through on a tennis stroke; the comments of the people around him were sharp, quiet, intense. The ball was now at the top of the board, knocking about furiously, and points were being racked up almost faster than the machine could tally them. To the onlookers' pleasure and Jody's dismay, it was the longest ball he had ever watched. It rebounded from side to side, hit a target, hit a bumper, hit more targets and bumpers, then careened down out of sight and was gone.

Everyone stared at the backboard. Many seconds passed before the machine finished computing the score. While it clanged and dinged and numbers raced forward so fast they seemed to trip over themselves, the player turned to Jody and looked at him as though the interruption had nothing to do with him, and he was sorry for it.

"No," said the newcomer, "but I guess if I can cook on land, I can cook on a boat. Does a cook on a Sun Town dragger just cook, or does he fish, too?"

On being told that he fished, Jody explained that he had been trying to get a site ever since he had arrived in town.

There was a cheer as the machine displayed the rewards for extraordinary performance. The player had not only amassed an impressive score—and decisively beaten the other player—but the machine had given him two free games. He turned to Jody.

"Wanna give it a try?"

"Nah. I've never played pinball."

"Then it's time you tried. Come on, it won't hurt you. See what you can do."

Someone nudged Jody from behind: "Go on. Whatta you got to lose?"

"But I don't get it!" Jody answered. "How did you win two free games?"

"I only won *one* of them," said the player, pointing at the lights on the console. "The other is what's called a 'match.' The machine throws out a couple of random numbers at the end of every game, and if they match the last two numbers of your score, you get a free game. Go on, give it a try."

Reluctantly, Jody stepped up to the machine. Someone pushed the reset button, the lights went on and off, and all the numbers returned to zero; a ball popped up in the shooter alley.

Jody stared at the bright lights and massaged the flippers tentatively, then with a sheepish expression pulled the shooter. Before he had it under control, the ball whirled around the top, slipped through the middle gate, and began ricocheting wildly from fire hydrant to fire hydrant. When it stumbled toward the flippers he stabbed the button on the side, caught it off-center, and hurled it at the rubber ropes on the left, where it bounced gracefully into the center of the board, hung there for a moment—and plummeted out of sight.

"You gotta reinforce it a little," someone said, behind him.

Jody turned and acknowledged the comment. With a metallic *thunk*, the second ball popped up in the shooter alley. Determined to do better this time, he pulled the handle back, and let go. Fearful of causing it to tilt and go dark, he began gently nudging the machine. He got more play out of this ball, but after some modest rebounding and knocking about, it seemed to lose interest and dropped through the space neither flipper could quite reach.

"Down the hatch," someone commented.

"Fish hole," someone else said.

The third and fourth balls went better, and he was even able to fire one of them back up to the top and send it through the gates again, but as if to mock his performance, the last ball got away from him and slipped through the no-man's-land between the flippers. He watched his score being tallied. In the ten- and hundred-thousand columns—the columns that had made the previous player's score so impressive—he showed nothing.

"Well, here's what you do," said the first player. "Come down to the pier tomorrow around four o'clock. Look for a boat called the *Windswept.*"

And with that, the entire group turned and lumbered out.

When Jody looked back at the machine, it seemed at once bright and gaudy, and cold and heartless.

He could not wait until four o'clock. He went to the pier around three, and nonchalantly studied the names on the prows of the various boats, or—when one boat blocked his view of another—went around and studied it from the stern. Suddenly he spotted the man he had encountered at the pinball machine: Ten or fifteen feet below the level of the wharf, he was fiddling with the net. It occurred to Jody that the man might well have forgotten about their meeting and, when reminded of it, give him the brush-off. He went over to a bitt wrapped with mooring lines, put his foot up on it, and tried to look as though he had just happened by.

The fisherman looked up at him. "Hey Cap'n!" he said. "This is the guy that wants to go fishin', and says he can cook!"

A weathered face appeared in the window of the wheelhouse, the door banged open, and almost directly across from him a fierce-looking man proceeded to size him up.

"Well, why 'ontcha come aboard."

Jody went to the rusty iron ladder on the side of the pier, let himself down, and hopped onto the boat's gunnel, then onto her deck.

"What's yer *name?*" said the impatient-looking man,

coming down the gangway and studying him as though he were a tuna hanging upside-down on a scale.

"Joseph Randall McGuire—uh, Jody," said the newcomer, kicking himself for sounding like he were giving a deposition.

"And I take it you've met Mario, here?"

The fisherman he had met in the Alibi came over and extended his hand. "And that's Grady and Asher," said the captain, motioning to two men who were mending the net.

"And *your* name is. . . ?"

The captain shot him an angry look, as if not to know his name was the worst form of impertinence. Jody noticed that the man's right eye did not move with the left, but stared straight ahead.

"I'm Manny Carrera. *Captain* Carrera to you."

Now a fourth member of the crew appeared at the top of the companionway.

"Hey Six-Pack, com'ere!" bellowed the captain. A squat little man dutifully joined the group beneath the wheelhouse.

"This is—*what's* yer name?"

"Jody. Jody McGuire."

"This is, uh, *Magoo*. He's gonna be taking your place. Gonna go out with us tomorra' and watch how you do it." The captain stared pointedly at the little man: "I was gittin' tired a' you anyway."

Ignoring the humiliation, Six-Pack extended his hand. "Good luck," he said, winking.

"Well, Magoo, you'd better get yerself some gear. I'm expectin' weather, so we'll probably be out just a day or two.

But get yerself down here tomorra' at five A.M. Five A.M. *sharp.*"

And that was it. As the others went back to what they were doing, Jody hauled himself up on the gunnels and up the rickety ladder, and began retracing his steps along the rough-hewn pier. Feeling triumphant over what he had accomplished, he turned back to wave to his new friends and to appraise his new quarters. But the crew had either gone below or were absorbed in their chores.

He spent the rest of the afternoon shopping for gear. His spirits sank as he wandered through Hatch's Marine Supply and studied the prices of slickers, bibbed pants, waterproof boots, work gloves. When the salesman assured him that it didn't pay to cut corners, he mumbled something about *first week's salary*, and wrote out a check for oil gear, knee boots—

"Gloves, *gloves*," said the salesman. "What you got here are *all right*, but instead of buyin' one pair like this—that're gonna get chewed up anyway—most a' the fellas buy five or six pair of these cheaper gloves, then while they're usin' one, the others can be dryin' out."

Accepting the advice, Jody revised the check to include five pair of cotton work gloves.

A sea bag—even a duffle bag—seemed an extravagance at the time, but when he arrived at the boat the next morning with his suitcase and sleeping bag, he was quickly made to regret not buying one. Excited by being up at four-thirty and putting out to sea for the first time, he studied the *Windswept* for a moment before going aboard, and watched the activity starting up in the muted light around him. The tide was high now, and though the boat was rocking gently it was an easy step across to the gunnels.

Above him, suddenly, the door of the wheelhouse nearly exploded off its hinges:

"Cain't come aboard here with that thing!" screamed the captain.

"What? This?" said Jody, staring at his suitcase.

"No sir! Cain't come on board here with that!"

Mario came out of the shadows, and the captain, acting as if a great disaster had narrowly been averted, slammed back into the wheelhouse.

"Why don't you just hand your stuff over to me," Mario said, quietly.

"Why? What gives?" whispered Jody.

"Just do as I say. Hand your stuff over to me, and we'll take it down below."

Mortified and humiliated, Jody tossed his sleeping bag over the rail, then put his suitcase down in a patch of blackness and knelt down next to it. The pleasure of putting out to sea for the first time could have been spoiled by few things so much as having to empty out a suitcase next to a piling and hand its contents over to someone else; aware that other members of the crew were stepping onto the boat behind him, he was thankful he could do it in early-morning darkness.

It was only after he had gotten his things handed across, and Mario had tossed them down the narrow stepladder into the crew's quarters, that he got an answer to his question.

"Because you don't go on board a fishing boat with a black suitcase," said Mario, slumping back on his bunk.

"Why? What the hell difference does it make?"

"A black suitcase brings bad luck. It's a tradition, I guess, call it superstition. Call it whatever the hell you want."

"A lousy black suitcase? Tell me, what difference does it make?"

"I don't know," said Mario, more firmly. "You just don't do it. You just *don't.*"

There were other things you did not do on a Sun Town dragger, and some Jody learned about in time to avoid doing them, and others he found out about the hard way. On the second day out, while they were working on deck, he began to whistle; Mario elbowed him pointedly. When Jody buttonholed him later to ask what he had done "*this* time," Mario explained that "whistling brings the wind up." "And another thing," said Mario, hunching over the rail during a quiet moment, "don't ever use the word 'p-i-g' on a boat. Say 'porcine creatures with curly tails,' if you want to, or 'little animals that go oink.' But don't use the word 'p-i' . . . don't use *that* word."

"But why?" Jody asked yet again, glancing around to see if anyone were listening.

"Why?" Mario took a moment to go back through old mental files, the accumulated experience of years:

"Because the boat is a lady, and she takes it as an insult."

"Okay. Is there *anything else* I ought to know? Think carefully."

Mario, resting on his forearms and watching the water sweep along the freeboard, began picking his teeth with his thumb nail. It was as if all this were such common knowledge that it was hard work even to try to remember it.

"Oh yeah, yeah. Don't ever stick a knife in a mast, or in a deck. It's bad luck. Bad luck for sure."

"Okay. No knives in masts and decks...," Jody said, wearily.

But there was one thing his mentor forgot to tell him, and Badeye—"Badeye" as he was known everywhere except in his own presence—never let him forget it. Jody had pulled the hatch cover back, one afternoon, and was helping the others lower fish into the hold, when Badeye stormed out of the wheelhouse and pointed furiously:

"How'dja put that thing down, down'nere!"

The crew turned and stared at him—who had committed the unpardonable sin of leaving a hatch cover upside down. As everyone hastened to tell him, it simply wasn't done, it led to all manner of foul-ups, and was the source of every kind of jinx and bad luck. And forever after, when he was feeling irritable or vindictive, Badeye made a point of reminding him of it. If the winch got stuck or the gears malfunctioned: "This woulda never happened if Magoo hadn't left that hatch cover upside down." When the net got caught on rimrack: "Would never a' happened, 'cept for Magoo and that hatch cover." If they went out and couldn't find fish, or found them but couldn't bring them up: "It was that hatch cover, Magoo, what'd I tell ya?"

The lessons began his first day out, and he couldn't tell which of them were teachable and which could only be learned from experience. The way the captain extracted the boat from the ranks of boats, that first morning, and turned 360 degrees in a space no wider than the boat itself. The way, after the deck lights had been extinguished, the town, the shoreline, the world so quickly receded and were forgotten. The way the fo'c'sle—which at first he misheard as "the folks' hole"—seemed so much more dungeon-like and claustrophobic as the sun came up and saturated the world with light. Most of what Jody needed to know he learned quickly. He learned the difference between eastern rigs and western rigs, between whalebacks and turtlebacks, between oil gear and chafing gear, between black backs, yellow tails, lemon sole, and dabs. He learned to fall asleep quickly, and stay asleep, as the *Windswept* bumped and groaned through quirky seas; he learned not to leap out of his bunk and dart up the companionway when the net's doors slammed against the bulwarks and threatened to come right through. He learned to relish the sight of the net, filled with silver and shedding water as it was manhandled by men in yellow slickers, he learned to respect the ocean and the different kinds of light it gave off as it rose and fell around them. In the inauspicious environment in which he was consigned to do it, he even learned to cook.

It was a bulky cast-iron stove beneath the companionway on which he was required to do his work; after Six-Pack pointed out a few of its idiosyncrasies and disappeared forever, he was left to make his peace with it. The stove was the kind of behemoth that might have run on wood instead of gas, a stove that would have been more at home in a mountain retreat or summer camp—from which it might very well have been salvaged. Although regarded with affection by the crew because it was the source not only of their meals but the fo'c'sle's only heat, it had one feature that made using it an unending challenge: it was never level. There was a rail around the top, which more or less prevented pots and pans from tumbling off, but there was nothing in the behavior of the sea to keep grease or butter from sloshing over the rims of skillets, to prevent the yolks of eggs from impishly sliding away from their whites, to keep soups and sauces from overspilling their pots, or to prevent the flipping of pancakes from becoming an almost comical test of ingenuity. If the syrup tipped over and Jody had to work while sliding in it—if he had to cook on days when hanging clothes swung at crazy angles—so much the worse; he soon learned which of his standards had to be relaxed, and which of his specialties had to be abandoned altogether. And to his surprise—and eventually, irritation—he got no sympathy for his plight. If he was required to purchase food, transport it to the boat, place it on ice, and prepare and serve it, he received no extra pay for his work, and beyond humorous reassurances that his ability to cook was what had gotten him the site, little sympathy from the crew.

Least of all from Asher Dubonnet. Of all the *Windswept*'s crew—Mario Mariano, Calhoun Bardell, Grady Wilson, and Asher Dubonnet—it was only Asher, the engineer and first mate, who from the start seemed irritated by his presence, only Asher whose crudity was not tempered by an underlying tolerance. If the neophyte made the mistake of saying, "Cap'n, I was thinkin' "—only to be interrupted by, "Magoo, I'll do the thinkin', you do the doin'!"—or if the captain, waiting to ding the bell to set the twine, stuck his head out the wheelhouse window and shouted, "Magoo, this here's a dragger and all you're draggin' is your feet!"—he soon learned that there was nothing personal in the remarks, the captain simply assumed the men were on board to work, and that aside from the amount of work they could do, one man was as good as another. If it was beyond the crew's capacity to transcend the unremitting physicality of life on board, to cut the atmosphere of hard labor with gestures of finesse or civility, there was at least a goodnatured, roughhouse quality about them that diffused tension and made life in small quarters possible.

For some reason, however, Asher Dubonnet took a dislike to him, and kept insinuating that it was only his ability to cook that had gotten him on board, furthermore that he was doing the one thing which from the point of view of work a cook must never do, hide behind his apron. It did not help any when the captain, having come down to supper from his quarters aft of the wheelhouse, announced that in a lifetime at sea, Jody's was the best food he had ever had. When Jody took the side of a black fisherman who had gotten into a fight at the Mermaid, Asher for the next several days made a point of referring to the winch drum by its slang name, the "nigger head." When he and Asher were working in the hold—the "slaughterhouse"—Jody found that when handed heavy things, the other hands often let go before he had a good grip on them. Finally, when the subject of survival suits came up over supper, one evening, Asher looked at him pointedly and said: "Yeah, but if you're gonna bring one of those things on board, you'd better bring a .45, too."

Gradually, Jody decided this animosity was something he could live with. If the spirit of camaraderie on the *Windswept* turned out to be less than he had expected, and the work of cooking for six men for ten and twelve days in a row considerably more, these were things to which he resigned himself. He gradually became convinced that he was pulling his weight on the boat, and that no one, including Asher, could tell him he wasn't, and he eventually discovered that if serving as cook was a labor of love, it also made him central to life on the boat and gave him respectability along the waterfront. These were matters he could sort out only while on shore, however. Life on the boat was an unremitting cycle of deck work, gear work, and galley work, and neither its rhythms nor the grim functionality of the surroundings were conducive to reflection. It was only when he was off the boat for several days running that he was able to stand back and look at his situation from the outside, to measure its realities against his expectations.

It was standing at the pinball machines in the Alibi that seemed to take him out of himself most quickly. Somehow, standing in the company of the others and watching the silver ball ricochet around the board mesmerized him, it consumed the energy in the front of his mind even as it allowed deeper reflection in the back. And when he played alone, he was dimly conscious of wrestling, in microcosm, the same elements of fate and chance that governed his life at sea. There, the rituals of performance and reward, promise and fulfillment, were so ubiquitous as to be confused and contorted; here, the penalties and rewards were immediate, instantaneous, and obvious. A record of performance was posted at the end of every play, and if he did not acquit himself well in one game, by the mere insertion of a quarter he could wipe the slate clean and start another. Fishing was an activity around which the deeper metaphors of human experience could be gathered, but somehow the work discouraged thinking about them; as Manny Carrera said, it was the "*doin'*" he was supposed to do, not the "thinkin'." But pinball, pinball at the end of a long trip, was something that called up all his mental and physical resources, that put him in touch with life as gamble, fishing as gamble, and at the same time enabled him to consider all the other risks and gambles that the fishing life routinely pushed from thought.

By the time the gray days of winter were giving way to hints of spring, he had gotten very good at it. Not only had he learned from what more experienced players showed him— how to use his body to reinforce the machine and gain control over the ball's movements, how to catch the ball in the flippers and cradle it while planning a shot, how practically to reach out and save a ball by slapping it onto the tip of one flipper and passing it over to the other—but he had carefully studied the rules, posted in small print at the bottom of the playfields. It was this more than anything that enabled him to rival the performance of the more experienced players, for although the rules were impossible to deduce from the jumble of lights and mechanisms, there was a coherent logic to each machine. Armed with his knowledge, he eventually began to think there was no mystery to the games at all, no mystery, that is, except the fundamental one: why some balls were fast and furious while others were slow and lethargic, why some could be bent to his will and commandeered around the board while others were stubborn and intractable, why some shot up the alley as though destined for glory while others carried a freight of bad karma, tumbling about without plan or purpose and merely putting in their time before yielding to the frustrating, agonizing fall to oblivion. For that was the rule that governed all the others, the fact that gave pinball its pathos and excitement, and made heroics possible, and defeat inevitable: The ball must sooner or later, no matter how long held in play, capitulate to gravity and fall through the tantalizing space that neither flipper could quite reach. It was a juggling act, a house of cards kept up by skill and concentration, and it was beautiful largely because its end was foreordained, and everyone knew it. And for this inevitable end, the fishermen of Sun Town had a ready-made vocabulary. "Fish hole," someone would say, when the ball had slipped suddenly or unexpectedly out of play. "Deep six," someone would murmur, describing the ignominious end to a triumphant session. "Man overboard," was the likely commentary on a ball that was wild and erratic, or a player who, from lack of concentration, was doing poorly. "Down the hatch, Davy Jones' locker, into the locker room." And when the ball was rebounding furiously, the commentary would often become enthusiastic, full of encouragement: "Uptown, gotta go uptown! Get her up to the bow, that's it. Keep her up there, keep her up in the whaleback!" When the ball didn't drop out of sight in one swift motion, but began a meandering descent, losing its rhythm, tiring out: "Uh-oh, get the bailing buckets. Better start bailin'! She's down in the bilges. Great, you got her back up on deck! Right up in the prow! She's goin' good now!"

Thus Jody lived in two worlds in Sun Town, the world of pinball and the world of the boat. By the time spring arrived, he had moved out of Mrs. Ganzi's boarding house on Water Street, and into a larger apartment. He had returned to Hatch's

Marine Supply and purchased a duffle bag and heavy-duty rubber gloves, and on cold days was wearing cotton gloves inside the rubber ones. He began phoning ahead to the supermarket, then borrowing Mario's truck and picking up as many as six carts of food at once, and after learning that it was the arrangement on some of the other boats, had insisted that the crew of the *Windswept* chip in for his services. He had gotten used to the boat and the boat's rhythms, to the personality of Badeye and the personality of the sea, to hauling back and reaping only stones or mud, or being so inundated with fish that they had to remove the bunker plates and sweep them directly into the hold. He had grown accustomed to coming into port after dark and pining for a good hot shower, but having to wait while the other boats unloaded, the fish coming up out of the holds one box at a time and being pitchforked about on the scales. He had resigned himself to being snowed in for days at a time, and wandering out to the pier and finding the *Windswept* looking like a wounded seagull, blizzard-blown and haggard, her bow a thick moustache of ice, her wheelhouse staring out beneath icicles that hung like sinister, bushy eyebrows.

It was in June, just before the annual Blessing of the Fleet, that he entered a select group to which few in the pinball crowd of Sun Town would ever be admitted. It happened during a week in which the sun had borne down relentlessly, making the painted surfaces of the *Windswept* hot and brittle and bringing unpleasant odors up out of the hold, even as it snuffed out the breeze that would have carried them away. Although the fishing had been good, Jody had kept a watchful eye on the ice supply, knowing that the faster the ice melted the sooner they would have to come in. When Badeye was called out of town, Asher Dubonnet, as first mate, agreed to skipper the boat past the viewing stand from which the prelate would pronounce his blessings. With the boat momentarily idle, Jody had several days to relax, to sit in the window of the Alibi or Whale's Tale and contemplate the town's annual transformation from an insular fishing village to a vast pageant of anonymous people looking for pleasure and diversion. And he had plenty of time to work out on the machine he most loved to play, and on which he scored most consistently. This particular collection of solenoids, bells, and thumper-bumpers was called Thor the Invincible, and though its theme was that of a fantastic hero triumphing over fantastic enemies, as there was to all the games there was only one real object: to keep the ball in play, to accumulate points, to beat one's previous score or that of a previous player. By now Jody had developed an intimate relationship with Thor. When he looked up at the High Score, posted in the corner, he saw the record of his own performance, eight hundred and fifty thousand points. His next great challenge was the score that would take him "over the top" and into a region of play where few players ever ventured: one million points.

It was the night before the Blessing of the Fleet, and having wrestled the machine for several hours, he was finding that he could almost make Thor the Invincible dance, he was practically flying the thing. "*Jody may do it,*" people around him said, quietly. "Look at that score. He may go *over the top.*" Mario —who in showing him his tricks had groomed him—was at his side, along with 'Houn and Grady, Spacey Stacy, Black Jack, and other aficionados. Several hours of play notwithstanding, he was quiet and self-contained within his bubble. With two balls still to go, he showed six hundred and seventy-five thousand points and three free games. In the recurring decision whether to shoot the next ball quickly, or pause and prepare oneself, he decided this was a moment when he should calm down and prepare himself.

It was the right choice. When the next ball swirled around the top of the board, he reinforced it through the only gate he had not lit up three times, then got an explosive amount of play out of the thumper-bumpers; the ball hit a kick-hole and popped out, he began a long-running dance with the flippers, going after targets he had already hit four or five times, and finally—just as the ball was about to slip out a side exit—managed to open a gate that routed it back to the shooter alley. He had a second go-round with the ball, and when it had at last slipped between the flippers gave the machine a moment to catch up with his scoring. Nine hundred and forty thousand points. Four free games. One ball still to play. He wiped his forehead on his shirtsleeve and crossed himself. If it had been craps, this is the moment when he would have breathed on the dice: The last sixty thousand points were by no means guaranteed.

But the gods or fate—or whatever explained his good luck, that day—were with him. Even before he had registered it, his friends were shouting: "Over the top! He's done it! He's gone over the top!"

By the time the ball had slipped down the hatch, he had racked up one million, one hundred and ninety thousand points.

Only the hundred and ninety thousand showed.

When it was over, he found that he was trembling. If the Alibi hadn't been full of unfamiliar faces, there would have been drinks on the house. As it was, there was talk—the machine seemed to go on ringing forever, there were so many points to tally—of a party or celebration, some commemoration for one of life's small but satisfying triumphs.

Jody passed the first of his free games on to Mario, and without really seeing it, watched the activity under the shiny glass. But the magic, the lustre had disappeared from the ball, and when he stepped up to try his luck with the fourth and fifth games he found that the board had cooled considerably; like 'Houn and Mario before him, he was not able to go above four hundred thousand points. The machine did not offer a Match at the end, and finally there were no more games to play; the console had settled back into blinking, faceless anonymity. Except for the new High Score, posted in the corner, it seemed almost to have forgotten.

Mario, who had been over the top twice in his career (and Grady and 'Houn, who had only come close) did the buying. The four wandered over to a booth that was being vacated by some tourists, and therefore had a faint air of desecration, and after some more toasts to Jody's victory, 'Houn said, "Well, Magoo, this has been quite a year for you. You got yourself on a boat, and you got your sea legs. Then, your first year in town, you went over the top."

"Here's to Magoo," said Mario, raising his glass.

"To the fishin', pinballin' cook!" said Grady.

Mugs were raised, and the sounds of celebration were gradually subsumed in the surrounding talk and laughter. The next day would feature the Blessing of the Fleet, the town's celebration of the fisherman's way of life, its solicitation of divine sanction for his continuing safety and prosperity. As more beers went down, the four fishermen began to whoop and howl. There was talk about women and talk about fishing, more talk about pinball—which generated new toasts to Jody— and suddenly 'Houn slammed his mug down:

"That's all well and good, Magoo," he said. "But what I want to know is, could you play pinball that good on the boat?"

Mario's eyes met Grady's, whose eyes met 'Houn's, whose eyes met Jody's.

Suddenly there was no drinking being done at all.

Although people in Sun Town wondered for years afterward how it was accomplished, there was absolutely no mystery to it. The four had had enough to drink to make them fearless but not reckless, and it was their cocky nonchalance that enabled them to get away with it. Shortly before the Alibi closed, Mario made a trip to the men's room, and half an hour after the bar had cleared out, he and Jody wandered down the alley at its side, where they were joined by Grady and 'Houn in the latter's truck. Being the smallest, Jody was delegated to climb through the bathroom window whose lock had been jimmied, then it was only a matter of letting the others in the back door, unplugging the machine, walking it out, and hoisting it up on 'Houn's truck. There were still plenty of late-night revelers on Bay Street who saw them, but it was precisely their failure to take elaborate precautions that led to a lack of curiosity. Mario had thrown a tarpaulin over Thor the Invincible, the fishermen were familiar faces in town, and soon, as though it were just another routine, waterfront chore, the machine was coaxed across the *Windswept*'s rails, and lowered onto her deck.

Now that the machine had successfully been "borrowed"—as Grady termed it—the party resumed. 'Houn produced a bottle of bourbon from his truck, and Jody—who as cook had a key to the doghouse—stumbled down the companionway and turned on the light. Alcohol and high spirits made the rest go quickly. The machine was strapped to the mast, its cord slipped through the doghouse door and plugged in, and then the men stood around and marveled at the spectacle, anticipating the moment when the boat's motor would be running, the inverter working, and Thor the Invincible—bright and cheerful as a Christmas tree—beckoning to its first player.

"Hey, wait a second," said Grady. "When the boat begins to roll, she's gonna tilt right out!"

"Hell, I can fix that," said Mario, who went to the locker on the side of the wheelhouse and got a screwdriver and a flashlight. Crawling under the machine, he went to work. "There're six or seven tilt mechanisms on these things," he said quietly, "one for everything from picking it up and dropping it to machine-gunning it with your hands. They adjust 'em to vary the amount of abuse they'll take, and the speed of the game. Hunh. This one's set pretty liberal."

"No wonder Jody went over the top!" said 'Houn.

It took Jody a minute to remember where he was, the next morning. He spied the orange extension cord dangling above him, then, through the companionway door, a patch of blue sky, after that the shiny flags and pennants with which the boat had earlier been festooned. *They hadn't really done it, had they?* He grimaced and rubbed the back of his head, and stared at the pin-ups on the bulwark next to him. Then he put his feet over the side of his bunk and climbed the companionway. *Oh my god. They'd really done it. Look at that thing. We really did it.*

It was a strange spectacle that thousands of spectators witnessed, that morning. After the celebratory mass at St. Peter's and the festive, float-filled parade to the waterfront, the town's fleet of commercial fishing vessels headed out across the harbor. When he saw the ungainly object with which the *Windswept* had been desecrated, Asher Dubonnet was incensed; after a heated argument with the crew, he threatened not to take part in the Blessing, at least not to let any of the festival crowd come aboard, as they traditionally did. Say what he would, in the center of the *Windswept's* deck, like a showpiece framed by the flapping pennants attached to the rigging and stays, there was a giant, outlandish toy. A vast crowd had gathered to watch Monsignor Casselli, imported for the occasion from some more reverent municipality, pronounce his blessing and sprinkle Holy Water; now the gaily festooned draggers came around from the far side of the harbor, and fell into line.

"And we know that God has the power, as Scripture tells us, 'to draw man up in his nets and cast him high and dry on the ground,'" the prelate intoned, his words echoing over the crowd on makeshift loudspeakers, his bright cassock ruffling in the breeze. "But it is a kind and forgiving God we beseech today, the God of plentitude, the God of the loaves and fishes, the God who, through his Son, called the Apostles to be fishers of men. . . ."

As Asher maneuvered the boat into the procession, Jody found the temptation irresistible. He flipped the switch underneath Thor the Invincible, and dropped a coin in.

"*Now* how 'bout those sea legs!" 'Houn exclaimed, as the ball began rolling about in sync with the boat's motions.

Asher stuck his head out the wheelhouse window and shook his fist and gave numerous orders, but there was little that actually needed doing. While the shiny vinyl flags and pennants crackled in the rigging and the sun sparkled on the whole bright pageant, the crew of the *Windswept* gathered around its drunken, unpredictable toy.

"*In nomine patri, filii et spiritus sancti, amen,*" the Monsignor intoned, dipping his aspergillum in Holy Water and sprinkling it in the direction of the passing boats.

If he had realized how close to the pier they had come, Jody would have stopped playing while they were directly in front of God's servant. But he had gotten a good run on a ball, and protested that he would quit the minute it disappeared.

"*In nomine patri,*" the Monsignor continued.

And broke off.

And lowered his eyebrows, and squinted in disbelief.

He turned to his side to find similar reactions all around him.

Having no choice, he eventually forced himself to go on.

"*Filii et spiritus sancti, amen.*"

FIVE

For the rest of his life Jody would wonder whether his behavior during the Blessing had a bearing on what happened the following winter. It was then that tragedy struck, and because of the superstition attached to boats and work at sea, there came a time when he began to see a relationship between the two. Was it some inscrutable law of expiation and retribution, or had a curse been placed on Asher because he had been skipper that day?

It happened after several weeks during which the town had been snowed in and the harbor frozen up. There were gale-force winds, at first, which Asher and the captain had to ride out in the harbor, then it began to snow: a smooth, quiet, relentless rain of white. By the time the sun returned, the harbor was full of pack ice, and the fleet was wedged in solid at the wharf. While the town began to dig itself out, and children gathered on the beach to marvel at a seemingly arctic landscape, the fishermen of Sun Town grew restless and irritable; there were fights in the bars, and several arrests. When the ice finally began to break up, and the Coast Guard had nosed a channel across the bay, the more ambitious captains took on supplies and ventured out.

Captain Carrera was among them, and for the first few days the only thing that marred his pleasure in the size of the catches—bag after bag requiring splits—was his irritation over what he had missed by being frozen up, so long, in port. Now they were striking it rich; it was as though the sea were rewarding them for the lost time, delivering up its bounty in restitution. The crew worked to the point of exhaustion, hoping to seem worthy of further blessings. Perhaps they worked *too* diligently, perhaps they had begun to get greedy; Jody could never decide. But on the fifth morning, when yet another bag was being brought up by halves and maneuvered across the rail, the boat hit a bump in the ocean and listed sharply. A winch man who had had a life at sea might have known to slacken off and let the bag ease down onto the deck, but Jody's reflexes were not that quick; he saw Asher heaving against it, and kept the winch in gear. Grady and 'Houn were being pushed backward by the bag, but Asher continued to wrestle with it. Suddenly the boat rolled violently, pushing him against the starboard rail. When it became clear he could not prevail against it, he let go of the bag, but didn't get out of the way, let go and was slammed backward against the rail. He sat down slowly, then lay down. Rolled over on his side.

Jody threw the winch out of gear, the net crumpled down inside the rail and was restrained, Grady and 'Houn rushed to Asher and knelt down next to him, Badeye slammed the wheelhouse window down.

"What's the matter with that man, down'nere!"

Grady, 'Houn, and Mario removed Asher's gloves and felt his wrists, then unbuttoned his oilskins and shoved their hands inside his jackets and shirts.

"It must be his ticker," said 'Houn.

"Or did he hit his head on the rail?" Grady asked.

"No, he didn't hit anything. I saw it. He didn't even

fall. He just backed away from it and sat down. Where's the first-aid kit?"

"Look, he's gettin' pale," said Mario.

Grady and Mario glanced at one another: "And there ain't no ambulance out *here* we can call."

"Let's lay him out and try CPR."

"Someone get a blanket from the fo'c'sle."

"Do you think we oughta take him down there?"

"No. It'll take too much time."

"Unbutton the rest of his clothes. Maybe we can pump the life back in 'im."

Badeye was on the gangway now:

"What's the matter! Somethin' the matter with that man, there? Hey Magoo, come up here and take the wheel!"

They worked on him, they pumped his chest. They tried mouth-to-mouth resuscitation, they took his pulse and looked at their watches, they talked about what to do. And the big, burly man showed no signs of reviving. Even though it allowed a blast of cold air into the wheelhouse, Jody opened a window and stood forward, looked down on the intense huddle of activity. The radio popped and crackled, but he knew that until given orders to do so, it was not his business to call for help. The minutes ticked by, the boat's lumbering motions suddenly aimless and without point. Jody continued peering anxiously through the window. Was this the result of something he had done, or not done? After what seemed like an eternity, a voice materialized among the static on the radio. Jody reached over and adjusted the gain.

"*Sea Pearl* calling *Windswept, Sea Pearl* calling *Windswept.* You guys there? Do you copy?"

Relieved by the thought of contact with the outside world, Jody took the wheel, pointed the boat into the waves, and grabbed the mike.

"*Windswept* to *Sea Pearl. Windswept* to *Sea Pearl,* yeah, we're here! Come in!"

"Well, how ya doin'? This is Ralph Duquesne. I *thought* you was in the neighborhood. Who'm I talkin' to?"

"This is, uh, Magoo."

"Well, howdy, Magoo! How you doin', partner? Is Manny around? Or is the old cuss out on the deck starin' in the hold and wonderin' who's stealin' his fish?"

"No, I think he'd *like* to talk to you!" said Jody. "We got a little problem here . . . and I think he'd like to talk to you! Hold on."

He stepped forward to the wheelhouse window:

"Hey Cap'n! I got Ralph Duquesne on the radio! You wanna talk to 'im?"

"Yeah, yeah. Okay!"

Badeye pulled away from the little knot of anguish and panic. As he hurried across the deck, 'Houn looked up at Jody and swiped his forefinger under his chin, then, lest there be any doubt, turned his thumb down.

Badeye stormed up the gangway, banged into the wheelhouse, slammed the window up, and took the microphone.

"*Windswept* to *Sea Pearl.* This is Carrera speaking."

"Manny? Issat you? I hope I'm not disturbin' your slumbers or anything, but I thought I'd seen you in the area yesterday, and I just wanted to say hello. You catchin' any fish, you old cuss? Over."

"Hey there, Ralph. Yeah we're doin' okay. I mean, nothin' to come runnin' right over here for, but, well, okay."

"Magoo says you got a little problem. Nothin' too bad, I hope. Over."

"Yeah, we got a fella on board that's, well, right sick."

"Who's that?"

"Asher. He's havin' quite a spell. Somethin's got into him, but I reckon he'll be okay."

Jody swung around and stared at the captain, who dragged the mike over to the starboard window.

"Sorry to hear it, old man. You gonna take him in, or what? Over."

"Naw, he's just got a little *touch* of somethin'. He'll be okay. You know Asher. If the fish are runnin', he ain't gonna be out of it very long. We'll take him down below, and let 'im rest up. Tell me, how *you* doin'?"

Jody stared at the captain, dumbfounded, but Badeye continued to peer out the starboard window. After some more noncommittal talk and banter, he signed off.

For reasons unknown to him—perhaps the captain didn't want him near the radio—Jody was ordered to exchange places with Mario. Then the rest of the crew, cold and shivery and dispirited, stood around on deck and tried to decide what to do.

"Well, what about the *Sea Pearl*?" said Jody, finding consolation in the proximity of the other boat.

"What about it?" said the captain. "She's ten or twelve

miles away. It'd take her more'n an hour to steam over here, and when she *got* here, what good could she do? She ain't got a doctor on board any more'n we do. Much less a funeral director. And it wouldn't put us any closer to port. Naw, it ain't *their* problem."

"Well, it *is* what you might call an emergency," said 'Houn. "Why don't we call the Coast Guard?"

"Now listen," said Badeye, "you know what happened two years ago with the Coast Guard, that time the twine got caught in the screw. They came out and got us, all right, an' charged me a hunnerd and fifty dollars an hour to do it. Charged me not only for the towing time, but for the time it took 'em to steam out. Three hours out an' three hours back. And dragged us right across that friggin' nun at the mouth of the harbor. Hell, how many times you think they've been *by* that thing? They oughta know. They put it there."

"Goddamn *Jewish navy*," said 'Houn.

"Nuthin' but a bunch a' Midwesterners," echoed Grady.

"And I really don't want a chopper comin' out and makin' a big deal outta this. We were doin' real good, we were doin' good jes' the way we were. An' it wouldn't help Asher now, anyway."

"Well, if we ain't gonna get a chopper or a forty-footer, we're just gonna have to take him in, aren't we?" asked Jody.

"Now *look*," said the captain. "We was doin' real good jes' the way we were! A coupla days ain't gonna make any difference to Asher, it ain't gonna help him one bit. And he's the one we're worried about, ain't he?"

There was a stunned, down-at-the-heels silence.

"But we *have* to go back," said Jody. "I mean, don't we?"

"Now lissen," said the captain. "I got ten tons a' ice on board. Three thousand gallons a' fuel. You can go back if you want to, but *I* ain't."

"What are we gonna do with Asher?" 'Houn asked.

"I *said.* I got ten tons a' ice on board. Hell, if we could get him back today, they couldn't bury 'im. Ground's all froze up. He'd just sit in a box out there at the funeral home, till spring. A coupla days on board here, down in the hold—where he spent so much of his life anyway—ain't gonna hurt 'im. Ain't gonna make a bit a' difference. If this'd happened while we were headin' in, people woulda said we'd done the best for 'im we could."

"But Cap'n!" Jody blurted. "You just can't take a man who's died in the line a' duty, and stick 'im down in the—"

"Now you lissen, Magoo! You cook good! You fish fair! But you think stupid! This woulda never happened, 'cept for you and that hatch cover, that time! You do as I say. An' that goes for the rest a' you."

Knowing that arguments with Captain Carerra could be prolonged but seldom won, the three crew members reluctantly did what they were told to do. 'Houn went to the whaleback and dug out a paint-spattered drop cloth, and handed it down to Grady in the hold. Trying to ignore the nature of their work —and the condition, becoming ever more apparent, of the person on whom it was being done—the crew removed Asher's boots and oilskins and, trying to treat the work as one more bit of shipboard drudgery, began dragging the body over to center deck. With Badeye giving orders—standing at the edge of the hold, or getting down on his hands and knees and peering in— they arranged themselves so that Asher could be lifted from the shoulders and eased over the edge. Suddenly made queasy by what they were doing, Jody went over and sat on the starboard rail. The figure of Asher being lifted from his armpits, his pale face slumping forward on his chest while he was nudged into the pit, reminded him of a Pietà, Christ being lowered from the Cross. Then he thought of something which, in reducing the matter to the mundane, enabled him to cushion the shock of what was happening and, temporarily at least, distance himself from it: *He never liked my beef stew.*

Wrapped in the paint-stained drop cloth, the body was placed forward in the boat's hold and covered with ice. When the loathsome task had been completed and the hatch cover replaced, the men huddled on deck in a cold, sour bubble of bad feeling, the heartless, vengeful mood of murderers; it was a mood that for the moment kept them from crying or talking, or even reminiscing. Sensing that it might relieve the tension, Jody suggested they go below for a mug-up, perhaps take the midday meal earlier than usual.

"Good idea, Magoo," said Badeye. "We could all use a break. But you know what happens to bottom fish when they hang in the net too long. Their constitutions can't stand it. So let's jes' deal with what we got in the net. An' the boat's runnin' anyway. It'd be foolish not to set the twine."

Too demoralized to protest, the crew put their work gloves back on, and Badeye went back up to the wheelhouse, and Jody returned to the winch. The bag was raised and 'Houn pulled the purse string, and the deck was once more awash in sparkling fish. Because the blood-spattered holds of Sun Town draggers resemble cattle stalls, they are often called "slaughter-houses," but from now on this bit of slang was carefully avoided. And because working in the hold was now a sinister reminder, indeed, felt like punishment, the work of icing and packing was rotated with scrupulous fairness. Still, each member of the crew had more association with the bizarre cargo than he wanted. The fish that were taken seemed more than usually dead now, and the process of packing and icing a distasteful task. Although fish crates were stacked around the body, camouflaging the sight did not make the presence of a dead man on ice any less disturbing; if anything, it turned it into a dark haunting *presence*. Dead fish, dead man: the hold had become a morgue, and though the crew were relieved to climb out of it, the *presence* in the hold threatened to transcend its confines and radiate through the ribs, planks, and bulkheads, and permeate the entire boat.

The fishing continued to be good, however, the weather remained crisp and clear, and the ice—to the crew's chagrin—held up nicely; even when they began to run low on food and fuel, it was not until they had filled every available box and every available space in the hold that Badeye granted their wish, and headed in. As he steamed around Kinriddy Point into the harbor, Manny Carerra willed himself into stubborn self-composure. Without going into detail, he announced that he was going to tie up as usual, then, taking refuge in a mood of grief and confusion, initiate the process necessary to get the body removed from the boat. He waited slightly farther out than usual, while the boats in front of him unloaded, then began maneuvering toward the pier.

Sal Drummond, the harbormaster, came out of the packing house and, waving good-naturedly as he saw the boat approaching, ambled over to the edge of the pier.

"Second time in thirty years Asher's been sick!" he called, over the noise of boat motors, winches, truck engines. "You don't suppose he's makin' a habit of it?"

Badeye throttled back and adjusted the wheel, and came to the wheelhouse door.

"Uh, how'd you hear about it?" he called.

"Ralph Duquesne told me! So how's the old wetback doin'?"

Grady and 'Houn, holding mooring lines, were standing stiffly at attention, and looked away.

"Uh, not too good!" Badeye called, stepping into the wheelhouse and nudging the motor into reverse. "Not good at all!"

Standing in his cold pool of light at the corner of the packing house, the harbormaster persevered.

"*How* not too good?"

Again Badeye adjusted the wheel and came to the door.

"Ril' bad, I'm afraid! Uh, lemme take care of this business here, and then. . . ."

Something was fishy. Badeye wasn't leveling with him. What did he mean, 'real bad'? And Grady and 'Houn were standing there like mannikins, staring at nothing, glassy-eyed as hell. What was going on?

Sal waved casually, and went back into the packing plant.

And walked out the opposite end, and to his office.

As he came up on deck, Jody saw the headlights approaching, and behind them, flashing lights: a police car followed by a rig from the rescue squad. Next a Coast Guard van arrived, and a second and third squad car. Badeye scrambled off the boat before the officers in the vehicles could board, and there was an intense conversation in the pool of light at the corner of the packing plant.

Now it was time to reap the harvest.

Asher was taken off the boat on a stretcher, and while the Sun Town *Star* reported that the catch was "confiscated," the indignity that Badeye suffered was worse than that. After the boat had been quarantined for two days while questioning went forward, it was taken back out to sea under the command of a Coast Guard lieutenant. While Badeye looked on, the entire cargo was brought up on the hoist, and under the watchful eyes of the Coast Guard officer and various police, state, and federal officials, dumped overboard. Then three nervous-looking swabbies climbed down in the hold and scrubbed it with disinfectant.

But why had Asher taken a dislike to him? Why had he made such a fuss when he brought his guitar on board? Why had he refused to show any appreciation for his cooking? Why was he always waiting for him to make a wrong move, just waiting—any time he screwed up—to pounce?

As if before an altar, Jody stood before Thor the Invincible and worked the flippers and pondered these things, stared distractedly at his score, inserted another quarter and started over. Occasionally he played with others, but more often he played alone, arguing and cajoling, treating the machine like a fortune teller, playing not so much against the machine as against himself, and always, in the back of his mind, searching for *reasons*. When a game was over, he was always ready to insert another quarter or, what was sweeter, to play the games he had won. If he were playing so well that he had the machine singing and dancing, there inevitably came a point at which it was no longer him against the machine, not even him against himself, but reflex against reflex, quickness against quickness, abstract stimulus against abstract response. Sometimes he felt he *was* the ball, he *was* the seductively lighted spaces among the blinking lights and playing surfaces, he *was* the interface between choice and chaos, freedom and predetermination. Did the pinball machine have a soul? he wondered. Did it cough up a Match—or loosen up and start producing free games—just when it knew his interest was flagging, just when, instead of inserting another quarter, he was about to walk away? Had it evaluated his skills and adjusted itself accordingly? Did it remember him from his last session of play, and welcome him back as a friend, or adversary?

Insofar as it put him in touch with himself and helped him puzzle out the truth behind the appearances, pinball became his crystal ball, his tea leaves, his Ouija board. He thought often of how he had been at the winch at the very moment his nemesis had been struggling with the net, and took consolation from the others' assurance that it was not his fault. He thought, also, of the way the town had responded to Asher's death, how it had rallied behind Badeye and been angered by the way his catch had been disposed of. From the response of the Sun Town *Star*, it was as though a favorite son, a hard-working, well-meaning entrepreneur, had once again been beaten by the System. When it became clear that Asher had had a heart attack and that no one could have prevented it, the town closed ranks around the matter and did its best to downplay and forget it. Like the time the crew had hauled Thor the Invincible out to the boat, the lack of true criminal intent resulted in no charges being filed.

Jody thought, finally, of the change that had come over Badeye as a result of his treatment at the hands of the authorities, his table-thumping and belly-aching about how the world kept a man down, how the world kept him from doing an honest day's work, his talk of selling the *Windswept* and retiring. It was going to be a while before he went fishing again, he told the crew. He was going to take some time off, and think it over.

It meant that for a while, at least, Jody was on the beach. A site on one of the other boats would not have been difficult to arrange; he had a reputation as a good worker and a good cook. But he had developed a grudging respect for Badeye, and felt that deserting him now would be an act of cowardice: He cooled his heels, enjoyed spending some of his hard-earned money, and tried to make sense of his confusion. And the thing that most helped him to do this was his addiction—for by now it was an addiction—to pinball.

"Uh-oh, I get the feeling technology won," said 'Houn,

coming up behind him, one afternoon, and finding him staring with a pained expression at a lousy score.

"It sure did," said Jody. "I was doing real well for a while—at one point I racked up three free games—but now she's gotten all moody on me. Can't make her do crap. You wanna try?"

'Houn put a quarter in, and Jody went over to the bar and got a couple of beers for them. When he returned, he found that 'Houn was playing without enthusiasm, just going through the motions.

When the game was over, he found out why.

"Come on over to a table," said 'Houn. "There's something I want to tell you."

Jody took his mug and followed.

"You remember that time, last summer, when we came up on that regatta, and there was one sailboat with her sails down? Runnin' along on her motor?"

Jody remembered how they had come within hailing distance of a Bristol 45, and how they had stood at the rail and shouted offers of help. The skipper had waved at them emphatically and said he had everything under control. Was he sure? Jody yelled, playing the Good Samaritan and practically volunteering the services of the dragger. Was he okay? "Yeah, I'll be fine!" the sailor called back, "if you'll just leave me alone!" Asher, who had been at the helm, changed course and veered away. "You don't get it, Magoo," he said later. "You never get it! That guy wasn't havin' problems with his sails, he wasn't under duress. He was runnin' drugs."

"Well, the way I see it," said 'Houn, "that's why Asher was always suspicious of you."

"Suspicious of me! Why would he be suspicious of me?"

"Well, Asher always had a fantasy of using the *Windswept* for a drug run. I mean a *big* drug run, fifty, a hundred bales. And you, bein' new and kinda green, well, he didn't think you'd go along with it. He was certain, some way or other, even if you weren't on the boat durin' the run, you'd find a way to jinx it."

"Jesus," said Jody, flashing on his first day at sea, his black suitcase. "Is this what Asher told you?"

"No. I just had a little talk with someone. Guess who."

"I have no idea who," said Jody.

"Badeye. Yep, I just ran into him in the Cannonball Café, where he was havin' coffee. And hell, he *needed* some coffee. I mean, the guy was stinko. I never *seen* him so drunk."

Jody whistled under his breath: "And he told you this?"

"Yeah. I mean, mixed in with the babble I *guess* he told me this. He said he had had similar offers before, and had always turned 'em down. But knowin' that he and Asher had fished together for a long time, they—whoever 'they' is—had begun to work on Asher. You know, begun puttin' pressure on him in hopes he'd convince the Cap'n."

"Yeah? So?"

"Well you know somethin'? I think the old man's right tempted!"

*

Your cut would be about forty-five thousand dollars.

The phrase reverberated in Jody's mind like waves pounding against the bulwarks of the boat. He had worked with Badeye on his ocean-going warehouse for two years, Badeye taking half of each trip's profits and claiming another share as a crew member, and now all that work, all those paydays, were being replaced by images of an overflowing jackpot, of money sweeping into their lives like water over the bow. The crew were sitting in the fo'c'sle, having completed only a meager tow but feeling good about their ability to work the boat one man short. The fo'c'sle, crude and rough from years of use, felt to Jody like a subterranean hideaway, a den of thieves in which nefarious plans were hatched, plots dreamed up. Although there was not another boat for miles around, the talk was quiet and intense, as though the surrounding bulkheads might have ears.

"How much warning would we get, you know, that the time had come?" Mario asked.

"Not a lot," replied Badeye. "This guy I mentioned—and all I know about him is his name's Tony—this guy would call and say, 'soon,' or 'toward the end of the week.' We'd lay up in port a day or two until we got an exact time, then for the sake of appearances we'd take on ice and do a little fishin' on the way out. We'd steam off to a spot outside the two-hundred-mile limit, then we'd rendezvous with a small freighter up outta Panama. Tony said he'd tell me what frequency they'd be on, so we could talk to 'em on the sideband."

As he sailed into unfamiliar waters, the captain was showing a side of himself that Jody had not previously seen. If, in the preceding two years, he had kept his distance from the crew, staying in his quarters aft of the wheelhouse when they weren't on deck, and not coming down to the fo'c'sle except for meals, he now seemed to bask in his role as ringleader and to take satisfaction in the planning and preparation it entailed. Having suffered a loss of face, and—so he thought—been reduced to ridicule over the Asher incident, having discovered that the world was not the place he thought it was and did not respect the values he thought it did, he had apparently, in one quick, pig-headed decision, turned those values upside down and was now out to beat the System, earn a hundred thousand dollars for one night's work, sell his boat, and retire.

"And where would we take the stuff in to?" said Grady, in an uncharacteristic gesture of civility sliding the coffee pot down the table toward the others.

"Well, Tony says there's an abandoned wharf south of Miles Inlet, near Port Kimball. I think I know where it is. I figure with the five of us workin', we could get the stuff loaded in about an hour, and taken off in a little less. Tony says he'll have a coupla trucks there, and some guys to help. An' he says he'll pay us cash. Didja hear me? He'll pay us *cash*. Right there on the spot. He mentioned some other cap'ns he's done business with, so I trust 'im." Badeye paused and looked away. "Yeah, I trust 'im."

"Tell me, Cap'n," said 'Houn, laughing with embarrassment at the intimacy of the question—it was the most personal thing Jody ever heard anyone ask him—"have you ever tried marijuana? You ever smoked dope?"

"Naw, I never smoked it. An' I never done it through the nose, neither."

"You've never done it . . . through the nose?"

'Houn's smile disappeared.

"Naw. An' I think if I caught any a' my kids doin' it, I'd lock 'em up in a barrel and feed 'em through the bunghole."

"Well, you're a good man, Cap'n."

Forty-five thousand dollars. The figure stuck in Jody's mind like a fantastic score on a glass-topped board game the likes of which he couldn't imagine; going over the top in pinball seemed suddenly very trivial. But it wasn't the money that led him to participate; as he stood at the machines in the Alibi and thought about it, the adventure registered with him more as a ticket out of youth and immaturity, and into manhood and experience. No, it wasn't the money so much as a question of loyalty to the men he worked with, of curiosity how Badeye would conduct himself, and how the boat—and he himself—would perform. The *Windswept* was a boat with a reputation now, and Manny Carerra the captain whose grit and determination were respected throughout town. No, it wasn't the escapade itself, and its reward or possible penalty; like the fishing life, these would forever remain unknown to those who lived on the beach. It was instead the credibility to be gained in places where such things mattered, the secured footing to be had among the gradations of gossip and scuttlebutt that established one's reputation in town. In the first personal conversation he ever had with Badeye, the captain assured him that if he didn't want to take part, there would be no recrimination. But this, too, was a throwing down of the gauntlet. Yes, he would do it for Badeye, he would do it for the boat; he would do it for a man who hardly knew what marijuana was, much less how it was used.

The operation took place during a hot, muggy week in July, and though every precaution was taken to maintain normal appearances, from the moment they got word the crew's nerves became as taut as mast stays. *Half a day's steam toward the Hensche Islands, then east out to sea. Time allotted to set the twine. Another half day's steam to the point of rendezvous. Transfer of the goods. Twenty-four hours' steam back, northwest, to Port Kimball and Miles Inlet. Two A.M., Friday, look for blinking lights.* They felt like pirates from the moment they cast off, and had to work hard to control their excitement; in view of what happened later, there was not much more about the trip out that Jody remembered. The seas were calm, a fog settled in as they went, and because they turned off their running lights they could only hope that anyone in their path had his eye on his radar. For the last two and a half hours, while their charts and electronic gadgetry told them otherwise, they were like passengers on an ocean crossing, hungry for home, hoping to see land over every swell and heaving shadow. The only relief for the frustration of straining their eyes against the darkness was going quietly in and out of the wheelhouse and peering at the radar. Because of the fog, it was full of clutter.

At last they came to the agreed-on Loran bearing. Badeye put the motor in neutral. Minutes ticked by.

Eventually, like a firefly in a mist, a light winked in the rolling fog. The captain pulled the wheel around and set a course toward the point where all eyes now converged. The light grew larger; there was a quiet voice on the sideband.

"*Buenas noches, my friends.*"

It was uncanny, thought Jody, the way the captain

brought the *Windswept* alongside the rusty wall of the small freighter. He saw the tips of lighted cigarettes even before he saw the boat—*five tons of marijuana, and they were smoking cigarettes*—and by the time a flashlight flickered above them, Badeye had cut the engine and was waiting while the waves did the rest.

Now, quick work. Lines were thrown down, the hatch cover pulled back, muted lights turned on; from the gangways above them came muffled voices. A cargo net was thrown down and tied in place, to form a slide. Without confirmation that they were ready, the bales of marijuana began toppling onto the deck of the *Windswept*. The crew tried to get into a rhythm, but the absence of any rhythm from above meant that to avoid being struck by the bales, they had to skip and dance as they worked. In a labor all too reminiscent of the work they were used to, Jody and 'Houn began dragging bundles over to the hold and handing them down to Grady and Mario. Badeye watched for a while with the disinterest of a man who had seen his boat loaded or unloaded a thousand times, then came forward and lent a hand. After twenty minutes, 'Houn and Jody took a turn in the hold, then the duties were rotated again. The work seemed to go on and on, sliding and lifting, lifting and heaving, until the crew were moving about in their own sweat, and grunting.

Suddenly it was over; no more bales came down the chute. The two crews stared at one another through the mist.

There should have been a celebration, thought Jody, *a ceremony at the completion of the work, a handshake, a toast, something.* But the cargo net was hauled up, the smoky lights extinguished, and there was nothing for the two crews to do but, from their respective levels, contemplate one another.

"*Vaya con Dios, my friend,*" said a voice on the sideband.

"You can let go the lines," said Badeye.

He had returned to the wheelhouse, and with his face barely visible in the lowered window was backing away from the rusty tub.

Ordinarily, alcohol was not allowed on the boat, but now that he was carrying a cargo of contraband, Manny Carerra made no comment when the first of several six-packs was produced. Tops were popped, and the cans raised in fatigued exhilaration. After a brief discussion of the transfer, Grady and Mario went down to the fo'c'sle for a rest. Jody remained at the door of the wheelhouse, and through the rolling fog tried to make his eyes focus. For a long while the captain said nothing. He sipped his beer and, eventually responding to some gentle prodding from 'Houn on the other side, said:

"Yeah, it went all right. It went good."

Presently, Badeye asked Jody to make him a cup of coffee. Except when they had been loading the goods, he had been standing at the wheel since sundown, and now his request for coffee indicated that he had no intention of taking a break. His resolve meant that Jody was up most of the night, for although lookouts were posted in bow and stern, no one seemed able to make coffee without creating a commotion and waking those who were trying to sleep. Still, they made it safely through the night, and when the morning sun did not dispel the thick blanket of fog, breakfast was served in an atmosphere of quiet celebration. Grady was assigned to the helm now, and kept the boat headed northwest toward the Hensche Islands. Badeye announced that he was going to get some sleep, and ordered that he be awakened at the sight of any other boat, or low-flying aircraft. When they reached shallower water they would set the twine, and proceed under the camouflage of their normal activity. Then they would steam on until dark, their destination Miles Inlet.

Although deck work now felt like an exercise in futility—although fish now seemed like a pitiful commodity compared to what was in the hold—it was not and they were not, for the process of setting out and hauling back, of sorting, cleaning, and stowing, not only disguised the contents of the hold—amid comments of "fishy-tasting joints," the pinboards were carefully adjusted to keep one kind of cargo from coming in contact with the other—but returned the boat to a routine so familiar that the crew could almost tell themselves they were out on the grounds doing a normal day's work. But no amount of wishful thinking could quite turn appearances to reality—the fleeting sight of another dragger proved far more fearsome than friendly—and for the rest of the afternoon the crew moved gingerly and with care, as though riding a powder keg. The fog stayed thick and low, and with Badeye at the helm again, they prepared for the final and most dangerous part of the run. The captain had had only a few hours of sleep, and as a matter of course Jody kept him supplied with coffee. While two men napped, or tried to, watches continued in bow and stern; proceeding more slowly than before, the boat lumbered through the inky water and rolling fog. As the drop-off neared, sleep became impossible; approaching land through shoals and sand bars had never seemed more risky. When not serving as watch, Jody climbed up on the whaleback and listened, or when he thought the captain might want something from the galley, went and stood by the wheelhouse door. The captain had a chart beneath the chart light and was studying it, familiarizing himself with landmarks, checking and double-checking it—so Jody thought—in an effort to relieve his tension.

The captain straightened up. Flipped off the light. And swung around. He went forward to the window and listened. He returned to the radar, stared at it, then went to the door, lowered his head, listened. He reached inside and pulled the throttle back, now turned the key and cut the engine.

In the distance there was the sound of another engine.

"It's the friggin' Coas' Guard," he muttered.

There was a brief stir down on the deck, then silence.

It was there, all right. The muffled sound of the other boat became slightly louder, then receded—whether because of atmospheric conditions or the course it was on, it was impossible to tell. The *Windswept* drifted quietly on the swells. The motor noise became fainter, a distant hum hardly louder than the air itself, then began getting louder again. Jody tapped the captain on the shoulder, and pointed questioningly to starboard. Badeye turned and pointed directly to port. *We're on a submarine*, thought Jody, *immobilized and defenseless. We're waiting while the enemy does his triangulations, decides where to drop the first depth charge.* The sound of the other motor became more pronounced, grew faint again; Badeye stepped quietly across the wheelhouse and stood in the opposite door. The *Windswept* creaked and groaned as she turned on the swells. Grady came and stood beneath them.

"They know we're here," whispered Badeye.

He stuck his head out the door and glanced forward and aft, looked up and surveyed the cloud cover.

Now the sound acquired a distinct personality. In the distance a searchlight was turned on and played across the smoldering water. It returned to its original position, made the sweep again, and was turned off. Seconds ticked by.

Then they could see the cutter's running lights, both red and green.

It was coming straight at them.

"Good!" whispered Manny Carerra.

The searchlight came on again, fierce and evil, Badeye stepped through the doorway into the wheelhouse, and the air crackled with the terrifying command from a loud-hailer:

"All right, this is the United States Coast Guard! We see you! Heave to and prepared to be boarded!"

The *Windswept*'s engine kicked to life and was throttled forward, causing Jody to collapse into the wheelhouse, dragging some tools and charts down as he went. The eighty-footer—preparing to pull alongside—was forced to turn sharply to avoid ramming them and, momentarily on a course opposite the one Badeye had chosen, swept across their stern.

"Tell everyone to get down and stay out of sight!" the captain yelled, stepping over Jody in order to shout at Grady.

Jody picked himself up and leapt out the door and down the gangway. The *Windswept* sliced through the water at maximum speed—a speed no match for the government's cutter—and the crew, crouching near the winch, were soon bathed in spray.

"Is he really gonna do it?" Mario exclaimed. "Is he really gonna try an' outrun 'em?"

"Hell, do you think he *can*?" said 'Houn.

"Hey, what other choice we got?" said Grady. "Oh shit, I could practically hear 'em rattlin' the chains!"

They raised themselves enough to see what the eighty-footer was doing, then glanced anxiously back at the captain. When the air thinned, the boat swung around sharply and they were back in thick fog. The cutter disappeared for a moment, and now the searchlight came on again and swept laterally across the water.

"Oh Jesus, he's gonna try an' do it!" whispered 'Houn.

The boat careened forward, and again pulled to starboard; there came a moment when the crew could see stars overhead, then the boat rolled forward into another bank of fog. Five, seven, ten minutes passed.

The engine stopped. The boat drifted to a stop.

"Oh Jesus, don't tell me he's lost power!"

"Naw, he's just decided to be quiet. Wants to see if he can hear 'em. And he doesn't want them to hear *us*. Oh shit, this is gonna be cat and mouse."

As though peering over the top of a foxhole, the crew raised themselves and looked over the rail, and listened. Sensing that some contact with the captain might be useful, Jody scuttled along the deck and up the gangway. Badeye was bent over the radar.

"If· they couldn't find me before, I don't see how

they're gonna find me *now*," he whispered. "There's so much clutter on this damn thing, theirs must be full a' clutter, too. That's why they waited and circled for so long. Here, take a look."

Jody applied his face to the cone, and found the scribe lighting up a mess of sheep's wool, a mottled patchwork that beggared description or interpretation.

"You're right, Cap'n," he whispered. "It's a friggin' mess."

And that is how it was for the rest of the night: a mess, cat and mouse on a dark formless sea, where most of the time they couldn't tell where the cat was, or even whether it was still on the prowl. Badeye went to the gangway on the side of the wheelhouse and listened, then pushed the ignition button and started the engine again. For a while he zigzagged as his instincts dictated, then he killed the motor and drifted for a few minutes, creating the welcome illusion that they had become invisible. From time to time he turned the radio on at low volume, and listened to the weather report. Often they heard, or thought they heard, engine noises, occasionally a suspicious shape appeared on the radar. The threat seemed to be everywhere and nowhere, behind every swell or alternately miles away; as the hours went by, Badeye became more and more obsessed with avoiding it. If they stopped for several minutes and drifted, he tried to make up for lost time by running at full throttle. If his sixth sense so dictated, he veered off course and took a roundabout way through water he didn't trust. If stars reappeared, he lurched for cloud and fog.

Whether because he felt better keeping busy or because

he was master of what little comfort was left on the boat, Jody shuffled back and forth to the wheelhouse, taking coffee to the captain, expressing concern, acting as liaison with the crew. The captain acknowledged him less and less as the night wore on, but inasmuch as it was his instincts, his seamanship, that stood between them and jail, Jody did not intrude; indeed, he found himself keeping silent watch with him, listening to him even when he was not speaking.

More and more, Badeye spoke only to himself: "Evasive action. Gotta take evasive action. Gonna lose those swamp jockeys. Everything was goin' good. Told Tony we'd be there about two."

Standing at the wheelhouse door and listening to the captain, Jody began to feel doubly invisible. It was as though there were no one else on the boat except Manny Carrera, as though he had tuned the world out and turned the chase into a personal contest. Icily controlled in his movements, there was a frenzied quality in his voice of which he seemed completely unaware. And then, at some point during the long vigil, when the monotony of the waves and rolling mist was beginning to make Jody feel vaguely unhinged, Badeye, looking resolutely forward, said: "Magoo, this woulda never happened, 'cept for you and that hatch cover that time."

Did he mean it? Or was he making an attempt at humor? The ensuing silence brought no answer, and the next time Jody slipped out of the wheelhouse he found himself thinking there was a madman at the helm.

Then a worrisome blip appeared on the radar screen. Or did it? The captain studied it, Jody studied it, 'Houn and

Mario and Grady came in and studied it. The captain removed the viewing hood and they stood around the screen like technicians in a missile control room. Among the clutter, the rotating scribe illuminated two distinct shapes: Coast Guard cutters? Freighters? Fishing vessels? The captain thought they were forty-footers from the Coast Guard that had been called out to join the chase.

"But why would they be maneuvering so close together?" 'Houn whispered.

Grady felt the images weren't clear enough to mean anything, Mario suggested they were products of the weather, possibly ghosts associated with the Hensche Islands; Jody, not wanting to question the captain, and not being able to decide, kept quiet. They were nearing the southernmost islands of the Hensche chain, with little more than two hours to go. Badeye said he was "not going to risk it," he was going to "put some distance" between himself and them, and "cut in closer to the coastline."

"But Cap'n," said 'Houn, "we ain't got time! I mean, the truck, the guys that are waitin' for us, they'll wait as long as they can, but they sure as hell aren't gonna be sittin' there at sunrise!"

"Besides, how can you be sure there's somethin' there?" said Mario. "Me an' Grady and Magoo, here, can't make it out. One minute it's there, one minute it's not. Maybe you're gonna take us out of our way for nothin'!"

Badeye was already hauling the wheel around.

"It's there. I know it is. An' we got time. Don't worry, we got time. I ain't gonna lose the whole friggin' crapshoot now. I'm goin' in where they'd least expect me, right in close to the shore. I don't like the feel a' this."

"But Cap'n!"

"I *said*. I don't like the *feel* a' this. Now git down on deck and keep your eyes open. Be good for somethin'. Told Tony we'd be there about two."

Disheartened, they shuffled out. When they were down on deck again, they began whispering among themselves.

"I didn't see anything, did you?"

"Hell no! Nothin' to worry about!"

"This goin' in close to the shore is gonna get our asses nailed!"

"Hey man, we ain't got time for this! We're late now! Suppose we get to the friggin' pier, an' there's nobody there! Whatta we do then?"

"If that sonofabitch isn't careful, he's gonna put us aground. There's rocks and shoals along the coast, down here. I know there are."

"You don't think he's gettin' a little . . . nutsy, do you? I mean, he's been standin' at that wheel an awfully long time, now."

"All I know is, whatever *he* saw on the scope, *I* didn't see."

Like a person who hears noises in the woods during the night, and can't identify them, Badeye had gotten skittish, gunshy; he had chosen to remove himself from the area. Was this the thing that was going to get them prison sentences, or were his instincts their last best hope? All the way in, he kept mumbling, "They're out there, they're lookin' for me. I know they are." In another forty minutes they were near land, *too* near land. Bell buoys clanged and bobbed, fog horns sounded from down the coastline, the circling eye of a distant lighthouse made their movements all the more anomalous. It was as though a magnetic force had caught Badeye in its field and stranded him between its two poles, sea and land. "The shallow-water boys are out there, I know they are. They want to play in shallow water, we'll play in shallow water."

"Hey, this is Hillerton!" whispered Grady, as the outlines of the shore became visible. "Half a mile down is Hillerton Harbor! He's takin' us right up through Quarry Reach!"

"This channel ain't made for a boat like this! If we was carryin' fish right now, we'd be scrapin' the bottom!"

"Shsssh!"

"I put the Point between them an' me," mumbled Badeye, as Jody stepped into the wheelhouse. "I'm keepin' my distance. Damn right I am. They wanna play in shallow water, we'll play in shallow water."

Crazed, something was making Badeye *crazed.*

"Maybe somebody better go up there an' talk to him," whispered Mario, when Jody was back down on deck.

The *Windswept*'s motor stopped, and the boat drifted quietly into Quarry Reach.

Badeye paced back and forth across the wheelhouse, listened, studied the air. Then:

"Magoo, you could bring me a cup a' coffee now."

"You sure you're doin' the right thing, Cap'n?"

"Magoo, I *said.* You could bring me a cup a' coffee."

Jody did as he was told, feeling that there was nothing

so pointless, at this moment, as creeping along the deck and down the companionway to make a pot of coffee, feeling that the captain had indeed gone mad. He heard the engine start up again, and the game of hide-and-seek continued. *Ninety-five bales, two and a half million dollars' worth of cargo on board, and at the last minute its delivery—and theirs—had become sabotaged by real or imaginary obstacles. The boat was like a mammal trying to give birth, who wouldn't drop her calf until she was certain she could do so unobserved. Two and a half million dollars' worth of cargo that had to be offloaded by first light, and they were lost and desperate for deliverance. And now the captain was as likely as not to run them right up into a salt marsh.*

The captain crept through other ports and inlets, curled around other small islands—"when the coast is clear I'll know it, they wanna play in the swamps, I'll play in the swamps"—drifted along on other water that would have been dangerous even on a night when the fog didn't limit visibility to ten or fifteen feet.

"If I had a gun, I think I'd put it to his head, and get us *outta* here," said 'Houn.

"My nerves won't stand too much more a' *this*, I tell you," said Grady.

Standing in the stern and studying the inscrutable world around him, Jody felt the motor rumble to a halt, and heard the swish of the boat's wake subside. All was still. Along the shoreline he could see diffuse lights and, above them in the distance, two fuzzy red beacons. One was the water tank on its rickety frame, the other the old fire tower; this would have to be Port Kimball. Now he could make out the profiles of sailboats on their moorings, and hear the melodious tinkling of slide-snaps against masts; he felt the heat coming off the motor beneath the wheelhouse. Or was it energy radiating from the man inside? *What was going on in there? And what further craziness could they expect from this Popeye the Sailor, this mad Ahab?* Realizing how precarious his relation was to the boat, its captain and crew, he suddenly felt very vulnerable. As cook they had treated him as a go-fer, and the result was he had worked harder than anyone else. And for what? For three days he had acted as page to a knight who was tilting at windmills, a man who seemed not only confused, but paralyzed. *Magoo, you could bring me a cup a' coffee now. Yessir, Cap'n, comin' right up! Magoo, you could do this, Magoo you could do that. This woulda never happened 'cept for you, Magoo!*

What was he doing out here?

He was in way over his head.

In over his head. . . . The sailboat. The motor yacht beyond it. The dinghy. The beckoning shoreline. Suddenly he was slipping off his boots and socks and shoving them under a pile of wire baskets, then ripping off his outer shirt and climbing up on the rail. He corkscrewed around and got a grip, then, digging his fingers into the scow's rough planking, let himself quietly down into the water; the wash of waves, the fog horns, the tinkling of snaps and sailboat rigging masked his descent. He hid beneath the stern of the boat and waited until the coast was clear, then raised his knees and gently kicked away from what felt like the waterlogged clapboards of an old barn, a bilge, a bulge—*was he the calf?*—and paddled slowly backward.

It felt wonderful to be free. Even the taste of the water was not unpleasant, but pungent and steamy, like clam broth. He paddled slowly and quietly until he bumped into a small boat; pulling himself around it and staying low in the water, he watched and listened until the *Windswept*'s engine kicked to life again.

The chugging of the engine slowly faded, and he was left alone in a liquid that felt more like broth than water. He turned and got his bearings, and began swimming toward the shore. Soon he had another boat to hold on to, and another, then, just when he had begun to fear he would never reach land, his feet struck bottom and he knew he was home.

As he walked along the beach, his new feeling of freedom was tarnished by the reality of his being cold, wet, and shivery. He came to a boathouse nestled against a hill and quietly opened the door, pawed around, and found a towel. He removed his tee-shirt and denim cut-offs, squeezed them out and dried himself; then he redressed, trudged up the hill, threw the towel down on a bed of pine needles and—totally exhausted—fell asleep.

It was still overcast, the next morning, but to Jody the air seemed refreshingly full of light. He walked into Port Kimball and sat on a park bench, and savored the sight of people going about their normal activities; then there was nothing to do but to hitchhike out to the highway, and down the peninsula.

"I'm going to Sun Town!" he called, to the man who eventually stopped for him.

"Well, hop in!" the driver replied.

After he pulled into traffic, he turned to Jody: "Do you live in Sun Town, or are you just going down for a visit?"

"Oh, I live there," said Jody, cautioning himself against giving out too much information.

"What do you do for work?"

He could not resist the temptation. "I'm a fisherman."

"You are, are you? Well, I have a lot of respect for fishermen! It's a risky business they're in. I know, because I'm from Sun Town, too. Wonderful town, though sometimes I think there are a lot of lonely people there. People in Sun Town, like people everywhere nowadays, I suppose, tend to bounce off one another. They find it difficult to make lasting connections, to find a spiritual foundation for their lives. There's so much *sand* around Sun Town, if you see my meaning."

The voice, the cheerful demeanor: where had he encountered it before?

Then he remembered.

"You're a priest, aren't you?"

"Yes. How did you know?"

"Oh, you picked me up a couple of years ago. Back when I was coming to town for the first time."

"I did? Well, you do look vaguely familiar. But I guess more people know me than I *know*. Which, of course, is not as it should be."

The priest's genial talk, his pride in the community, his ramblings about rootedness and the need for foundations, eventually lulled Jody to sleep. When he awoke, fog still blanketed the highway. Father Mahady dropped him on Bay Street ("we have two Masses on Sunday! why don't you join us?") and Jody trudged the rest of the way on foot, his head filled with confused thoughts of the night's work and images of a hot meal, a warm shower, a dry bed.

He found it impossible to sleep. A feverish desire to

know the outcome of the night's activity warred with a need to remain invisible, a desire to forget with a desire to reestablish his presence in town. He got up, dressed, and went out into streets that were filled with oblivious tourists. As he loped down Bay Street, however, he could not shake a feeling of phoniness and hypocrisy; when he came abreast of the Alibi, he heard the jukebox and friendly laughter, then the jingling of the pinball machines. He stopped and peered in the window. From the rear, the bright, gaudy machines beckoned to him; exactly as it had a thousand times before, the screen door banged shut behind him.

"Hey, Magoo!" someone called.

"What's the fishin' like?" someone else said. "And what are you feedin' 'em these days?"

He circulated among the crowded tables, patting people on the back and saying hello. Keeping an eye on the machine until it was free—*he had to think, he had to think*—he went over and took possession of Thor the Invincible. Soon he was back in form, and had the machine clacking and ringing, and either it was being kind to him or he had an added edge of tenacity and purposefulness, for soon he was losing himself in it, shaking out his tension, racking up points and playing with the kind of elegance and finesse that 'Houn would have appreciated.

'Houn, who, as he got ready to let go the next ball, was standing at his side. . . .

"Tell me I ain't seein' you," said 'Houn, quietly, menacingly. "Tell me this ain't you standin' here. And *definitely* tell me this ain't you standin' here two games up on a pinball machine."

Taken aback, Jody stared at him.

"Yeah, it's me," he said finally. "Uh, *how'd it go?* Did you, uh, *complete the job?*"

When at last 'Houn spoke, it was in a tone of barely controlled fury:

"Well, given the state *Badeye* was in when we last had the pleasure of your company, and given that we've been on the verge of *losin' our friggin' minds* ever since you disappeared, let's jes' say that the rest of us *did what we had to do.* Hey man, where the hell you *been?* We didn't know whether you'd fallen overboard, *jumped* overboard, gone and ratted on us, or what! Ol' buddy, I don't know what your story is, but if I was you, I wouldn't go too near the boat an' try an' tell it."

"But what about the stuff?" Jody asked, leaning over the machine to secure it. "Did you get it . . . unloaded okay?"

'Houn still seemed unable to believe his eyes.

"Yeah, *they* were there. And *we* were there. And let me tell you, the work had to go forward without any jimjackin' around. But it all got done, no thanks to *you.*"

With this revelation, Jody relaxed a little.

"And you got back up the coast okay?" he asked, quietly.

"Yeah. *Somehow* the old man got us home."

Jody had to fight to keep from sounding like an inquisitive child:

"So you came in and unloaded . . . as usual?"

"No, not *as usual.* Not *as usual* at all. Badeye was talkin' about callin' the friggin' Coas' Guard and havin' 'em come down to the boat so no one'd think we'd had another crew member *die* on us. We didn't know whether he'd done it or not.

Do you know how it felt to be standin' around wonderin' whether they were gonna come down and go over the boat with a fine-tooth comb? Just cause a' *you?*"

Jody lowered his eyes:

"I guess that takes care of *my* share. . . ."

"I *guess* it does! You ain't *got* a share! Man, you blew it! When we finally found your friggin' boots and shirt back there, and realized you hadn't fallen overboard, but jumped—that was it! You were out!"

Out. Free but Out. What was worse, that he had let them down, or that he had decided to take part in the first place? Out, and at the same time in over his head. Dizzy, reeling almost, his eyes wandered across the florid surface of the patiently waiting Thor.

"Tell me one thing," he said. "Do you think there was something—or someone—out there that Badeye was right to try to avoid?"

'Houn thought about it.

"Probably. Yeah, probably. I'd have to say there was. I tell you, that guy's got amazing instincts. That guy's one hell of a cap'n."

Sensing a softening in 'Houn's tone, Jody raised his eyes and tried to make amends.

"Hey, I got two free games on this thing, you want one? Come on, whattaya say? For old times' sake."

He smiled hopefully, and thumped the glass of the pinball machine.

'Houn wasn't buying.

"Now you listen to me, ol' buddy. There's some people

around, right now, that aren't gonna be real happy to see your face. Why don't you do yourself a favor? Get out of town for a while, get the hell out until things cool off. Maybe you'll get lucky. Maybe, after a while, the others' nerves'll settle."

"What, exactly, are you saying?"

"What I'm sayin' is, maybe you'll get off without a *gun* bein' put to your head. How 'bout it?"

Jody stared down at the glass:

"It's that bad, huh?"

"Damn right, it's that bad. And you'd better be thankful you ran into *me* before you ran into *them*. You don't know how deep in you are."

In, but Out. Jody felt like a fish at the bottom of the net.

"So maybe I could talk to somma the guys, and after a coupla days, I could—"

"No, I'm talkin' now, *right now*. An' just be thankful you ran into me before you ran into *them*."

"But what's the big rush? I got a coupla free games on this thing, and there's some other—"

"Hey, man, I'm tellin' you! If the boat had rolled over and went down, I woulda tried to save your life, right? And you woulda tried to save mine, right?"

"Right."

"Well ol' buddy, *I'm friggin' tryin' to save your life*."

With that, 'Houn turned and walked off, slammed out the door, and disappeared into the crowded streets.

Jody looked back at the bright, patiently waiting machine. He cast his eyes across its friendly, beckoning board and patted the glass affectionately. She was primed, tuned up, seasoned and ready to go. Thinking of what he would tell his landlord, his family, of where he would go and how he would get there, he looked lovingly at Thor.

It pained him to do it.

"Hey!" he shouted, turning to the noisy, laughter-filled room, "I got a coupla free games on this thing! Anybody want 'em?"

SIX

In the Lifeboat Lounge, this Fourth of July Weekend, Felix is struggling to keep up. He owes a whiskey sour to Debbie Fensen, a light Vermouth to Sharon Lowd, two frozen daiquiris to Roy Oberholzer, and a bottle of Chardonnay to Lee Castleton. He has to stay focused, and keep moving.

"Hey, I got my car fixed!" someone shouts. "Thanks for the recommendation!"

"Glad to hear it worked out!" Felix calls back.

"It was some little doo-hickey in the carburetor! Joe said all he had to do was run some air through it, and when he put it back together it worked fine!"

"Yep, Joe's a master!" Felix calls, turning his back on this man he doesn't remember ever having seen before. He moves smoothly down the bar to the ice sink.

"It's wumpty."

He stops to collect from a man who is waving bills at him.

"What?" he says, turning.

"It's wumpty."

"It's *what*, for chrissake?"

"Wumpty!"

"*Oh*. You want another *drink*."

"That's what I said."

With a *can't-you-see-I'm-busy* expression, Felix picks up Grubby Eddy's glass, goes to the cash register, waves acknowledgment to a waiter at the end of the bar, makes the drinks on his mental list, returns with the first man's change, and pours a drink for Grubby Eddy. There is a look of childlike innocence about Grubby Eddy, and their eyes meet in mutual forgiveness.

Like a piece of furniture, Grubby Eddy sits with total impassivity, as if under a bell jar. But there is a hint of amusement in his eyes. *Le mot juste*, he says to himself, staring into his drink. *No. Le mot juiced. Hey, everybody, the joint is yumpin'. And the gang is—the Genghis—all here.* The light in the TV flickers, and he looks up. He sees a cat licking its lips at a bowl of cat food, and reflects on the amount of pet food consumed, each year, by humans. The ad fades, and another begins; Grubby Eddy forces his eyes away from the TV. *Been winkin' all drink*, he says to himself, *I mean drinkin' all wink*. When he looks back at the TV, a female newscaster is staring at him oh-so-significantly, and from within her own glass bubble telling him what he imagines are very significant things. He studies her makeup, her blouse, the malocclusion she cannot quite disguise, her forced air of sincerity. *Doesn't give a damn about what she's reporting*, he thinks, *hardly knows the locations of half the countries she's referring to. Doesn't know who's fighting who, or why; she's just performing. That's it, read the script, ma'am, just read the script.* He overhears a phrase from down the bar, and stares at the reflections in his glass. *A clarity benefit, yes, that's what we need. A clarity benefit.* He glances up again, this time at an image of starving children. *Cats eat, children starve. There has to be something wrong with that, somewhere.* He ponders the shiny reflections and reaches out and grips his glass. One long satisfying swill, and the glass is empty. He raises his arm and catches Felix's eye.

Down the bar, a conversation is under way about the fireworks display of the previous evening.

"They must have gotten damp," Bill Macklin says, ruefully. His pleasure in the laughter he evokes is undermined by the fact that as a real estate broker he is concerned with the town's image, and knows that a perfunctory display doesn't do anything to enhance it.

"Maybe some of the kids got to 'em out there on the Point, and tampered with 'em," says one of his companions.

"I don't think they hired a very good outfit this year," someone else chimes in.

"No no, it was the same company as last year," Bill Macklin replies.

And so the talk goes on, with none of the pundits willing to admit that no matter how good budget-cutting feels at Town Meeting on a blustery night in March, come Fourth of July and its fireworks display, the only things anyone cares about are *large* and *long*.

"We raise quite a bit of money at our charity benefits," Sylvia Meeks continues, two stools away. "We had a bake sale and an auction this year, and I'm going to encourage the group to experiment with a 'Monte Carlo Night.' There's this nice man I talked to, Tony or something, who's going to help me with it."

Mrs. Meeks tries to enlist Kitty Solomon's interest in her projects, then their conversation turns to travel. "I haven't traveled *much*," she says. "Herbert's view is that our lives are a vacation right here in Sun Town. But I *have* done two hundred miles on my Exercycle."

Beyond them is a man with a wad of bills in his hand talking to a much younger, very pretty woman. The fact that he is standing, and she sitting, lends weight to his pronouncements. He speaks confidentially for a while, then his emotion explodes to the surface:

"Dammit all, my wife's nothing but a born-again virgin!"

"Oh, are you in gutta-percha?" says the man with the carburetor problem. "My brother-in-law used to be in gutta-percha. Had one of the biggest factories in the world. Did you know gutta-percha becomes soft and pliable, when it's heated? It used to be used in dental work, to make tooth impressions, and in horses' hooves to protect them from irritation. Because it has great insulating properties, it's also used in electrical applications. Like the first transatlantic cable. Did you know that the first transatlantic cable is still in use? Bet you didn't know that."

The well-heeled man and his date stare at one another in disbelief.

"Yessir. They used to import gutta-percha in syrupy balls wound around sticks, but the natives who gathered it were paid by the pound, and my brother-in-law said they occasionally found rocks and bones—even skulls—wrapped up in it. But he's no longer in business. New products forced him out. Everything's done with plastic, nowadays. Neoprene. Amalgams. Synthetic resins."

"Honey," says the standing man, turning in such a way

as to block out the intruder, "whattaya say we go back to the motel?"

Doug Brindle wanders into the lounge, and moves quickly to the seat the young woman vacates. He casts about for Flipper McDougal, and is disappointed not to see him.

"Can I get a draft?" he says, when Felix comes over.

"Sure. Open the window."

Doug doesn't laugh. His novel is not going well. More precisely, his novel is not going at all. His original plan, to trace the fortunes of a large southern family through many generations of its history, has begun to seem too ambitious. He doesn't have enough models on which to base his characters, and he's beginning to think it would be better to narrow the focus, perhaps portray a marriage that is on the rocks. If he did that, he could give the couple a beautiful daughter, and get in some romantic interest. He has a model for her, at least. His old girl friend.

"So, do you live in town?" says the man on his right, still smarting from the world's lack of interest in gutta-percha.

"Sure do. Wouldn't live anyplace else."

Doug is relieved to be able to put his meditations on hold.

"Some town, isn't it?" says the man. "Whatta you do for a living?"

"I'm a, uh . . . writer."

Doug's revelation carries a solemnity appropriate to those who feel deeply, and suffer greatly.

"You're a writer, huh? Gosh, that's terrific! Good for you! *I* wanted to be a writer but, well, I had a wife and kids. And frankly, I just didn't have the discipline for it. I'm the active type, I can't sit still for two minutes but what I get antsy. I've done very well in my business, however, and it's amazing the things I've seen along the way. In fact I've always thought it would make an interesting story, you know, for others coming up, for folks who wanted to know what it was like. But I'll be damned if I could write it myself. I've got the stories, all right, but I don't have, you know, the words. But now, you and me, maybe we could team up. I'm sure I have a book in me, and maybe if I gave you all the information you could just, you know, put it into words."

The man's enthusiasm, his deferential air, are seductive, and Doug again feels alive with the literary life.

"What do you do?" he says.

"I'm an industrial photographer."

Doug recoils. His shoulders slump.

"Like, I got this commission one time for a display presentation about egg cartons. I'm not talkin' about your little cartons that eggs come in, I'm talkin' the machines that form the shipping boxes, the *dies* we call 'em. Now, the company that makes these machines is run by a guy named . . . well, I can't tell you *that*, 'cause he's a well-known guy, and you've probably heard of him. But what we'd do, see, is change his name. Camouflage it. That's the sort of thing I'd rely on *you* for. But I digress. Anyway, so I get out to this guy's factory, but he isn't there. . . ."

The story Doug is hearing doesn't have quite the dramatic intensity he had been hoping for; by his expression he tries to show that he is not interested. Someone nudges him

from behind: Flipper McDougal, his means of escape? He
turns to see a smiling man holding out his arms in an attitude
of . . . behold!

"Hey-a-y!" the man exclaims, when Felix comes to take
his order. "This is quite the boat you got here! I haven't seen a
boat like this since I got out of the navy!" He slaps the dory's
gunnels (on which, stem to stern, the arms and elbows of the
faithful are propped), stands up on the foot rail and leans
forward. "Well, her beam-ends need to be tightened up some,
but I think with a little work I could get her back in the water!
How much are you askin' for her?"

"Oh, she's a great little boat," Felix says, forcing a smile.
"Uh, what can I get for you?"

"Now, since she's a great little boat, and we got a great
crew in here—and I'm the skipper—why don't you fix me a
spar varnish and water! Naw, make it a Seabreeze!"

When the interruption has concluded, Doug Brindle, to
his dismay, finds that it has not served to distract the man on
his left.

"So I'm standin' in this guy's office, see, when who
comes in but this really gorgeous-lookin' dame. I mean, she
doesn't just come in, but sorta *slinks* in, you know, like she's
some sorta model or stripper, or something. And hell, she *coulda*
been a model; you shoulda seen those knockers! Believe me, she
really had it in the dairy case! Now listen to this. Are you listenin'?" The man jabs Doug with his elbow. "Listen to this.
'Maybe you'd like to take a coupla pictures of *me* with that great
big camera of yours,' she says, and she props herself up on the
boss's desk and sticks her chest out. 'And who, may I ask, are

you?' I say, you know, tryin' to keep my cool. 'Oh, I'm Mr. . . ,'
well, I can't tell you *that*, 'I'm *Mr. X's* secretary.' So we talk for a
few minutes, and then this guy comes in that I call 'Mr. Muscles'
(you can change the nickname if you want to). Well, 'Mr. Muscles' goes over and kisses the dame, and asks her if she's all
right, you know, like I've been puttin' the make on her. Then he
turns and stares me up and down, and I'm thinkin' I'm gonna
get my damn *clock* cleaned. Now, you shoulda seen this guy. You
listenin'? He's wearin' a tee-shirt and jeans, and I'm tellin' you,
that tee-shirt was bein' stretched nearly to bustin'. I mean, this
guy had a body like a garbage bag full of door knobs."

Doug looks away, and sees Flipper McDougal taking a
seat at the end of the bar.

"Uh, look," he says to the eager raconteur. "This is all
very interesting, really it is. But I'm afraid there are other projects I'm working on, right now. Maybe you could find somebody else who'd help you—"

"Hey now, it doesn't all have to be about industrial photography! I realize industrial photography isn't the most glamorous subject in the world! But I got plenty of other stories!
Like the things that've gone on in the union. You wouldn't *believe* the things I've seen go on in the union. And if you and me
was to collaborate, I could smooth 'em out, then you'd just have
to write 'em down."

"I'm afraid I don't have time. Besides, someone's come
in, an associate of mine, that I have to discuss some important
business with. If you'll excuse me—"

"Hey, don't you think we could work together? Hell, I
think we'd make a helluva team!"

"No. Sorry. Can't do it. Now, please, excuse me. I have to have a few words with my associate."

"You sure? Would *he* wanna do it?"

"No, I'm afraid he's busy, too."

Doug Brindle thinks, *this is it, I'm not going to say another word.* Backing off the stool, and commending himself for resisting this attempt to pry him away from his more lofty ambitions, he sidles through the smoke and bodies toward the friendly companionship of Flipper McDougal.

The noise he hears nearly makes him dive for cover.

From the kitchen comes the clatter of breaking dishes. Following Debbie Fensen through the Out door, Courtney Johnson had sensed that she didn't have her tray balanced properly. He watched her try to steady it, then as it tipped backward, lurched forward and—holding his own tray clear—buoyed it back up. Two platters shot past him, however, and crashed to the floor. Now Debbie stands with her back to the door, tears forming. Dave Lindholm peers beneath the plate rack, scowls, and turns back to his range; other waiters and waitresses, stepping around the mess and heading out the In door, offer consolation. Finally Debbie gives in, puts her head down, and weeps uncontrollably. Servers filing into the kitchen with a *who-did-it* expression only make matters worse. When she eventually regains a semblance of composure, she realizes that two of the dinners can be salvaged, but she must confront Dave and Lenny with the culinary masterpieces that must be redone. Dave studies the orders on the wire, and pretends to be oblivious. *So it happened,* he thinks; *no use rubbing it in.* Debbie looks at him as if he were wielding a razor strop.

"Hey, it's only dead fish!" he calls to her. He glances at the dupes on the wire and waits for her to smile. His *sous-chef* comes over:

"Hey, didja hear the one about the society lady and the party she gave at Thanksgiving? She's got all her guests at the table, see, and the butler comes in carrying a great big, magnificent turkey on a platter. But a cat scoots between his legs, he trips, and the whole thing goes over—splat—right on the floor! The society lady doesn't bat an eye. 'Wickerstiff,' she says. 'Please have this little unpleasantness cleaned up, and then bring us the *other turkey*.'"

It takes Debbie a moment to get it, during which she relaxes and her face softens.

"So sprinkle some parsley on those vegetables!" Dave orders, "and take out the two dinners you have. Tell 'em *somebody in the kitchen* dropped somethin'. We'll have the other two plates up by the time you get back."

Under the chefs' gentle prodding, Debbie smiles, wipes her face, and goes to do it.

Lenny flashes Dave a look of horror:

"'Dead fish,' huh? Didja ever come upon that Oriental dish where they pan-fry the whole thing, live, first one side, then the other, so it's still wigglin' when it comes to your table?"

"Hey man, I'm a cook, not an animal tamer!" Dave calls back. "And frankly, I'm not partial to sushi, either!"

As Polly Schreiber picks up an order of fettucine and a couple of artichokes from the steamer, she overhears the repartee between the two chefs. At one of her tables is an oriental couple who have made sure to let her know, right from the start, what discriminating diners they are, and how sophisticated is the food in their own country. *Now the couple are acting like culinary judges before whom she must prove herself. Oh well,* she thinks. *It takes all kinds.* As she makes her way through the dining room, the new waitress—*a figure Dutch couldn't resist*—grabs her by the elbow.

"Golly," says the girl. "I've drawn a complete blank. Do you remove dishes from the right, or from the left?"

With a figure like yours, who cares? Polly thinks. *No, fair is fair. You're a good worker, and totally lacking in vanity.*

"Oh, it's simple!" she says. "It's like politics! You *serve* from the left, and *remove* from the right."

The girl repeats the formula as though committing it to memory. "But I don't see what that has to do with politics," she says.

They smile and go their separate ways. As she returns to the kitchen, Polly notices that the oriental gentleman is fiddling with his artichoke, poking and stabbing it as though it were a snapping turtle. *Aha!* she thinks, and makes a mental note to give him a word of instruction. Mike Passini, the busboy, however, is at her side, and whispering that he has a story he must, he absolutely *must* tell her.

Apparently Roy Oberholzer is at it again. The waiter to whom Dutch had had to give his "flip-flop" speech had gotten the message, all right, indeed is now so adept at badgering people that the other servers consider him the master of "Discipline Dining." For the others, mimicking Roy behind his back has become a favorite pastime. "What? You don't like your food? You eat your dinner! If you don't eat your dinner, you'll be punished! And don't take all night about it! I have other customers waiting for this table! You do as I say, you hear me, or I'll get my whips! You wouldn't want me to get my *whips*, would you? You wouldn't want me to get my *whips and chains*?"

Then there was the Saturday night when Roy got confused, and reversed two patrons' orders. The first had already taken a bite from his, but Roy raced across the floor and grabbed it out from under him. "That's not yours!" he shouted, and—hurrying to the second diner—snatched *his* dinner and replaced it: "*Here's* yours!" Then back to the first, who sheepishly accepted his replacement.

"So I'm clearing the table next to where he's taking orders," Mike Passini says, "and I hear this woman ordering a steak. She wants it *very* rare, she's super-concerned that it's not going to come out rare enough. She keeps nagging Roy about it. 'I want it positively blue,' she says. Roy dutifully notes it down. Someone else orders something, and she interrupts again: 'I don't care if its *heart* is still beating.' Everyone finishes ordering, and she starts in yet again. Finally Roy loses his patience. 'Madame,' he says, drawing himself up, 'I will instruct the chef to place your steak very briefly between the legs of a deeply suntanned, adolescent boy.'"

Polly breaks into laughter, suppresses it, and they split apart, each wondering who to tell the story to next.

"Have I got one for you!" Polly says to Lee Castleton, who is loitering behind a ficus tree. "Remind me later!"

Lee does not show any interest.

"Hey, what's the matter with you?"

"Oh, nothing. I've just got a bunch of sitters and

talkers, regular campers. I can't seem to budge them. And as our fearless leader says, 'time is money.'"

"Ah, you need to take a refresher course in Discipline Dining! Talk to Roy! Meanwhile, don't worry! 'They also serve who only stand and wait'!"

Polly sashays into the kitchen, parks her menus by the door, clips her dupes to the wire, grabs a serving tray and stops at the bread locker, then ladles dressings onto several salads. She hoists the tray up, threads her way out of the kitchen, and heads out to Table 3. She serves up her orders, and turns to go and check on the oriental couple.

Oh my god.

The entire artichoke has disappeared.

Hearing strains of "Summertime," Lee Castleton glances across the room at Ed Shakey. She appreciates the advice he has given her recently. Dutch had been showering her with attention for about a week, and on Tuesday had offered to drive her home. "Why don't we stop at my place for a nightcap?" he said. *How could she have been so naive? How could she not have known he was going to make a pass at her?* He had not been very subtle about it, in fact had said there were lots of other girls who could be "accommodating." He hadn't exactly come right out and said her job was on the line, but that was pretty much what he meant. Luckily, she talked to Ed, who reminded her that Dutch had "a reputation" and she shouldn't take it seriously, in fact she should come to work just as if nothing had happened.

Fortunately she had taken his advice, because nothing *had* happened, and Dutch had acted more embarrassed than anything else. But Ed has his own marital problems, she learned: a wife who resented his being out six nights a week, and felt he wasn't giving her enough help with their baby. So she and Ed had gone out to Chowderville's, a few times, and danced. What a consolation to have a friend like that.

As she returns to her duties, Lee again glances across the room at Ed, but Ed has his eyes on the keyboard and doesn't see her. Still chafing over the way the previous evening's fireworks display had disrupted his music, he concludes "Summertime," and begins "Mean to Me." He had practically been trampled by people scurrying to the windows for a view, and when the fireworks were over, the only thing anybody wanted to hear was "Happy Birthday." After that, there was a call for "God Bless America," and that in turn roused all the other teary-eyed sentimentalists. "Do you know 'America the Beautiful'?" one lady asked. "How about 'It's a Grand Old Flag'? Well you *must* know 'I'm a Yankee Doodle Dandy'!"

No, lady, I don't know 'I'm a Yankee Doodle Dandy.' My repertoire is limited to about five hundred tunes, and inasmuch as I don't get many calls at high school assemblies and YMCA campfires, there're a few I'm a little rusty on. But you'll be glad to know that a real piano player is coming in soon. I'm just sitting in, see. But this other guy knows every song ever written.

Ed discreetly scans the room.

"Play something we know the words to!" someone calls.

A lady whose figure suggests gargantuan appetites approaches the stand. *Oh lord, don't let her sing,* Ed thinks. She hikes herself up on the stand, and as if she were settling a bet made at her table says:

"Do you know 'I'm a Ding Dong Daddy From Dumas'?"

"No, I don't know that one," Ed replies. "Sorry."

"Oh, sure you do! *Everybody* knows that one!" The lady wags her finger at the keyboard as if all the elements of the tune were lurking there. "Just start it; it'll come to you! I'm sure if you get the first few notes, the rest'll come to you!"

Ed holds his ground. She persists: "You don't know 'I'm a Ding Dong Daddy from Dumas'? You know, 'I'm a ding dong daddy from Dumas, do you wanna see me do m'*stuff*?' " Helpless now, she looks imploringly at the folks at her table. Ed begins another tune, and finally, like an elephant decamping from a circus stool, the woman steps off the platform and returns to her seat.

To prove that despite temporary lapses he is a bona fide piano player, the genuine article, he hauls out the frills and trills, and concludes the set with "Misty."

As he gets up and wanders across the restaurant, people smile at him.

"We love your music!" someone calls. "Come over here, will you?"

Ed goes to the speaker's table.

"You play very, very nicely," the lady says. "What do you do for a living?"

Ed is taken aback. "Well, this *is* my living," he says, finally, and moves on.

He must get out of there—even if it means forgoing a

drink at the bar. Remembering that he promised his wife he would get a few things at the grocery store, he waves to Felix, eases through the knots of people waiting to be seated, and wanders out onto Bay Street.

At thirty-seven Ed already exhibits the features of the species, *Career piano player, bar and restaurant*. He carries his hands like tools on loan, his fingers curling up inside his palms, and like noodles, his arms hang limply from rounded shoulders. There is a tentative quality to the way he walks, a fastidiousness that comes from having to protect his means of livelihood from damage or destruction. As he heads up Bay Street and past the village green and Town Hall, he is both a world unto himself, and a sort of soft and pudgy public commodity: like the seashell art, beach towels, and saltwater taffy he passes, something for sale. His destination is the Beach Variety Store, but the earrings in a shop window catch his eye; he goes over to have a closer look. Should he buy them—or some other little gift—for Helen? At the top of the window there is a stained-glass ornament dangling from a plastic suction cup. *Pacifier*, he thinks. *Remember to buy pacifier*.

As he rejoins the sea of humanity and again becomes engulfed in the crowd, he is alternately fascinated and repulsed by what he sees: teenagers with punk haircuts; girls with raccoon eyes; gay men walking what appear to be gay dogs; kids on bicycles and skateboards; women pushing baby strollers filled with beer; people with ice cream, fishing rods, knapsacks; muscular men in lettered tee-shirts—EVERYONE HAS TO BELIEVE IN SOMETHING, I BELIEVE I'LL HAVE ANOTHER DRINK. I LOVE EVERYBODY, YOU'RE NEXT. IF IT DOESN'T FIT, FORCE

IT. *But why is Helen being so moody and irritable?* he thinks. *She has a good voice and a modicum of training, but does she really have the talent for a career in musical theater?* Among the potpourri of smells, he detects the aromas of hot dogs and cotton candy, stale beer and warm fudge, hamburgers and pizza, musk oil and patchouli; as he heads to the curb to make room for a car with hood scoops, he gets a whiff of bayberry candles, scented soap. *But suppose she doesn't make it through the summer? She's already getting restless, and talking about going back to the city. Is it time she saw a therapist?*

He passes Smuggler's Alley, where some manic-looking kids are hovering over spin-drip paintings, and glances in the video arcade next door. As he approaches the Gaslight Café, a pianist—it must be Dicky St. Regis—is just concluding a sing-along with some loud, bombastic chords. Ed finds the spectacle loathsome, but from professional curiosity—or rather, instincts of territoriality—stops to make an appraisal. As usual, Dicky is all giggles and fluff. Controlling a roomful of people from behind an out-of-tune spinet piano is not easy, but Dicky is doing it. He carries on some banter with the people closest to him, then shouts: "Are there any newlyweds in the house? Raise your hands!" Finally a couple near the window meekly complies. "Hey, it's nice to see you up and around!" Dicky squeals. "Now here's a song I wrote one night while waiting for a round of applause; it's called 'I'll Be Your Franklin Stove if You'll Be My Duraflame Log.'" The audience winces and groans, and Dicky, looking misunderstood—thenwinking and preening—vamps an intro.

Feeling better about his own talent, Ed moves on.

Ignoring Vodka Man and some other bums in the alley

next to it, Ed finds a consoling refuge in the Beach Variety Store. He waves to the woman behind the counter, whom he has known for years, and makes his way among the narrow aisles, picking up dog food, tuna fish, a pacifier, a box of diapers, and toilet tissue.

"How are things at the Dockside tonight?" says the woman at the cash register. "You busy?"

"Jammed. Absolutely hammered. The whole town's crazy-full-up. The center of town is a regular zoo."

The woman leans forward over the counter and speaks confidentially:

"Say, you didn't hear anything about a big drug shipment coming in on one of the fishing boats, did you?"

"No. I don't get much gossip sitting behind the piano. And I don't use the stuff myself."

His eye falls on the headline of a newspaper. TROOP BUILDUP CONTINUES IN WAR ZONE. Against his will, he glances at the headline beneath it. FATHER MURDERS WIFE AND FOUR CHILDREN, TAKES LIFE. He tries to put the headlines out of mind. The woman bags his purchases. He wishes her well, and pushes through the screen door, and out to the bustling street.

"Thank you, thank you very much, ladies and gentlemen!" Dicky is screaming, as he re-passes the Gaslight Café. "I'm going to change the pace now, slow things down a little." *Change the pace. Slow things down a little.* Was there ever a piano-bar player in the history of the world who didn't *change the pace, slow things down a little*? "My next song—and this is serious, folks—is about a young boy with a terminal illness who my mother and

I found living all alone in the woods. The boy had been diag-
nosed with a disease of the lymphatic system, and my mother
and I took him in, and made it our sacred duty to nurse him
back to health. We were eventually able to get him the help he
needed, and now the doctors say his future is—yes, you guessed
it, ladies and gentlemen—bright! This song, then, is about the
most powerful force in our lives! Love! Yes, I'm talking about
love!"

Feeling a little overwhelmed, Ed returns to the Dockside, squeezes through the crowd in the foyer, and places his
bag beneath the reception desk. He shakes out his fingers and
tries to decide what he will play first. All he can conjure up,
however, is the maze of faces, the hustle and bustle on Bay
Street. It is one of those times when he can't think of a single
tune; the thought that he has never known more than a handful
of tunes paralyzes him. As he sits down at the piano, there is a
vague heightening of anticipation. He almost comes up with
something, but its title is occluded by the words, TROOP
BUILDUP CONTINUES IN WAR ZONE, FATHER MURDERS
WIFE AND FOUR CHILDREN, TAKES LIFE. He tries to relax. He
knows that in practically any of his pockets he will find old set
lists, and these will give him the inspiration he needs. He
reaches in his shirt pocket, and unfolds the paper he finds there.

Dog food
Tuna fish
Diapers
Pacifier
TP

He feels like he has been sitting there for hours. He gazes across the room and sees Lee Castleton smiling at him. Oh, why not? What could it hurt? There are new people in the room, and besides, who's listening? He adjusts the bench, begins a leisurely introduction to "Summertime," and suddenly his mind fills with lots of other tunes he wants to play: "You'd Be So Nice to Come Home To," "My One and Only Love," "I Don't Want to Set the World on Fire." Then he will go down to E flat and do "Tenderly," "Moonlight in Vermont," and "Isn't it Romantic."

As he begins to play, the atmosphere in the restaurant brightens; there is an intimation of peace, order, and harmony, a reinforcement of the sense that dinners are coming smoothly off the line, and that people may relax and enjoy what is being prepared for them. Ed invents a melodic filler, and another and another.

Bright, bouncy music fills the room, and with the festive nonchalance of the *Titanic*, the show goes on.

SEVEN

It stands like a shrine in the hot sand and bright sunlight of Oyster Shell Road, Joe Gallagher's service station does, and the cars and tires littering the asphalt around it, the parts piled on the hill behind it, might be the gifts of pilgrims, the residue of sacred rituals that have gone on for centuries. Although the building is of simple cinderblock construction, there is a hint of Art Deco about it which makes it a memorable presence upon the landscape; the antique signs and lettering, and the way the plate glass windows frame anyone working in the office, enhance this effect.

As they pull into the station and their car sputters to a halt, the building is so bright that the young man and woman who emerge from it must shield their eyes from its glare. They peer in the office window, then move uncertainly toward the dark, cave-like bays. Because everything is bathed in grease and shadow, the darkness within is disorienting, at first; it takes a moment for the couple to realize that two men are at work. At the rear of the bay, one is masked by a car's upturned hood; the other is visible only in legs that kick and turn beneath a car raised on jack stands. On the back wall, between a rack of fan belts and an assortment of hoses and gaskets, there is an out-of-date calendar showing a discreetly draped pin-up; nearby, over a bench piled with tools, there's a sign saying CASH MAKES NO ENEMIES, LET'S BE FRIENDS. Beneath it (as if understatement could not be trusted), there is another: POSITIVELY NO CHECKS.

In the way that air seems thicker inside a church than outside, and the stillness more still, the coal-black forge exhibits an almost theological peacefulness, a tranquility seemingly frozen in time.

Now there is a message from some faraway place where the gods are at play: "Full count, runners at first and third. Carson on deck."

The voice recedes, and the wayside shrine fills with the miscellaneous cheering, rustling, and whistling of an anonymous crowd.

"Top of the fifth," the voice says, as though speaking from, and describing, a game played twenty years previously. There's a sharp *crack*. "It's a long fly ball to deep left! Way back, way back—what a drive, this one could be gone!—it goes into the stands about seven rows in! Home run!"

As though the couple needed this burst of excitement in a far-off stadium to break the ice for them, the young man finally says:

"Uh, 'scuse me. Anybody home?"

The legs kick and turn beneath the near automobile, and a metallic pounding begins. Eventually the other man backs out from under the hood and, wiping his hands on a greasy pink rag, comes forward.

"What can I do for you?"

There is an air of the surgeon about the man. Because people come to Joe Gallagher only when they have problems, each pointing to his car and asking, in so many words, *can this child be saved?*, he has developed an impervious, businesslike manner. Practical to a fault, Joe doesn't believe in making repairs designed to last a hundred thousand miles on cars that have only ten thousand miles left in them, and will scavenge parts from the junkers on the hill behind his shop if they will do the work of new ones. Knowing that nothing lasts forever, he nevertheless enjoys trying to beat the odds. He would rather keep an old car going than do routine maintenance on a new one, and regards his work as an endless process of patching up: his war with attrition. The older the car, the more he likes to work on it, which is why people in Sun Town who tinker with cars—street rodders and do-it-yourselfers—regard him as their friend and mentor. Despite the notices on his walls, they know how casual he can be about money.

Being new to the town, the newcomers don't know that, about a year ago, it was discovered that thousands of gallons of Joe's gasoline had leaked into the town's water supply. The town had seen lean times and changing times, it had seen honky-tonk and commercialism replace picture-postcard solitude, it had seen land values fluctuate and personal values somersault, but this was its real loss of innocence, this was the judgment it feared most: that the problems people moved to Sun Town to leave behind were destined to follow, that contrary to its self-image, there was little difference between it and the rest of the world. Where the talk of the town had previously turned on fishing, in-laws, and high-school sports, it now reflected concern about tetraethyl lead and benzene, rashes and headaches, brain damage and mental disorders. The town had begun getting its water from an auxiliary wellfield, but because the field had to be overpumped in order to meet demand, the sodium content had reached worrisome levels; a summary of parts-per-million was now a weekly feature of the Sun Town *Star*. What was the world coming to when you couldn't go to the kitchen sink, and simply fill a glass with water? What was the world coming to when supermarkets *sold* water? While Joe sat in his office and ruefully watched, state and local officials turned up by the carful, and probed and tested; meanwhile an argument went forward about who was at fault. Joe protested that he pumped gas primarily as a convenience for his shop customers, and that doing so wasn't even profitable; it had never occurred to him to replace his old pumps and tanks. He had recently changed distributors, he explained, and hadn't noticed the loss of gasoline. Because so many lawsuits were threatened, a lawyer for the company that supplied Joe's gas was hired, and because so much depended upon his interpretation of the data, Joe hired another lawyer to deal with *him*.

Now he stands at the threshold of the bay, turns the pink rag over in his hands, and listens to the young man's description of his problem.

"Every so often, for the last couple of days, she would simply konk out. I thought maybe it was the pancake thing on top of the motor, the generator I guess"—*air filter*, thinks Joe—"so I took the top off and looked in it. Then when I put her back on again, she seemed to run just fine. But yesterday afternoon she developed a knocking sound—how did you describe it, honey, a kind of 'pinging' in the back—I think it's something in the axle"—*one of the universals, perhaps a wheel bearing*—"but I decided to keep driving anyway. Well, we were coming over the

bridge, yesterday, and I realized that the pinging had stopped."
Piece of metal in the brake lining. Finally got worn down.

"I think it's the spark plugs," says the young woman.

"So we stayed in a motel, overnight, and set out again this morning"—the young man shoots a furious look at the girl, as if it were clearly not the spark plugs and he had said so all along—"and I was thinking maybe I needed an oil change. For a while we didn't have any more trouble, but—sure enough—today around lunchtime she started konking out again. And you know what I found? I found the car runs better at high speeds than at low! If I'm speeding along on the highway, she does just fine, but the minute I slow down—and especially if I stop—that's when I have trouble! We just did make it into town, here, and you, uh, well, you were the first gas station we came to."

Realizing his torrent of words hasn't produced much by way of explanation, the young man trails off. Now the mechanic under the second car slides out on his body dolly and mumbles something about transmissions.

"There's a shot, a line drive to right!" says a voice from some faraway place where the gods are at play. "Doesn't quite clear the wall! Hits the wall and takes a bounce! But Carson is going to reach second standing up. That means the tying run is on, and there's still nobody out."

As if his mind had been on transmissions all along, Joe steps into the shadows and says something to his assistant. As he turns back to the anxiously waiting couple, he waves to Bill Packard, who is going by in his pick-up.

"Why don't you start 'er up?"

Pleased by the attention he is receiving, the young man

goes and gets in the crippled car. He turns the motor over and over until it finally catches; when it begins to fade, he guns it to a roar. It starts to quit, and he catches it and nudges it back to life; it starts to die again, and he catches it. But this time no amount of pumping the pedal, and no amount of pleaful glances at Joe, are sufficient to save it. He turns the key again.

"Hold it right there," Joe orders.

"Could it be water in the gas?" the girl says.

The young man gets out and looks anxiously at Joe: *Can this child be saved?*

Joe turns the rag over in his hands, and wipes a smear off his forearm:

"When was the last time you had a tune-up?"

The couple stare at one another. There is an awkward silence, then the young man says:

"Uh, what's a tune-up?"

"Ball four!" comes the voice from the grease-stained radio in the back. "He walked him! Merrick is going out to the mound now, he wants to talk things over. Yannos and Scorsman are warming in the bullpen."

You have a volatile liquid that you've refined from oil: it's only natural you'd try to put its volatility to use. You mix some air with the liquid and produce a gas, you apply a spark to the gas and—boom—you get an explosion. Slowly it dawns on you that you can use the explosion to push on something, to do work. Joe removes the air filter from its pan, throws it in the trash, and, unconsciously trying to assuage his irritation at the young couple's ignorance, gives to himself the lecture he would like to give them. *Let's say you use the explosion to push on a piston inside a cylinder, and with a connecting rod transfer its movement to a crankshaft; why, you've turned the crankshaft a little!* He glances over the engine compartment for obvious signs of problems, and takes a screwdriver out of his pocket and pries the distributor cap off. *But what are you going to do with the exhaust that's left above the piston? Well, maybe the piston could push it out as its momentum carries it upward again.* He inspects the distributor cap, nudges it to the side, and disconnects several spark plug wires. *But you can't push the exhaust through a port where new gas is coming in, so you'd better have one port for gas, another for exhaust.* As he inspects the points, he continues addressing his thoughts to a mental image of the young couple. *Maybe some rods connected to the crankshaft could operate valves that would open and close the ports at the right—the precisely correct—times. You could have a smaller shaft do this work, a camshaft we'll call it, and connect this camshaft to the crankshaft.* He stares at the points, and frowns; as he walks over to the parts cabinet, he hurls them in the trash. He runs his finger down the boxes, finds what he wants, and after rummaging around on a shelf nearby, locates a set of spark plugs and a condenser. *Torque*, he thinks as he replaces each of the spark plugs. *Just enough, but not too much force.* He adjusts the gap on the points, replaces the condenser, snaps the spark plug wires back in place, then the distributor cap, and goes and gets in the car.

Magazines and trash litter the front seat, and he shoves them out of the way. *Trail mix*, he thinks, glancing at the crumpled package. *The only trail these kids know is probably the Interstate.* He turns the key in the ignition, and the motor runs roughly.

He catches it as it quits and revs it again, then lets it return to idle. It coughs and sputters to a halt. *Gas flow*, he thinks, irritably leaning over and retrieving a magazine he has knocked off the seat. *Peace Through Nonviolence*, it says. He hauls himself out, goes to the front of the car, and, leaning over the engine, pries back the choke valve and nudges the throttle arm. There is a whiff of gas as fumes drift up; he backs out from under the hood and wipes his hands on his rag. *Peace Through Nonviolence. Yeah, sure, is this engine nonviolent? Pistons are slamming down with two tons of pressure, the crankshaft's turning two thousand times a minute, and a hundred times a second, sparks are flying out of the coil. You stand in the wrong place while you're revving the motor, and a fan blade can fly off and go right through your neck. Put your hand on the carburetor at the wrong time, it'll blow your fingers off. A jack slips—or the car ain't solid on the lift—and the damn thing'll crush you. You think cars aren't violent, just stand under a bridge on a busy highway and listen to 'em. Believe me, when a machine has a capacity for danger that must be carefully controlled, it's violent.*

Regulating the motor using the throttle arm, Joe yanks the wire off the number one spark plug and holds it close to the block. In tiny bursts, a spark arcs across to it; it looks at first like a good clean spark. *And if one day they go to electric cars? Why, it'll be the same damn thing. Kids like these won't have any idea how they work, or how to fix 'em. But they'll be drivin' 'em, oh yes, they'll be drivin' 'em. And they'll be talkin' all the while about peace and nonviolence, and gettin' up with expensive high-tech music instruments and singin' about the simple life, the good old days. And when their cars, their instruments and amplifiers break down? Why, they'll bring 'em to some old fool like me to fix 'em.*

*

On a cold January night exactly six months before, Bill Packard had been sitting in his living room contemplating the fire on his hearth. He was well aware that the heat lost up the chimney was as great as, or greater, than what the fire threw into the room, but it pleased him to see the flames dancing quietly, exuding their cheerful warmth. He made no connection, furthermore, between the fires he was paid to extinguish and those on his hearth. He reasoned that the fire chief's fire was no different than the postman's mail.

Bill studied the burning shards of wood, scraps from a construction site that John Savoy brought him, and noticed how smoke puffed out in tiny geysers, how flame, as it reduced pieces of trees to flimsy latticework, revealed their interior structure, how shards of burning wood had separate and distinct personalities. Here was a ghost, there the outline of a bird, here a laughing face, there a goblin. Was there an unconscious revenge in seeing matter consumed by flame? he asked himself. An illicit pleasure in generating these little rituals of destruction? No, it was more primordial than that. It was the pleasure of seeing matter transformed into heat, comfort, and coziness, the intuition of a connection to primitive folks—the visceral experience of the equation: fire equals survival. He could hear wind crackling in the trees outside, and whipping the power lines; a stark white moon, investigating everything like a cold menacing eye, revealed how brittle and fragile the world had become. There had been something frightening, that night, in the combination of bright light and piercing cold, something that cast thoughts as well as things into sharp, clear outlines. Company: one could not have too much company, on a night like this, and a fire on his hearth was the sort of company Bill found very consoling. *Inside, outside. Me, us, here. Them, there, elsewhere.* His house, with its plume of smoke wafting into the night air, was little more than a tiny hut on a vast plain, and the distance between the inside and outside of a lighted window never greater.

Now his pager squealed: "Fire at the corner of Bay Street and Smuggler's Alley," the dispatcher said.

Suddenly, he was all business. He replaced the fire screen, put on a heavy sweater and his fireboots, and called to his wife upstairs. He walked quickly to his truck, yanked out the engine-warming cable, and got in; the rest of his turnout gear was on the seat beside him. There were blasts from the fire horn on top of Town Hall, the honks of a crazed or wounded animal: three honks and then silence, three honks and then silence. In the distance, doors slammed, cars and trucks materialized in the streets; through the denuded trees, red lights twinkled and sirens wailed; from near and far an urgent commotion pierced the tranquility of the town. Now there were flashing lights on Crescent Street, as bulky engine and ladder trucks filled it with their rumble and sent vibrations up the side lanes. There were voices, quick, nervous, and efficient, on Bill's radio.

Now they converged. Men who minutes before had been snug inside their homes pulled hoses from accordion folds, worked wrenches on frozen hydrants, adjusted lights, donned air packs. At the rear of the fireground, electric meters were pulled, propane tanks unplugged and dragged away; axes and pike poles were applied to stubborn doors. At first, the fire appeared to be confined to the ground floor of the building, but this floor housed a shop full of baskets, candles, and paper goods. Bill looked up and appraised the direction of the wind. Bare tree branches clicked and scraped, eerie white clouds sailed smoothly, effortlessly across the sky. *The town on a night like this was a tinderbox, a powder keg, and everybody knew it. And nowhere were the structures more closely sandwiched than in Smuggler's Alley.* Through his excitement, through his sleeve ends and boot tops, he could already feel the cold.

The interior attack began. The hiss of steam sounded over the muscular whine of the pumpers, and the smack of water against flame generated thick smoke that engulfed the firefighters as it was sucked out into the night air. There was more steam—purposely generated—but more fire; it played hide-and-seek among the walls, leapt up with stark clarity and was beaten back, only to dart up somewhere else. In fractured slices of black, red, and orange, men moved among the hoselines, took turns at the nozzle ends, crouched in the side entrances, studied pump pressures, discussed alternatives. As if it were a large complicated toy, men climbed onto the turntable of the aerial ladder. It rose slowly off its cradle and began turning; there was a flicker of light in a third-story window, and a fireman with a pike pole climbed the ladder to investigate. Bracing himself against the ladder, he jammed the pole through the window, and shards of glass crashed down into the street. A fireman with a charged line moved to replace him.

Like a trick match which, when lighted and blown out, bursts into flame again, the fire was tenacious and unpredictable. It would yield to the blanket of water being played on it from several directions, then some new storeroom full of crated giftware would ignite, and the building would again fill with dancing light. Forty minutes went by, during which the surrounding trees whispered quietly and the fish-eyed moon moved slowly across the sky. And men and machines, drawing water at the maximum rate possible, could only stay even with it. Icicles formed on dormers and eaves, water poured off the firemen's helmets, cascaded down the alley in shiny rivers, froze in slippery puddles. Now sheets of flame curled up the outside of the structure, threatening the adjacent buildings, and a deluge gun was played on it. At one A.M., the Sand Bar Discotheque emptied out, and a huge crowd—aware for the first time of what could only be considered a *better show*—gathered at the edge of the scene, talking excitedly, shivering. Half an hour later, when the interior of the building was dark and Bill believed he had the fire knocked down, the building's owner, Herb Solomon, arrived and told him the cockloft was full of wicker, candles, and lamp oil. At that moment, an intense orange light filled the vents that had been hacked through the roof, flames reached like snakes' tongues out the gable ends, and like an exploding volcano, the top of the building went up.

It was as if the lid had been blown off the entire town.

Three hundred yards to the bay, Bill said to himself. *Throwing everything we have at it, but what we have isn't enough. Plenty of capacity in the apparatus, but damn eight-inch mains don't yield sufficient pressure. Pumper number three hemmed in by the apparatus on the street, not a good situation. Impossible to reposition the apparatus and keep pumping. But if pumper number three could draw from the bay. . . . Three hundred yards, across the street and down Fisher's Boat Yard. Not an easy pull. Eighteen lengths. Have to drag the line by hand. Five, seven, eight minutes. The men already tired.*

When Joe Gallagher arrived at the scene, that night, what he witnessed made him very uncomfortable. It was the contagion, the sheer contagion of it. *Feeding on itself like gossip*, he thought. *Fanning the flames of smoldering anger.* He stood in the shadows behind the perspiring disco dancers, and as the fire burned in his eyes, it seemed to accuse him personally. Feeling unwelcome at yet another town disaster—feeling his very presence might be a bad omen—he had resolved, when he left his sister and brother-in-law's house, to go straight home. Spotting the flames from as far away as Millrace Road, however, he had realized the town's entire waterfront was in danger. Now he stood in the freezing shadows, crossing his arms and clamping down on his gloveless fingers. *For six months, now, the undercurrent of bad feeling wherever he was known. The talk, the suspicion, the anger and resentment. Water water everywhere, the children sang, but not a drop to drink!*

"Hey Joe," said a cop. "Come over here, wouldja?"

Startled, he wondered if even here—even now—he was going to face recriminations.

The cop motioned him to the front of the crowd:

"They got a little problem with pumper number three," he said, putting his hand on Joe's shoulder. "Any chance you'd give 'em a hand?"

Joe quickly appraised the flames on the roof, and beneath falling cinders and foul-smelling spray, scrabbled down Smuggler's Alley; he could see that pumper number three was the last defense against the fire's spreading laterally. But its hood was up. He joined the knot of firemen standing at the front of the truck.

The radio crackled with orders from Bill Packard. The pumper captain quietly explained the problem to him.

"Okay, fellas," he said. "Step aside. Let him in there."

Joe raised his foot to the bumper, and hoisted himself up to confront the motor.

"Three and two," says a voice from some faraway place where the gods are at play. "In the month of July, Calderra, who bats left, is hitting three-twenty-eight."

"Well I'll be damned."

Joe says it out loud, as though irritated at, even a little disappointed in his discovery; there is a stillness associated with problem-solving in the shop, a meditative, theological peacefulness. Having ruled out the other causes of the problem, Joe has a shop blanket over his head, and with the car's hood pulled down over him is studying the problem in darkness. The car's engine idles roughly and begins to fail. As he nudges the throttle arm, the blanket slips from his shoulders. He steps back, adjusts it, and bends forward again.

At the top of the coil, a spark is arcing inside a crack. Farther down in the engine, another spark is leaping from the battery cable to the block.

"Well, I'll be damned," he repeats. Yanking the wire out of the coil, he kills the motor.

"There's a one-hopper to the shortstop, this should be an easy out. Britton has it and throws to first, and that retires the side. With five hits that pushed three runs across, the score is seven to one."

"Why, he practically saved the entire town!" people said, when the story of the Great Fire—the myth concocted out of all the little stories—came to be constructed. "If it hadn't been for Joe Gallagher, the entire Alley might have gone up!"

"And the way the winds were, taken the entire water-front with it! A fire like that could have leveled every building for ten or fifteen blocks!"

"And then jumped across Bay Street!"

"It's just lucky Bill Packard ran a feeder line to the bay, because they were drawing all the water they could! They were at the point where all they could do was cross their fingers, and pray!"

"This whole town's nothing but matchsticks; it wouldn't take much to wipe it right off the map!"

"And if Joe hadn't gotten pumper number three going, they would've laid all that line for nothing. They would never have had the water they needed."

"But why did it take Herb Solomon so long to arrive? Those guys ended up having to fight two different fires. Anyway, it's just lucky that Joe was around, and was able to get that pumper going."

Although accounts of the fire appeared in the Sun Town *Star* for weeks afterward, when other issues began to reclaim their importance Joe Gallagher's name was no longer mentioned in connection with the contaminated wellfield. Instead it was said that "gasoline from an underground storage tank" had "leaked into the aquifer near the Graham Hollow Wellfield," and that "while studying proposals to effect a clean-up," the town was "considering legal action." A lawyer for the town argued that responsibility for the leak lay not with Joe, but with the company that supplied his gas and owned his tanks. It was obvious to everyone that Joe's means were inadequate to the lawsuits that were threatened, and gradually the town began to close ranks around him, to view him as the innocent victim of large, impersonal forces. Besides, in being where he had been, and doing what he had done for the town, he had for all practical purposes redeemed himself. No one had enjoyed standing in judgment of him, after all. And if a community couldn't stand by one of its own, what kind of community was it?

In the half-light Joe backs away from the car, wonders whether he has a coil in stock. A battery cable, yes, but does he have a coil? As he goes to the parts cabinet, he reflects on the way coils induce voltage changes, and how they occasionally develop cracks on their caps, like the one on that pumper, the previous winter.

"Hello in there!"

The voice is insistent, impatient.

"Be right with you," Joe says, completing his survey of the parts cabinet, and adjacent shelves. He picks up a rag and wipes his hands, and comes forward.

"What can I do for you?"

With a distressed look—as if to say, *can this child be saved?* —the man announces that his car is burning oil. To prove it, he goes out and starts the motor. He races it, and white smoke pours out of the exhaust pipe. Joe notices that the alter-nator is squealing. He walks over to the driver and tells him to cut the engine.

"I'm afraid there's something wrong with my generator, too," says the man. *Alternator.*

Joe opens the hood and notices that the firewall is covered with oil. He feels around the oil pump, checks to make sure the spark plugs are tight. A reflection from a tiny puddle near the water pump housing catches his eye.

"Come over here," he says. "I think you got *two* problems. You're not *burnin'* oil, your oil is gettin' out here, through this worn-out head gasket. That's what's makin' the mess. See? Even your fan and air conditionin' belts are wet. And it's gettin' in the bearins' of your alternator, and that's what's makin' it squeal."

The man looks at him, bewildered.

"Now you're probably usin' too much transmission oil, too. Am I right?"

The man regards him as if he were a shaman, or witch doctor.

"The transmission oil is somethin' different. I suspect your transmission oil is leakin' into the crankcase through your vacuum modulator, and gettin' burnt up inside the motor. That's what's producin' the smoke in your exhaust. I won't know for sure 'til I drop the pan."

"Bottom of the seventh," a voice says from the grease-smudged radio in the back of the shop. "First game of the doubleheader. We're tied at one."

The man, who wears a gaudy neck medallion on a gold chain, takes out a wad of bills and waves them at Joe:

"Any chance you could get right on it? I'm only going to be in town a day or two."

Loping into the station now, as though to a watering hole in the desert, the young man and woman reappear. Finding their car exactly where they left it, they initially assume that Joe has not had time to look at it, worse, that it's beyond rescue. They step around the man with the neck medallion, and follow Joe into his office.

Joe explains what he found, and what he did.

"I checked for a noise in the rear end—you said there was some pingin' or clickin', or somethin'?—but everything looks okay. Brakes are okay, wheel bearins' are okay, universals are fine. Differential's got oil in it. I took her out and drove her some, and she runs real good."

"That's great!" says the young man. "How much do we owe you?"

Joe consults the work sheet by the cash register, and hands the couple the bill. "You needed a new air filter, new battery cables, and a coil, along with plugs, points, and condenser. So that's one-eighteen twenty-four for parts, sixty-four dollars labor. Total of—"

"Can I give you a credit card?"

"Nope. Sorry. Don't take credit cards."

"Why don't you take credit cards?"

"Don't have a credit card machine."

"How come you don't you have a credit card machine?"

"Don't take credit cards."

Joe smiles: *Any more questions?*

The young woman reaches into her purse, and pays in cash.

"Well, we're here, so let's do it!" says her partner. "Why don't you fill 'er up?"

Joe hands the couple their keys, and they go to their car and pull forward to the sleek new pumps on the brand new service island.

"There's a single to right," says a voice from some faraway place where the gods are at play, "played nicely by Coleman. Krieger rounds the bag, and holds."

Dutifully, Joe goes out and pumps the gas.

EIGHT

In the lounge of the Dockside, Denise Lefevre is celebrating Bastille Day with more than the usual patriotic fervor.

"Let's see, I had a madras, then I had a Manhattan. What's next? Oh, I know! How about a margarita?"

There is a howl of laughter from those around her. Felix looks at her skeptically, and she titters like a child with a box of chocolates.

"Oui! C'est bon! Gimme a margarita!"

Not that Denise started at the beginning of the alphabet; by now no one can remember where she *did* start. It's just that downing drinks, this way, is so madcap—and the potential for amusement such an improvement on television—that there is no reason not to drain the skit to its dregs. The regulars begin dilating on what should follow the margarita.

But they're getting out of hand, Felix thinks. As he stocks the bar and prepares for the evening's onslaught, the man who must function as scoutmaster, social director, drink wizard, and policeman feels he is being backed into one of the roles he likes least, that of the disapproving adult who makes everyone else's fun possible. He invokes one of his cardinal rules, *the bartender must run the bar and not let it* be *run*, and notifies Hi-Beams—who is reaching up to the television in the corner—that *he* will change the channel. He pulls a carton of empty beer bottles from beneath the ice sink, and steps up onto it.

"Curve ball, strike one," says a voice from some faraway

place. A batter is knocking dirt off his spikes. "We're in the bottom of the fifth."

"You may be, but I'm not!" someone jeers from the end of the bar. "But I'm gettin' there! I'm gettin' there!"

Felix flips the channel. From the level of its tires, a car is shown bouncing over a rock-filled creek bed. There is an image of a shock absorber, then the words, BUY ONE SHOCK GET ONE FREE.

"Just what the world needs!" someone shouts. "More shocks!"

Standing on the box, Felix plays their game for a minute or two more, then, to make a point, leaves the picture where it is: a soap opera.

"Hey Felix, you know any bar jokes?" Spacey Stacey calls.

"Yeah. I'm lookin' at 'em."

"Aw Felix, come on."

Things quiet down when Dutch wanders in. He takes a seat at the end and begins tapping his fingers on the bar.

"Is everything all right?" he asks Felix.

"Yeah, everything's fine. You want something?"

"Oh, gimme a glass a' soda, I guess. You're *sure* everything's under control?"

Dutch had come in through the kitchen and found his newest pearl diver still working on last night's dishes, but standing in a puddle of soapy water. He was a real smart aleck, this one; prodded for an explanation, he had replied: "In order for something to get clean, something else must get dirty." And the other day, when he had explained to his crew that they were all in the same boat and had to work together, the kid had piped up: "Yeah, but the boat's got a hole in it." Always something, in this business, always something.

Dutch has other things on his mind, however, and after moving down the bar kibitzing and patting people on the back, he goes into the men's room to check the temperature of the hot water, which has been creeping up. While he's drying his hands he reads the instructions on the electric hand dryer. "1. Shake excess water from hands. 2. Push button. 3. Rub hands under nozzle. 4. Dryer stops automatically." And beneath this, in tiny surgical letters, someone has scratched: "*5. Dry hands on pants.*" His face reddens: someone who works for him? For weeks they had debated whether to install electric hand dryers; you would have thought it was a debate over arms control, or abortion rights, or something. Over everyone's objections, he had finally had them installed. And now this. *Always dealing with crowds. Masses of people. Always having to plan for worst-case scenarios. One or two people wash their hands, fine. Fifteen or twenty people wash their hands, weird things begin to happen. Fifty, a hundred people use the bathroom, things go insane. Somebody decides to wash his hair or clean his dentures—who knows what they do?—or leaves the water running, and it overflows and he has to get a plumber to remove the stopper mechanism. Well, at least it's better than what happened at Chowderville's. Guy got stuck in the men's room, couldn't figure out how to unlock the door, and panicked. Tore the entire door off its hinges.*

Irritated by this newest desecration of his restaurant, Dutch goes back in the kitchen and arbitrarily throws his weight around, then, having met with too little resistance to feel satisfied, returns to the lounge. "Hey babe," he calls to Susan Breedon, the sculptor he's had his eye on. "Nice to see you." (Like to see more *of* you.) "What're you doin' this summer?"

"Oh, shakin' sheets up at Herschel's Guest House."

Daydreaming about shaking sheets, Dutch ensconces himself at the bar, and is puzzled when Denise Lefevre's request for a Negroni provokes a burst of laughter. Presently he is joined by a man wearing a large pinky ring and a glossy neck medallion. There is something about the man that Dutch finds unsavory, and after motioning to Felix, he backs off his stool.

The man grabs him.

"You Dutch Dugan?"

"Maybe I am, maybe I'm not. You from the IRS?"

"Well, that's the last thing I am. Name's Tony. We talked on the phone a couple a' times. I'd like to help you with your restaurant business."

"Thanks, but I don't *need* help," Dutch counters. "If you knew how long I been in this busi—"

"You don't *understand*," the man says. "I want to help you with your *restaurant business*. You could at least let me tell you what kinda help I can provide." He takes a sip of his wine and stares at Dutch menacingly. "Now, I realize there're people in here you may not want knowin' your business, so maybe we could go over to one of those tables."

Dutch wants none of it. "Hey pal, if you knew how long I been in this racket—"

"You didn't *hear* me. Why don't we go over to one of those tables, and have a little talk."

In a manner he finds difficult to resist, Dutch finds

himself being ushered away from the bar, and to a table in the corner.

"But I tell you, business isn't that good!" he is soon having to say. The "protection" he is being offered—which amounts to nothing more than someone's agreeing not to torch the place in exchange for a share of the profits—leaves him with an urge to jump up and run out of the restaurant. "Look. I run an honest business, and there just ain't that kinda money!"

The stranger patiently takes a sip of his wine:

"Now come *on*, Dutch. We know how many dinners you're doin'. We know what kinda money there is. Business is good, your business is *good*. That's why we want to become partners with you. —Oh honey!" he calls to Debbie Fensen, who is setting up in the background. "Bring me another glass of wine, will you? It's the Chianti. Thanks, darlin'!"

"But I'm *tellin'* you," Dutch repeats, holding his ground, "business isn't even as good as it was last year. Last Saturday we did only about forty lunches, a hundred and twenty-five dinners. Usually on a Saturday, at this point in the season, we'd do—"

"Now come *on*, Dutch, you can talk to me. 'Cause I'm here to help you. But don't insult me, okay? Don't start givin' me phony numbers. We know how many dinners you did, last Saturday—and Friday and Thursday, and any night in the week, for that matter! You see, Dutch, we got friends in the laundry that does your little cloth napkins. Now the mathematics is simple. One meal, one napkin, am I right? So don't start lyin' to me. Don't start lyin' to someone who wants to help you with your restaurant business."

When the interview has concluded and Dutch has

agreed to pick up Tony's tab, he finds his earlier concerns being swallowed up in fantasies of germs and impurities, spiders and bloodsuckers, leeches and parasites. He returns to the bar for a vodka, and after a while realizes that Denise Lefevre has her arm in his, and that he is being asked for an answer to a question. He backtracks, tries to reconstruct the conversation.

"Okay, yeah. Yeah, sure," he says finally, looking at Felix. "Give her a piña colada."

Once again, the bar goes up.

"Well, would you look at that! Dutch is actually gonna buy someone a drink! He's broke down an' is gonna buy the nice lady a drink! Hey Dutch, you okay? Somethin' the matter with you?"

He hears almost nothing of what follows. He resolves to go home and take a shower. But before he gets in the shower, he lies down for a nap.

In his nightmare, the Dubnow kid has returned to work at the restaurant. To give everyone a relief from his incessant chatter, Karen has asked him to sweep the front walk. He does so, but covers the broom with dog droppings. He comes inside and begins sweeping in the dining room, bringing what was outside *inside*. Patrons coming into the restaurant are asking, "flagstones still being repaired?" Karen tells Dubnow to go to the storeroom, get some doggie bags, and distribute them among the tables. SANIBAGS, they say, FOR THE DISPOSAL OF SANITARY NAPKINS. Now a chorus line of servers is doing a fan dance across the restaurant, but instead of fans they hold cloth napkins. *No one seems to notice except Dutch and a man with a gaudy neck medallion, standing in the shadows.*

The slap of water in the shower returns him to himself, and as he dresses for work he regains his self-composure. *Of course. It's a restaurant he's running, isn't it? How could he not expect all manner of creeps and weirdos to walk through the front door? Besides, what does this Tony person amount to but a bit player in a torrid melodrama? Well, this was his town. He had plenty of friends—and friends in the police department. Just how scared was he supposed to be?*

Having reduced Tony-the-Extortioner to a footnote in the ongoing melodrama of the restaurant business, Dutch dresses with the swagger, the cockiness of a bullfighter. He puts leashes on his dogs — *how'd you like to have a few words with my Dobermans, Mr. Tony?* — and saunters out to the streets of Sun Town. At the Dockside, he ties the dogs up on the patio—the quintessential statement of *this is my yard*—and goes around to the kitchen door. The sight of the employees going about their tasks is consoling to him, and he stops to offer a word of encouragement to the know-it-all dishwasher.

"Place looks good!" he says. "Now that wasn't too painful, was it?"

"Nah. And anyway, pain is its own reward."

Dutch pretends not to hear, waves to Dave and Lenny, and edges through the knots of waiters and waitresses, applying solicitous pats to one or two of the latter. He shuffles through the swinging doors and out onto the stage.

"Hey, we're pretty hot stuff!" Dave calls, when the chefs are alone again. "We use real potatoes!"

"Yeah! From a real can!" Lenny calls back.

"And we wouldn't think of serving leftovers!"

"Not until the next day!"

When they see him coming, it is apparent to Kathy Shively and Karen Willis that Dutch is in One of His Moods.

"You know, I've been thinking" he says, as if he has not been thinking at all, but merely fastened onto the first subject that has come to mind. "We ought to figure a way to siphon off the energy here at the front entrance. We have to think more about pacing the crowd, so that on nights like this when there are people backed up and waiting, we'll have control over the dynamics of the situation. Think of it as like wave motions, which paradoxically also act like particles. I mean, this ficus tree doesn't have to be right here, does it?"

Karen and Kathy—who are dealing not with energy and wave motions, but a large crowd of hungry people—bury themselves in their work, Kathy in the reservation book, Karen at the credit card machine. The women whose job it is to run the restaurant while letting Dutch think *he* is running the restaurant realize that it is one of those occasions when he is going to try to redesign the place from the ground up.

"And I've made a decision, Kathy. Kathy, are you listening? I've made a decision. You know these large parties that come through and leave pathetic little tips? Especially the tour groups? Brenda was saying the other day that she had a party of twelve who spent over three hundred dollars and left a *seven-dollar* tip! And then there was that group, last week, that wanted everything on separate checks—"

Yes, they know. And left a four-percent tip. And their bus driver backed the bus into the brick wall on the side of the building, and put a crack in it. It was all they could do to keep the kitchen help from going out and throwing tomatoes as the bus pulled away.

"So here's what I propose. Let's institute a fifteen-percent service charge for parties of eight or more. I think eight's a reasonable number, don't you? Now Karen, if you'll have some little tabs printed up, we can insert them in the menus so there won't be any confusion. Can you take care of that for me?"

Sure, Dutch. And I'll single-handedly stop the arms race and find a cure for cancer. But right now, there're people waiting out front who are hungry for dinner. And you're slowing everything down.

Confident that his orders have been understood and will be carried out, and reminding his hostesses to keep an eye on the lobsters in the foyer, Dutch wanders off to see what else he can do to make the restaurant run more efficiently. So thorough has he become in his review of his troops that he even stops with a word of encouragement for the piano player.

"You sound good!" he says, catching Ed Shakey between tunes. "I really like the way you execute the piano! Everything all right in your sector?"

It is Dutch at his most paternal, and Ed wonders whether it's a good time to ask him to have the piano tuned. But with his uncanny instinct for such things, Dutch flashes him a V-for-victory sign and scuttles off.

Ed is having a very satisfying night. Earlier, a man had come up who said he was a movie producer and Ed's sound was just what he wanted for a movie he was working on, and promised to get back to him. Later he received a couple of very generous tips. Now he plays one of his favorite tunes, "My Ship," and follows it with "Lucky To Be Me." As he goes into the latter, however, a feeling of melancholy grips him. *Why is it that the times when I'm most pleased with my playing are rarely the times when anyone is listening? Like my arrangement of Lucky To Be Me: it's a good arrangement. But it's gotten predictable. I don't feel like I'm really creating. Maybe other people can hear what I put into it, but I can't. And that makes me feel like I'm hoodwinking the audience. No matter what I do, it seems like it's never enough. Is that what makes me, as Lee said, a misanthrope, a sourpuss?* Ed moves into a minor key and, thinking of Lee, does "Summertime." *They should hear me when I'm alone, like in the middle of the night when I've had a few, and am really playing. But when I'm playing at my best, there's rarely anyone around. Not other musicians. Not Lee. Not even Helen.* He concludes "Summertime" on a note that feels slightly too lugubrious, and glimpses Lee in the distance. *But why is Helen acting so strange, so uncommunicative? Is it postpartum depression? Or is it the way the baby is restricting her freedom? I'm doing everything I can, aren't I? Changing diapers in the middle of the night, generally trying to take the pressure off? But if I don't work six days a week, what are we going to do for money? She knew when she married me that this is the way a working musician lives: out every night, and home late.*

He is playing "Someone to Watch Over Me" when Lee arrives on the stand with a Cup of Coffee. Ed looks surprised.

"You wanted this, didn't you?" she says. "I thought, when you glanced at me a minute ago, you were signaling."

"Yeah, sure. Thanks a bunch," he says.

Dammit. I've got to lay off the sauce.

"I told Felix it was for you, and the least Dutch could do is buy you a drink now and then. So it's on the house."

"Many thanks. Any chance we could go out for a drink, later?"

Lee smiles flirtatiously: "You're sure this isn't going to get you in trouble?"

She steps off the stand and hurries back to her charges.

"Oh, miss!" a man at one of her tables calls, "would you put your finger in my coffee?"

"Uh, sure," she says. "Isn't it hot enough? Is there a problem?"

"Yeah. It's not *sweet* enough."

The man smiles and Lee smiles back. Everyone at the table smiles, except a woman who looks like she's had a lifetime of this sort of thing. Lee promises to bring them their check, and flies off to the brood on her right.

"Do you have carafays?" the young man inquires, transparently trying to impress his date.

"Do we have—what?" Lee replies.

"Carafays. Carafays of wine."

"Oh sure. Sure we do!"

"I had a doozy last night," Sharon Lowd says, when Lee approaches the bread locker in the kitchen. "Apparently the woman didn't want to ask for a doggie bag, so she was putting her melon in her pocketbook. I *think* she had already consumed the sherbet, but I'm not sure."

Hands move quickly; baskets are lined with napkins, rolls go in, butter is poked with forks, dumped onto butter dishes.

"How about this one?" Brenda says, next to her. "I just gave a check to a guy and a girl who were looking dreamily at one another over a wishbone. She stared at him sadly and said, 'I wish things had been different.'"

"No, come on. Really?"

Brenda turns to Lee. "Hey, didja hear? Dutch is gonna institute a fifteen-percent service charge for parties of eight or more. Good news, huh?" She finishes and moves off, and after a moment—like a paratrooper going out a jump door—Lee follows.

"One carafay for Miss Castleton," Felix says genially, "one cara*fay* of cha*blay*."

Felix moves smoothly up and down the bar, the crush of people in front of him relieving him of the need for personal interaction. This is the way he likes it, these nights when the demand is not so great that he can't keep up with it, but when his involvement with any one customer can be kept to the minimum. Not only are the tips better on nights like this, but his duties divide perfectly into the amount of time available, and he can put himself on automatic. The motions move themselves, the choices make their decisions, and eventually, like a croupier at the gaming tables, he becomes invisible.

Tonight the gamblers are very talkative.

"He told me he was a hot-shot university professor, but from all I can tell the only chair he ever held down was a chair at the Alibi!"

"When she finally dragged herself out of here, Denise said her stomach felt like the floor of a canary cage."

"I knew this minister, once, who had three daughters: Faith, Hope, and Joanne."

"Hey Jerry, I hear you had a birthday! What'd you do on your birthday?"

"Drugs."

"Let me explain to you about fishermen, ol' buddy (it is 'Houn, from the *Windswept*). "Fishermen are people who name their boats after their wives, daughters, and girl friends, then go down in their holds, fill 'em full of fish, swab their decks, coddle 'em, fight 'em in rough seas, hold onto 'em for dear life— then put 'em up on stanchions for the winter and leave 'em high and dry."

"The nice thing about being a veterinarian is, you can eat your mistakes."

Did he really say that? Felix backtracks. No, he can't have. Felix dallies a moment, but the speaker has turned his back. Smoothly and efficiently, he moves down the bar, cleaning and tidying up as he goes.

"Hidey-tidey."

The voice is impish, mischievous, mocking.

"I said: 'hidey-tidey!'"

"Hey, you makin' fun of my efforts to keep the bar clean?"

"No," says Grubby Eddy. "I was simply observing that it's a great night for *skinny* people to go *skinny*-dipping."

He motions to one of the waterfront windows.

"Oh yeah, yeah. One of the highest tides of the season. Full moon. You wanna drink?"

Sure, why not? What else am I here for?

Feeling like he is in a crowded elevator and more people are pushing their way on, Grubby Eddy elbows the person next to him to reclaim his space, and returns to his dialogue with a world he can neither quite shun nor quite accept. He tries to determine the relationship between the behavior he sees around him—the little mannerisms and interactions—and the realities of the larger world, even the realities of war and politics. He knows (but can't say how) that these little instances of self-expression, a man's way with a woman, a woman's way with a cigarette, determine the character of a society, and by extension translate into global destinies. In the behavior he sees around him, he thinks he can detect the entire range of human character, in the mannerisms of waiters and waitresses, hostesses and busboys, the key to truth and beauty. He knows (but can't say how) that the large meanings break down into this and this, and that and that, and makes a practice of following the chain of causality from surface impressions to their metaphysical import. Although he admits these flashes of insight—which seem so momentous when he is drinking—are fleeting and evanescent, he knows that the health and well-being of entire nations could, with the appropriate tests, be read in the thoughts and daydreams of the Little Man, a man like himself sitting in a bar having a drink.

Reluctantly, he glances up at the television. Through the nimbus of talk and laughter he can isolate individual words and phrases, can almost will his ears to reach out and choose the one sound he wants to hear; it's as though the waves of noise around him could be made to separate and pull back, and the one desirable sound come to him through the stillness. And then this conceit is shattered. "Senior administration official," he hears. "Eyewitness news, in-depth report. Made with the help of nature." *Dammit, everything's made with the help of nature! Asphalt, shoe polish, styrofoam—everything! They'd better not start showing little animals scurrying around on the desert floor! They'd better not show us baboons picking ticks off one another! Goddamn snowy RE-grets!* He slouches down and averts his eyes, swears he will have no more to do with it. As he lifts his drink, however, an impish voice says that to be angry is at least to have feelings. And besides, who else does he have to talk to? If he doesn't talk to the television, who *will* he talk to? Hating himself for acquiescing to his own degradation—and for the lies he must tell himself in order to convince himself he *isn't* acquiescing—Grubby Eddy looks up again at the flickering lights.

Jack Freund, the sidewalk portrait artist, comes in now, and takes a seat next to him. From long experience, Grubby Eddy knows that Jack is sinking into his usual thousand-yard stare, a dazed, exhausted mesmerization with whatever is in front of him, probably the one-eyed pirate across the bar. Jack has come to the Lifeboat Lounge, no doubt, because this is the place where, with the fewest steps at the end of his work day, he can get a drink. Grubby Eddy visualizes him in his sidewalk booth, under the bright floodlights, visualizes the penetrating stares of the onlookers as Jack tries to capture, one after another, the likenesses of people he has never seen before. *But what does he do when he begins having trouble with that nose, that ear lobe, that shadow around the corner of the mouth? What does he do when he realizes he has made a mistake, but can't start over? How would it look if he tore the drawing off his easel, threw it on the ground, stamped on it? How would that go over with the doting parents, the admiring lover? No, he must continue drawing, for there is no turning back.* And in that

germ of insight, Grubby Eddy finds the key to the man's character. *There is no turning back. There are no second chances. No hand
will reach miraculously down out of the heavens and alter the offending
line, the imprecise color. Because there is no turning back, there is no re-
demption, no forgiveness.*

Grubby Eddy feels something unpleasant rubbing off
on him. The strict controls Jack lives under—the self-punishment required to keep him performing, of which he can only
rid himself with drink—seem all too familiar. When Felix
comes, he smiles and holds up his hand.

"All set?" Felix says.

*All set? Why don't you say it like it is? Have you drunk your-
self into a stupor yet? Have you drunk yourself as far into oblivion as
you're going to go?*

He slides off the stool and, carefully avoiding the eyes
of Jack Freund, wanders out.

Flipper McDougal comes in now, and considering it beneath his dignity to battle his way through the crowd to the one
available stool at the bar, trades a few words with Polly Schreiber and meanders back out. A minute or two later, Doug Brindle—who had hoped to find his friend here—comes in, and
considers himself fortunate to get the vacant seat.

Doug looks downcast, haggard. He has been trying to
get going on a novel about a man and a woman whose marriage
is on the rocks, but has decided he doesn't have enough experience to carry it off. Such a plot might be too narrow, in any
case. It would be better to begin with something formulaic, a
murder mystery perhaps, or, if he wanted to work on a broader
scale, a novel about international terrorism. What would be the

ingredients of such a novel? An oil sheik. International smuggling of arms, or maybe drugs. Radioactive materials. Government intrigue at the highest levels. . . .

"A penny for your lies."

"What?"

"I said. Your *dog* die or something? Jesus, you're no fun! Relax, loosen up! Lemme buy you a drink! My name's Toby Pettiford."

The man extends his hand as if used to a world that eagerly awaited such information.

"Doug. Doug Brindle."

"So what are you thinking about, all wound up in yourself like that? Wait, don't tell me. I know. Lost your girl. Am I right?" The speaker looks at Doug with an expression that suggests that no matter what the problem is, he's seen it all before. "Well, I'm gonna find *me* a girl in this town, and if I can find one for me, I'm sure I can find one for *you*. So stick with me, partner. And I'll tell you another thing. They gotta lot a' beautiful boats on the waterfront, here, and I intend to make friends with someone who owns one. Now, if I could make friends with a girl—or *two* girls—that own a boat. . . ."

The speaker glances at Doug to determine whether the prospect is generating any interest.

"Had a boat myself, one time."

"Oh yeah? What kinda boat did you have?"

"A thirty-two-foot fixed-keel sloop. The 'Jolly B' she was called. Sailed her down to the Caribbean, one time, with a coupla women for crew; almost didn't make it through the Bermuda Triangle. Got caught in a tropical storm and broke her up on a reef. Man, she was a beautiful boat."

As they talk along like sailors thrown up in a rum joint on a South Sea island, it becomes apparent that Toby Pettiford has done a great many things. He has been a sailor, a scuba diver, a pool hustler, a pilot, a radio announcer, a ski instructor (*when does he sleep?* Doug asks himself), and along the way has known, worked for, or been close to this one, that one, and the other one. As his list of accomplishments lengthens, Doug begins to feel like he is sitting next to an expanding balloon around which he must creep if he is to inhabit the same space. There is even a cause-and-effect relationship in this, his own diminution following from Toby Pettiford's self-aggrandizement. Toby continues to regale him with adventures until, suddenly, his air of amusement is replaced by a tone of defensiveness.

"Whatta *you* do?" he says.

Doug wonders whether he has done a single interesting or noteworthy thing in his entire life.

"I'm a *writer*," he replies, in a slightly apologetic tone.

"You're a writer? You write? Hey man, I live it! I live it, baby, I'm tellin' you! Don't give me 'writing,' 'cause I've lived it! Damn straight I have! 'Write it. Wrote it.' Don't tell me you 'wrote it,' baby, 'cause I've fuckin' lived it!"

"Hey Doug," someone calls, "you comin'?"

Warily, Doug turns around.

"Time to go dancin'!" an acquaintance says, smiling at him. "The bus is leavin'!"

In a town that takes its playfulness very seriously and

tolerates every form that playfulness takes, one of the cherished rituals is going disco-dancing at the Sand Bar. Obviously, there are thrills to be had in town that are more exotic than disco-dancing, but often they seem to *start* with dancing. Until now Doug wouldn't have been caught dead on a dance floor; the gyrations seem to him uncivilized, the noise deafening, the whole activity crude. But now as a modest exodus begins around him, and a stranger threatens him with humiliation and abuse, Doug's desperation conspires with defiance to make him take the plunge.

"Hey, where you goin'?" asks Toby Pettiford, as if he were just coming to the good part, and Doug certainly wouldn't want to miss *that*.

"Mystery leg," Doug says, using the local slang.

"What?"

"The wiggle and the jiggle. Uh, a private party. Sorry, I gotta go."

Leaving Toby Pettiford fuming at his beer, Doug throws a tip down, catches up with the crowd heading out the door, and follows them up Bay Street to the Sand Bar.

He hears the *boom-boom, boom-boom* first, then feels waves of heat radiating from the front door; it's as if a huge crowd had gathered to operate air hammers and rock drills. Murals of shipwrecks greet him as he enters, and the floor is shaking; it occurs to him that it's not too late to cut and run. But the people in front of him are saying, "It's okay, he's with us," and a bouncer is looking him up and down and saying, "I don't care, I never seen him before, five dollars," and an impatient crowd is piling up behind him. *Well, I guess if you want experience, you have to pay for it,* Doug thinks. He hands over the money, and goes in.

The noise all-enveloping, the heat all-encompassing; it takes a minute for his eyes to adjust. *I never did like amusement parks and haunted houses,* he thinks. He tries to get downwind of the loudspeaker next to him, but people are packed in so tightly he feels like he is moving through jungle underbrush. "Uh, 'scuse me," he says, several times, before realizing he cannot be heard. When he arrives at a clearing, he turns and looks for the folks he had come with; they have been swallowed up in the crowd. He studies the dance floor, where heads are bobbing, bodies jerking, and discovers that the music, or rather the beat—*boom-chugga, boom-chugga, boom-chugga, boom-chugga*—sweeps everything before it, gives meaning to all it touches—whether the flashing lights, the revolving pinpricks of light from the mirror-covered globe on the ceiling, the smell of marijuana, or the blacklight—now strobe—that flashes in stop-time and freezes the dancers in jerky, ghostlike poses. The record ends and without dropping a beat, another begins. People drag themselves off the dance floor; others, as if stepping onto a skating rink, take their places. He feels the beat pounding against his chest, and decides it has the tempo of a deliberate walk. Unable to hear himself think, he steps out of the shadows and picks his way across the room—*boom-chugga, boom-chugga, boom-chugga, boom-chugga*—and dots of light slide down the walls, making the room spin dizzily. When he gets closer to the center of the action, he discovers that not only couples are dancing but groups of three and four, and that farther along, the dancers are mostly men: men without shirts, men in tight cut-offs, men entwined in one another's arms. He wonders if he is supposed to be there. He retraces his steps and finds a place at the bar. He has a foothold now, and as he watches the action—*boom-chugga, boom-chugga, boom-chugga, boom-chugga!*—he finds the excitement and exuberance overriding his defenses. Not that he has any desire to participate: he is too much of an observer to expose himself like that. No, it is enough to stand at the bar and watch the kaleidoscope of movements, meanings, and expressions. Here is a guy with a fishing hat and corncob teeth, there a biker who looks like he's suffocating in his leather jacket, across the way a little knot of non-dancing servicemen whose crew cuts give them all the *savoir-faire* of skinned cats. Beyond them is someone he knows is a cashier at the supermarket, and over there a local postman; there's a funky black dude with a porkpie hat, a guy in cowboy boots, a couple of lesbians with punk haircuts, and somebody he thinks is a fisherman—*boom-chugga, boom-chugga, boom-chugga, boom-chugga!*—and all are dancing and all seem happy, if not ecstatic.

The men's room is a different story. At the end of a dimly lighted passageway, bright fluorescent lights throw men into sharp, garish relief. Several preen in front of the mirrors, others drink from small flasks, in one of the stalls there is a noisy, moist, self-involved sniffing; a few men stand around as if they were waiting for someone, or had noplace else to go. Something about the scene makes the activity on the other side of the wall seem like good clean fun. To his relief, Doug's place at the bar, and his beer, are waiting for him. Among the wild gyrations, he now starts to detect the subtleties of style and movement that make some dancers more interesting than others. The main distinction is between dancers who hold or touch their partners, and those who don't; beyond this, there are the body movements: the yo-yo's who jerk up and down, the flight-deck controllers who send signals to landing airplanes, the marionettes who shake their hands at the ceiling, the reckless ones who dance a little with everyone on the floor, the specialists in angular momentum, the sylphs who ride on gentle breezes—*boom-chugga, boom-chugga, boom-chugga, boom-chugga!* The lights come up again, eliciting new cries of pleasure, tiny polka dots wander up and down the walls, whiffs of marijuana drift through the mist and heat. Doug turns and finds the man on his left smiling. "Wild, isn't it!" he says over the noise. The stomping and churning go on, and when the man again catches his eye, Doug smiles, too: "Cheers!" he says, raising his glass.

The man moves closer to Doug:

"Hey pal, wanna make a little money?"

Doug shrugs in a way that says *doesn't everybody?* and turns back to the madcap craziness.

The man signals to the bartender, orders a beer, and points to Doug:

"This'll be over in a few minutes! Let's talk!"

Doug drinks with enthusiasm, watches the show, and feigns protest when he is handed a second beer.

"So, do you live here in town?" the man in the neck medallion says, as they thread their way through the crowd and out into the cool night air.

"Wouldn't live anyplace else!" Doug replies. "Whew, that's some scene, isn't it!"

"I'll say. Com'on over here. Here's my little baby. Just had some work done on her. Climb in the front."

Doug hesitates, wonders what he's getting into. But the man's charm is seductive. *Well, if this is experience,* he thinks, *let me have it. But careful. Greeting card salesmen and insurance adjusters don't drive cars like this.*

"Y'see Doug, I work for a firm that does market research, and we're interested in how many people are dining in the various restaurants in town. Do you ever go in the Dockside?"

"All the time."

"Good. We're looking for someone who could give us a report on the number of dinners they typically serve. It's essential that our research be done anonymously, which is why I'm asking you. All you'd have to do is sit at the bar for an hour or two, keep track of what you see, and write down the figure. It's easy work, Doug, almost anyone could do it. But I'd see that you got a nice little hunk of change for it. Whattaya say?"

"Sounds easy enough to me."

"And if you produce, Doug, I could probably get you some other work. Hey, I think we could make last call at Chowderville's! Wanna try?"

"What's to lose?"

As they enter Chowderville's after a brisk ride through town, Doug waves to Ed Shakey, who is standing arm-in-arm with Lee Castleton.

"The full moon is really beautiful, isn't it?" Ed says, as he escorts Lee out onto the deck.

"Incredible."

The bright bulging moon, shining over the harbor with theatrical intensity, lends a consoling warmth to the cool night air, outlines the bay in front of them and renders the lights curling around the harbor soft and twinkly. Because it sends a line of sparkles directly across the water at them, it seems to single them out.

"'Lunacy.' Comes from 'lunar,'" Lee comments. "I've felt crazy for the last three days."

"Did you ever notice how the moon seems to get larger as it sinks toward the horizon?" Ed asks, putting his arm around her. "You'd swear it was bigger when it's close to the horizon than when it's way up in the sky."

As they stand like spectators at an air show, knowing few things in life are more beautiful than this, Ed gently tightens his grip. As he escorts Lee along the sea-fragrant streets, the ethereally peaceful streets on a night when the only sounds come from far-off buoys and bells, anything seems possible. They avoid streets that intersect with his own, and go up School Street, and across on Quesnel. Her pace is unsteady, now, and although she has cleared her thoughts of the night's work, she is already anticipating tomorrow's. She does not encourage him to follow her down the walk to her cottage, but he does so anyway. She looks at him sympathetically and says something about how much she likes his music, but she does not encourage him to take her hand, to look into her eyes, to say things more intimate than she has energy left to deal with. He bends to kiss her, and she does what she must to comply. He squeezes, she resists. He stands back and implores. She resists.

In the end, their parting is warm, easy, friendly; *in*

resistance there is at least complicity, Ed thinks. She waves from her door and, feeling like he's one of the best piano players who ever lived, he skips up the walk. *But the party's over,* he tells himself, and begins to whistle the tune.

For some it is over. For others, there is still the matter of cleanup. The stage must be swept, the sets returned to their original positions, the props stored in their proper places if the party is to resume tomorrow. At the Dockside, Dutch is puttering about in the darkness. Even though he is not doing anything important, he finds it enjoyable to fiddle around in this, his second home, to savor his success and to hear in the stillness the echoes of a busy, profitable day. Peering through the portholes of the kitchen door, he is reminded that he is *not* alone: In the still-bright kitchen, the crazy clean-up man with the scar on his face is getting ready to scrub the counters and walls, mop the floor, do the scutwork that requires only muscle and time. *But why does he raise his arms and shake his fists at the ceiling? Who the hell is he talking to?* Like a spy in his own house, Dutch crouches and watches, feels like a peeping tom but tells himself this is his prerogative, wonders whether the man goes into the food, or investigates the cash register. *But he's a good worker. He may be half nuts, but he's a good worker. Maybe, in work like this, it's better when they don't think too much.*

Suddenly Dutch remembers he has one more chore, after all. It's the night when the rug-cleaning people are coming in. He backs away from the kitchen door, and goes to the front desk and takes a handful of change out of the cash register. Moving among the tables and chairs, he bends over in the lingering moonlight, then goes and busies himself in the harder-to-reach places: under booths and in out-of-the-way corners, behind fixtures and plant stands. In the end he will have dropped about a dollar and a half.

He knows that rug will be clean.

NINE

Standin' at the doors of the choppers. Standin' at the seven-six-twos, lookin' for 'em in the swamp grass. Find one, blow 'im out of the water. Mutterin' Death, they called us. Go out at night with the lights on, draw their fire, see their muzzle flashes and go after 'em. Lightnin' Bug. Some name. Then defoliation. Gave 'em no place to hide. Easier to spot 'em if they had no place to hide. Only You Can Prevent Forests. That's what they said. Then the White Mouse got me, 'cause a' the pills.

As he works, the kitchen clean-up man talks to himself, every so often stepping back—he is scrubbing the backplate of the grill—and shaking his fist at the ceiling. He dips and squeezes and wipes. His thoughts counterpoint the rhythm of his arms.

The White Mouse got me. Put me to work sweepin' the barracks. Sweepin' and sweepin', but the floor already clean. Find a pebble, sweep it from one end to the other. Turn around and sweep it back again. Standin' at the seven-six-two. . . . Christ, how many people did I kill.

Though he is fit only for solitary work, and some instinct tells him that, here at the Dockside Tommy does not consider himself alone. He has a friend, and if the friend does not say anything, at least he does not accuse him, does not ask him questions about shooting people in swamp grass, or taking pills. The friend—a tiny field mouse—appears on the counter, now, but at first his presence angers Tommy. He feels like he is shooting wildly, or the ship is taking groundfire. It is only a blur he sees behind the bucket of rags. He scrubs behind the grill for a while, then tiptoes over and swings around and angrily yanks away the bucket. The field mouse cowers, shrinks almost to nothing, it has no cover, no place to hide. It darts along the wall and returns to the corner, darts along the other wall and returns. Freezes. No twitching, no movement of eyes, almost no heartbeat. It is as defenseless as that soldier they ran through the swamp grass, running him until he couldn't run anymore, running him until—exhausted—he just stood there looking up at them, shaking his rifle in defiance. They hosed him with the guns, and he just exploded. Blew up all over the place.

Tommy imagines himself up in the sky again, staring down at this defenseless mouse. He feels like a giant; if he were to shout, he supposes that the mere sound of his voice would blow the creature off the counter. He leans forward, contorts his face with mad intensity, extends his arms as though he were sailing through the sky: an angry, vengeful god firing thunderbolts from every trembling finger, spraying the creature with gunfire.

He returns to work—and the mouse is gone. He scrubs for a while, angry at himself for reasons he cannot understand; eventually he is overcome with remorse. He takes a butter dish from a nearby shelf, goes to the silverware bin and gets a knife, walks to the reach-in and opens the door. *One stubborn little gook, shaking his rifle in the sun, a fiddler crab no higher than the sole of his shoe, waving his pathetic little claw.* There are shards and crumbs on the edges of the desserts he sees, scrapings on the rims of plates. He removes a crumb here, and a crumb there—being careful not to disturb anything fit to serve—a dot of chocolate, a sliver of almond, a bit of meringue, a raisin; he picks the morsels that look most delicious. He arranges the banquet on the butter dish in a way that seems attractive to him, and places it on the counter where he always leaves it: behind the rag-filled bucket.

Eventually there is a commotion at the kitchen door; it is the rug-cleaning crew. As they bang through the kitchen with their equipment, Tommy stands in the corner, protecting the spot where his little friend may be having his snack. Futilely trying to ignore the intrusive rasping from the other room, he works for two more hours, then, making sure the door has locked behind him, puts the trash and garbage out, and leaves.

It is three o'clock in the morning. The still, quiet air cushions all sounds, and makes the few that remain seem out of place; it is as if by some unwritten rule the world had temporarily turned its back on Sun Town, and allowed it to revert to a scrappy fishing village governed by the rhythms of sky and water. All the more reason, then, for the movements of those still awake to seem anomalous: whether the stragglers wandering up Bay Street from the bars and restaurants, the young men and women sailing along, ghostlike, on clicking bicycles, or the men loitering under the piers with vacant, hungry expressions. Despite the appearances of peacefulness and quiet, nothing is inconsequential at this hour. Everything contains hidden purpose, so much so that entire short stories could be written based on whose cars or bicycles will be seen where, in the morning.

On Crescent Street, Tim Mullen is sitting at his ham radio transceiver. As Tommy the clean-up man lopes up Bay

Street, his body is the passive recipient of a burst of high-frequency radio energy.

"CQ CQ, CQ CQ, CQ DX," Tim announces, into his microphone. "This is WA1YYI. CQ CQ, CQ DX."

Tommy sees the flashing lights of an ambulance up ahead, and associating it with Military Police vehicles, retraces his steps and turns up School Street.

"CQ CQ, CQ DX. This is WA1YYI. CQ, CQ DX." Tim doesn't take for granted what is happening. He knows his signal is bursting out of his antenna and radiating across the harbor at nearly the speed of light; traveling horizontally until it hits a layer of charged particles high above the atmosphere, it is bouncing back to earth, then rebounding into the atmosphere again and skipping its way across the darkened land, the continent, the world. Tim is still fascinated by the way his antenna can pull radio signals down out of the sky, his receiver isolate the one desired and, after breaking it down and amplifying it, cause it to materialize in his speaker. At any hour of the day or night, all the world awaits him: civilian and commercial traffic, foreign languages, music in exotic rhythms, political propaganda, radioteletype, Morse Code. Even when incomprehensible, he finds the constant obbligato of beeps, moans, and squeals evocative, and therefore pleasing. "CQ DX, CQ DX," he calls, by his choice of code signaling his desire to talk only to someone at a great distance. As he turns the dial on his transmitter and debates whether to listen or to call on a different frequency, he remembers his introduction to wireless communication, namely, the Christmas he received his first CB rig. Still a child at the time, and without knowing what he was doing or understanding anything about radio, he had set up the antenna, plugged the unit in, and pressed the mike button. Mimicking the things he heard on the street, he had called:

"Breaker breaker! This is . . . *Dyke*!"

There was a silence, then:

"Come in, Dyke!"

Who was speaking?

"Who is this!" he blurted.

Pause.

"This is . . . God! Have you been a good boy, today?"

Shaken, he had turned the unit off, and sought refuge in a chair in the corner. Only when he was much older did he understand that Mr. Keneally, next door, had received his transmission and was having a little Christmas-day fun with him.

"CQ, CQ, CQ DX," he says again. "This is WA1YYI."

As he waits for a reply, he remembers how Mr. Keneally explained that anywhere a radio signal was being received, it was also penetrating the trees, cars, buildings, and people around it: every radio and TV transmission, every CB, fire, and rescue signal, every aeronautics communication and satellite downlink. The millions of transmissions were pulsing outward from dishes and dipoles, Yagis and longwires, beams and booms, magmounts and rubber ducks, and penetrating one's body without one's knowing it, and as if one were not even there.

"CQ, CQ DX. This is WA1YYI. . . ."

At the corner of Bay Street and Puritan, John Savoy and Pat LeRoche, the two EMTs on the rescue squad call, are not thinking about radio waves coursing through their bodies. Hovering over their patient, John has resolved to treat the case

(Code 66 on Code 3) like any other. *I'll go right by the book*, he thinks. He and Pat have tried mouth-to-mouth and chest compressions, and now he has the defibrillator paddles out, and has loosened the shirt on the comatose body. Quickly he connects the heart monitor. There are too many people in the room; he orders them out. If defibrillation works, they'll transport the patient to the rig and connect him to telemetry at the hospital. *I'll go right by the book*. He adjusts the oxygen and demand mask, reaches for jelly, coats the paddles, adjusts the settings on the monitor. His eye moves from the defibrillator to the patient's face, and as he concentrates on following correct medical procedure, he feels, yet again, the sting.

"Who's to say ten thousand, a million—even a hundred million—cycles-per-second is a great number?" Nat Keneally had asked Tim, when he was studying for his ham license. "In some cases, a single *second* may be a long time, a slow—almost plodding—period of time. Think of the hummingbird that beats its wings fifty, eighty, as many as two hundred times a second, think of the frequencies up in the billions—the gigahertz—and how they compare with the poor millions, the poor thousands."

As he applies the paddles, John Savoy, a building contractor, remembers the year he hired Tommy Stubbs to dig trenches, carry forms, and mix concrete. Tommy had been a hard worker, and reliable to a fault. But Tommy scared people. There was that strangeness about him, the unsightly scar on his face, his erratic hand motions. When nailing up forms or walking wheelbarrows through dirt and mud, he was unbeatable. But confronting people one on one? He scared them. His wife asked him not to leave her alone with Tommy, said she didn't feel comfortable around him. Oh, there were plenty of people he affected that way, Steve Marsilius among them. Given the chance, this hot-shot detective would have had Tommy up on any number of charges. Marsilius had come to town determined to make a name for himself, and having plenty of unsolved crimes to choose from, decided he would get Tommy for at least one of them. It got so he couldn't drive by a site where they were working without smiling, as if to say: *I see you, Tommy, I know who you are, I'm waiting, I have time.* But because he had trusted Tommy and given him a job, Tommy had become as attached to him as a puppy dog, and would have followed him around all day out of sheer loyalty.

"CQ, CQ, CQ DX," Tim calls from his ham shack on Crescent Street. "CQ, CQ, CQ DX. This is WA1YYI."

Then came that period when he was out of town, most weekends, visiting his ailing mother. He had made up reasons, each time, to discourage Tommy from coming to the house and scaring his wife; he had hated to do it, he had hated to *lie* to Tommy—but how stupid had he been! *Everything okay with you, partner?* he had said, upon returning from one visit. *Yeah yeah,* Tommy replied, looking confused and crazed. *I know'd you was worried about yaw wife, so I hung around, and watched out for things. But everything must be okay, 'cause I saw Steve Marsilius comin' outta yaw house at five o'clock this mawnin'. . . .*

"CQ CQ," calls Tim Mullen, "CQ DX. This is WA1YYI."

Out of the corner of his eye, John Savoy registers the gurney's being positioned at his side. He looks again at this man who is sucking oxygen and fighting for his life—this man who had an affair with his wife—and acknowledges Pat's report that contact has been made with the ER at the hospital, and they are waiting to monitor. *But it's a fifty-minute drive, all the way down the peninsula. I will do everything I can possibly do. I'll go right by the book.*

Among the knot of onlookers outside on the sidewalk is Russell Dinsmore, of the women's apparel shop, Russell of Spring. The sight of the gurney's being wheeled down the walk and into the ambulance terrifies him, but he lingers and watches anyway. *This must have been what it looked like the night they took Win away,* he thinks. It had been only a casual pickup, and Vincent would have been furious if he had known about it. On the other hand, Vincent was acting pretty trashy himself, lately. He hadn't even known the boy's name. Winston? Winthrop? Window, Window—*Dressing?* What a beautiful body he had had! Probably just drifted into town looking for trade, but suddenly there they were, holding hands at the Forklift Bar. The next day, they had gone to a tea dance at the Rod and Rudder Club, and after that to the Mad Hatter's Ball; because Vincent was away, he had brought him home. And now he was dead, poor boy. *Oh, the gays of Sun Town are dropping like flies. There's Perry Morello, down to skin and bones, and Marty Magnuson walking with a cane, and Arthur Gerris looking like death warmed over. Is it time to have myself checked? No, I don't want to know! But what about Vincent? I have to have myself checked, don't I? For Vincent's sake?*

The doors of the ambulance close around the body, and with lights flashing the rig pulls away. Telling himself he must definitely have himself checked, Russell heads home to his lover. *Uh-oh, who's this angry-looking fellow?* he thinks, moving to the opposite side of School Street so as not to have to confront Tommy Stubbs.

Filing down the narrow sidewalk, and being momentarily assaulted by the red flasher of the ambulance, is an older couple. Julian deSilva and Lorraine Quinlan are returning from her mother's house, and because she has ignored the question all evening, he is again trying to come to some understanding of why Lorraine will not marry him. Had they not been faithful and devoted friends for many years? Were they not as comfortable together as old shoes? Were they not comfortable even as a threesome, him, her, her mother? Why, then, was she holding back? Why was she content to let them appear to be three doddering people, two middle-aged, one old, who did nothing but while away the evenings in a stuffy house while life raced on around them? Could they really go on this way, he secretly wanting one thing, she another?

As always, her evasion has dismayed and irritated him; it was as though she knew something she would not explain—as though she knew something she could not admit even to herself.

They watch the ambulance pull away, and Julian takes her hand. It is not children he wants, he whispers (he has said it many times). They are too old for that, and besides, he has no interest in children. But wouldn't she derive comfort and consolation from having a permanent partner? Ought they not at least share the pleasure of companionship? Lorraine says something about recognizing John Savoy and Pat LeRoche, and then her father's words are in her ears again.

Your inheritance will be quite considerable, but you will receive it only on one condition. You must not marry before your mother dies. She will need your continued care and support if she is to derive any happiness from the remainder of her life. You will have many years in which to enjoy the fortune I have amassed, but until your mother dies, I insist that you remain single. I have named an executor who will come forward at the appropriate time; he will know whether you have conformed to the terms of my will. Now, if you should meet someone whom you love and wish to marry, I can only counsel you to be patient. Do not tell him of your obligation, or why you are postponing your marriage. He will not understand, and furthermore will only resent your mother, my loving wife. That, in turn, will distract you from providing the kind of care and support she deserves.

Oh, dear sweet Julian, how patient you are! Yes, we will marry one day, we will! But not yet! Not yet, dear Julian, not yet!

When the couple reaches Railroad Square, Lorraine notices the boxes and bags that overflow the trash shed at the Dockside Restaurant.

"Isn't it a pity," she says, "that someone can't find a way to use leftover food. You'd think that they could find a way to distribute it to the poor and needy. Think of how much food gets thrown away, every day. I don't mean food that's been handled, of course, but things that are still perfectly edible."

Julian grunts and stuffs his hands in his pockets. At a time when he is feeling rebuffed by the woman he loves, the world's routine injustices are not something he wishes to contemplate.

Lorraine persists.

"Really, Julian, why can't things be better organized, so that when the means exist to satisfy the needs of people who have little, those persons would receive them and not have to go without?"

As they are made to wait while a garbage truck turns and backs along the side of the restaurant, Julian is gripped with a feeling of sourness and futility. Its warning beeper sounding shrilly, the truck backs slowly out of their path, momentarily framing them in its headlights.

"CQ CQ, CQ DX. . . ."

Tim Mullen inadvertently causes another radio signal to penetrate the couple, the truck, the piled trash, the restaurant. Through his window he notices the bright lowering moon, and recalls the time he and Mr. Keneally bounced a radio signal off its surface. Doing so was tricky, and the 23 Centimeter Band notoriously difficult to work, but somehow they had managed it. Mr. Keneally had consulted his lunar charts, adjusted the az-el mounts on the parabolic dish in the back yard, and fired up his transmitter. He had pressed the mike button, they had stared at one another and at the loudspeaker, and about three seconds later—in the exact duration of the signal they had sent—there was an unmistakable *ssssst*.

The memory of it gives him an inspiration. Using his five-watt, 2 Meter transceiver, he fires up the repeater in Town Hall, the remotely controlled transmitter designed to receive and rebroadcast signals at greater power. He hears it identify it-self in Morse Code, and makes some adjustments that patch his telephone into the circuit. But who will he call? There is no one up at this hour. For the sheer pleasure of seeing the system work, he reaches for the touchtone pad and dials his own number. The signal is transmitted at 146 million cycles-per-second to Town Hall, the repeater connects it to the telephone system, and on the table next to him his phone rings. Foolishly—as though touching paint clearly labeled WET PAINT—he grabs it.

There is no one on the line.

Or rather *he* is on the line, the final link in a perfectly closed circle.

"No, I want to know!" Lorraine says, as she and Julian pass through the headlights of the garbage truck. "I have a right to ask it! Why do those who have so much waste it, while others suffer and go without?"

The anger in his voice startles her. He has never spoken to her this harshly:

"Dammit, Lorraine! It's politics! You know that! You know what it's like trying to get anything done in this town! It's politics, pure and simple!"

Having silenced the telephone, Tim Mullen glances at the moon as it slowly dips beneath the horizon, and decides to try one more time. He swings around to his transmitter.

"CQ, CQ, CQ DX. . . ."

TEN

By the time it was over and he had left, that gray day in March, Barbara Crosby, the Town Clerk, was beside herself. She breathed deeply and worked up her resolve and, papers in hand, marched across the hall to the Town Manager's office.

Agnes Morley, Jim Kiernan's secretary, looked up and knew instantly that something was wrong.

"Agnes, I have some bad news."

Agnes raised her half-glasses, hanging from a beaded cord around her neck, adjusted them to her face, and with schoolmarmish deliberation accepted the papers Barbara handed to her.

"My, *my*," she said, squinting up over the rims, "you're right, this is. . . ."

Barbara glanced into the inner sanctum:

"Where's Jim? I think we'd better show this to Jim."

"I'm afraid he's out for the afternoon," Agnes replied. "He went out to confer with Joe Gallagher, and make an appearance at the nursing home." *And stopped for a drink with Sal Drummond, he did, but no need to go into details.*

"Well, what are we going to *do*?" Barbara asked. "I know. Let's show this to Bill."

For the two custodians of the town's business, sharing the papers with someone—anyone—seemed like the best thing to do. Agnes made some adjustments on her computer, got up, and the two hurried down the drab, high-ceilinged hall to where a sign said: TOWN PLANNER.

"Damn, I didn't even know that was his *name*," said Bill Magnuson, hunching over his drafting table.

"And he smelled of alcohol when he brought these in!" said Barbara. "Why, he could hardly stand up!"

There was a knock at the door, and Spencer Davis, the Town Counsel, looked in.

"Am I intruding? Sorry, I didn't know you were busy."

"No no, come in," Bill encouraged, looking at the others significantly, "come in and have a look at *this*."

Sensing the mood in the room, Spencer Davis put aside the subject on his mind—Jack Burnham's difficulties with the Zoning Board—and made himself receptive to what was apparently more important news.

"Hunh. These look like valid signatures, don't they? My god, the damn thing looks bona fide, doesn't it?"

"Well, what are we going to *do*?" Barbara repeated.

"I don't see that there's very much we *can* do," replied the Town Counsel, in a glum tone of resignation.

It would be as true to say that the news moved through the walls of Town Hall from one clerk and secretary to another as to say that people went about *telling* it, for the average citizen, applying for a building permit or paying his taxes, would not have known a crisis was afoot, would not have known that a great commotion was going on beneath the outwardly smooth appearances of municipal functioning. If, for the rest of the afternoon, the bureaucrats of Town Hall resembled a classroom full of students getting unruly while Teacher was out of the room, a person on a casual errand who happened to be near the Town Manager's office at four-thirty would have had a better sense of the day's development, for it was then that Big Jim Kiernan returned and, by a chastened Miss Morley, was given the news. It was not so much that the Town Manager's response could be heard from one end of the building to the other, or that his voice actually blew the walls down, as that this was precisely the effect he would have wanted.

"Mr. Kiernan?" Agnes Morley said, her voice cracking. "Barbara brought some papers over this afternoon that I think you'll want to have a look at. She had to leave early, and asked me to bring them to your attention."

Big Jim grabbed the documents impatiently, glanced at them, recoiled, and returned to the top and began reading them again. His eyes narrowed, he bristled from head to foot, then, in a voice that could be heard all the way down the hall to the License Department, issued his response.

"*Are you shitting me!*"

No, they weren't. As careful examination showed in the days that followed, the signatures were legitimate and had been entered in sufficient quantity, the form was the correct one and had been properly filled out, the letter—if not the spirit—of the law had been honored, and there was simply no getting around it:

Vodka Man was running for selectman.

When his words had faded from the air, Big Jim stormed around Miss Morley's desk and into his office, and slammed the door. He sat down in the high-backed chair which for so long had cradled his deliberations and from which, *ex cathedra*, he had issued his pronouncements, and swiveled around to his private window on the world. *Who needs this?* he thought. Parting the blinds with his fingers, he could see Sylvia Meeks paddling along on her bicycle, Jack Burnham sailing by in his ark of a limousine, Dutch Dugan rounding the corner in his van; near the cannon on the town green, as usual, some kids were horsing around. Meanwhile, the sidewalk parade of winter-weary residents went on. *Fools*, he thought, of one and all. For nine years he had peered through these blinds, spying on a world which, more than any other person in town, he controlled, and compared to the papers and conversations that moved across his desk, never had the view had any more reality than a shadow-play. *Fools*, he thought again, angrily yanking the cord and closing the blinds. He turned back to his desk, and to the affidavit. It was not just the twenty-five signatures, it was not just that *twenty-five registered voters*, some of whom he knew personally, had decided to nominate Lamont Benedict—*Lamont Benedict, for chrissake*—to an important position in town government, it was not just that by doing so they were attempting to rob him of the majority by which he dominated the Board of Selectmen, the majority by which anything had ever gotten *done* in town: It was worse than that. It was that by encouraging—teasing was more like it—by teasing Vodka Man into running for office, a man who would sell his coat in the dead of winter for a drink—a man who, if he weren't on the streets, was probably drying out in the lock-up—by teasing *the town drunk* into running for office, a group of voters were throwing up their hands and announcing they were fed up with town government and—this is what stung the most—with him in particular. He might have survived challenges to his leadership, over the years, he might have survived more than one attempt to effect his removal from office, but with two of the selectmen already set against him, and representing a faction in town that concurred, he could not survive this.

What to do?

There were some hesitant, scratching noises at Jim's door, noises such as a zoo attendant might make before stepping into a cage with food.

"Yes, Agnes?"

"Mr. Kiernan, I've finished the DEQE report, and your letter to Dr. Burnham. Unless you have something else for me, I'll be going home."

"That's fine, Agnes. I've got everything under control, and tomorrow's another day."

"And, uh, Mr. Kiernan? I'm sorry about this, uh, unexpected development."

"Now don't you worry about a thing, Agnes. There's nothing in this for any of us to worry about."

Exhausted by the implications of what certainly lay ahead, and afraid if she lingered he might change his mind, Agnes forced a valiant smile, and closed the door.

What to do?

By the time he trudged down the Town Hall steps, the next morning, and across the village green to Claggett's Drug Store, the cup of coffee Jim was intent on was not only part of his strategy, but a vital necessity. Unable to put the matter out of mind, the preceding evening, he had stopped at the office of the attorney Charles Swann, and they had gone out to the Sundowner for a drink. Thus fortified, he had stopped at the house of another man of unquestioned loyalty, Burton Latch, the Building Inspector. *Why had no one told him the plot was underfoot? How had it been planned and carried out so quietly? Who was behind it?* His wife had made him a drink and listened to his tirade, then he had gone out to Bill Langevin's for more consultations, some poker to take his mind off the matter, and more drinks. In each of the places he went, and in each of the conversations he had, the advice was the same: He was going to have to make peace with Duane Claggett.

If he had moved his office chair far enough to the left, Jim Kiernan would have been able to see the corner of Claggett's Drug Store. To go there in person, however, was to leave a world where people spoke one's language and had one's safety and well-being at heart, and to venture across a no-man's-land to another where these things could be undermined at the slightest provocation. Crossing the village green, his head throbbing as he pondered the shenanigans of an out-and-out drunk, Big Jim felt as though he ought to be carrying a white flag, felt as though he were going to a place where tribal councils were constantly under way and where, though its outer fortifications be breached, the cosmetics and lotions and shampoo with which the rival camp was stocked contained poison darts and secret detonators, or served as camouflage for attackers who were just waiting to strike out. For Claggett's Drug Store, a town institution for seventy-five years, was the province of the town's most conservative element, the families who, having made their money out of the town's growth, didn't want to see it changed any further, who—no matter what it was, for it was always something—didn't like what was "happening" to the town and whose intense, gossipy powwows were carried on under the watchful eye of their leader, the pharmacist at the rear of the store—*and Chairman of the Board of Selectmen, for chrissake*—Duane Claggett. There were other breeding grounds of talk and gossip in town, places where conversation bubbled and plots were hatched, and being as politic as the next man, the Town Manager knew where and when he was welcome, and where and when he wasn't. In this case, it was a source of satisfaction to him that on most items, including prescriptions, the pharmacy on Oyster Shell Road was significantly cheaper. Not that he and Duane Claggett lived in separate worlds, or that their paths never crossed: far from it. Both at the weekly meetings of the Board of Selectmen, that Duane chaired and in which he was the chief respondent, and in numerous other matters of town business, he and the fastidious pharmacist were thrown into constant, if not association, proximity. But it was only the minimal rules of civility and decorum that kept one from dropping all pretense and calling the other a prudish, humorless, self-righteous stick-in-the-mud, and the other from dropping his mask, choosing his words carefully, and calling the first a cheat, a loafer, a liar, and an out-and-out crook. The two, in short, would ordinarily not have had anything to do with one another beyond what was required by their official duties, but with Lamont Benedict looming as a wild card in the scrambled deck of town politics, the Town Manager had to admit his counselors were right: some bridge-building and compromise were in order. Hoping he had the look of man who was unarmed and defenseless—and reasoning that for a fresh hot cup of coffee he would do just about anything—he opened the door to Claggett's, cheerfully held it as two fussy-looking ladies passed in front of him, and went in.

He was there, all right. In his prissy turtleneck, his dainty white lab jacket, he was busy with his pills and bottles—*happier than a child with toys*, thought Jim—on his platform in the back. Proceeding nonchalantly, the Town Manager strolled down the fluorescent minefield between products designed to calm and cleanse and soothe and beautify, and was conscious of a faint stir among the ladies at the soda fountain; it was as if a known criminal or potential shoplifter were among them. When he reached the rear of the store, the woman at the cash register glanced anxiously over her shoulder at her boss and stepped back, as though fearing a volley of cough drops, bunion pads, and pill bottles.

"Mr. Kiernan," said the pharmacist. "What can I do for you?"

Well, I'm sure as hell not here to get a prescription filled, so don't give me that dry-as-dust, medicinal tone.

" 'Morning, Duane. Uh, something's come up that I thought we ought to talk about. Wonder if I could buy you a cup a' coffee."

The pharmacist looked down at him like a judge sizing up a defendant. They had been through this routine four or five times, over the years, and Big Jim tried to look like he didn't have a gang of his boys out front, lying in wait for the ambush.

"Uh, sure," said Duane. "Let me just, uh, finish this order here, and then. . . . Why don't you go up to the soda fountain, and I'll join you in a minute."

"Or I could take you out," said the Town Manager, doing the next part of the dance the way he always did it.

"No-no. Go up front and I'll join you. That way I'll be on hand in case someone needs me."

"Fine," said the Town Manager. *In the Hall of the Mountain King*, he thought, his head throbbing patiently.

He ambled back up front, and seeing two wives of local businessmen abandoning their places at the counter—*no no, ladies, remain calm, there's not going to be a shootout*—smiled with professional cheer and hauled himself up on a stool. The departure of several other people allowed him to choose two stools on the corner and thus put some distance between himself and his adversary. *Wouldn't you know it. Duane gets a chance to do some real wheeling and dealing, some backroom politicking, and he once again arranges to do it in this picture window, right in this fish bowl, so everybody in town can see what's going on. Has to have everything proper and aboveboard. The Little Minister who's afraid to be seen in public with That Woman. . . .*

"Yeah, coffee please," he says to the counter girl. "And why don't you give me a couple of those glazed doughnuts. That's right, those on the end. Thank you."

"And you can pour me a cup, too," the pious stickler says, materializing at his side. "Only you'd better make mine decaf."

It takes a minute for their orders to arrive, during which the two men studiously avoid looking at one another and during which, try as he might to review the bidding and evaluate his hand, the Town Manager's thoughts—provoked by the word *decaf*—keep returning to the person he's about to spar with. *It's his missionary training,* he thinks. *Is it Mormon? Jehovah's Witness? Whatever it is, he's never shaken it. He acts like he's a missionary to the entire town, and can dole out self-righteousness the way he doles out prescriptions; he thinks he's the custodian of the town's soul, and can run his pharmacy like a church. He seems to think the remedies for the town's problems can be broken up into tiny units and placed in capsules, and handed out one by one. But his scientific mind, his puritanical need to say* no *to everything—isn't that the first word a child learns,* no?*—gives him a groundhog's view of the world, provokes him to endless legalistic quibbling over every question and thorny issue. Meanwhile, the important decisions get postponed. This town had better drag itself into the modern world or it's gonna have real problems. But no, not Duane. He always has one principle or another going for him, and he's so stubborn in the way he appeals to 'em that it makes everybody else look wishy-washy, hypocritical; nobody knows how to challenge him on anything. It's as if he's on a white horse, or as if someone else—his father? his grandfather?—lives inside him and does his thinking for him. My god, the man's never laughed, he's never loved, he's never lived. Well, I'll start at the beginning; maybe if I give a little, he'll give a little. At least there's no one listening in on us. Guess we scared 'em all away.*

Big Jim had other problems on his mind, that morning, as he sat at the counter of Claggett's Drug Store clutching his coffee. For one thing, there was the problem of the town's water supply, caused by the leakage from Joe Gallagher's storage tanks. For another, there was Jack Burnham's threat to leave town, owing to the Zoning Board's refusal to give him a variance for a house on Kinriddy Point. *Can't afford to lose another doctor, that's for sure.* There was also the problem with the new sewage treatment facility. Nat Keneally had already quit the

Board of Selectmen over it. *Hell, the engineers have said—said re-
peatedly—that everything will be fine once a few kinks are worked out.*
And now Vodka Man was running for the seat vacated by Nat.

Finally, and most worrisome of all, there was the problem that had arisen with the funds from the town's parking lots.
Though he was slowly getting the sewage problem under control, at least its effects sufficiently camouflaged to mollify public
opinion, the irregularities that had developed in the parking lot
fund had come close to being the thing that ruined him.

"The problem seems to be the way the receipts are
coming in from the waterfront lot," Warren Hogue, his Police
Chief, had told him. "I'm afraid Armand Lucette and some of
the boys have developed, shall we say, sticky fingers. But I don't
think there's any need to raise a great hue and cry about this, I
think we should just go over to the Dockside, some night—just
you and me—with some binoculars. Dutch has a storeroom upstairs next to his office, and we could not only count cars, but
see what's going on down in the booth."

On a suffocatingly hot Saturday night the previous August, they had ensconced themselves in the upstairs storeroom
of the Dockside. Jim had trained the binoculars on the ticket
booth, and they had sat there for a long while without saying
anything, the Chief clasping his knee in a corner or exercising
an option about which he had pointedly not inquired, puffing
on cigarettes. Because of the heat coming up from the Dockside kitchen, the place was stifling.

"Don't you want to have a look?" Jim had said, eventually.

"No, you do the honors," the Chief replied. "Don't worry, I'm here when you get tired."

Big Jim had dabbed his face with his handkerchief and returned to the window, dutifully counting cars and making notes on a note pad.

"Warren, do you think there's any possibility the funds are being rerouted *after* they leave the attendants' hands?" Jim asked. "You know, being rerouted somewhere in the Treasurer's office?"

"It's possible, anything's possible," the Chief averred, as he lit yet another cigarette. "But as I told you, I think the most likely place for the money to get siphoned off is right here where it's being collected. These are the only people *I* have any reason to suspect. At least so far."

The two had returned to silence, and eventually the Chief, as if doing some mental detective work, had interrupted a drag on his cigarette:

"When Armand brings the money in, in the morning, he gives it to Agnes. Is that correct?"

"That's correct," Big Jim replied, keeping his eyes against the binoculars. "Armand usually comes in just after eight, and the Treasurer's office doesn't open till nine. Hey now, Warren, you're not implicating Agnes, are you? You're not implying that *she'd* dip into the till, and then do all the record-tampering that'd be necessary to cover it up? I can't think of anyone I'd trust more. I'd trust Agnes with my own child."

He had turned and stared at the smoky silhouette of the town's chief law enforcement officer; it was as though his own honor were at stake.

"No, I guess not," the unflappable voice replied. "I'm just trying, you know, to put two and two together."

The dark stuffy silence resumed, and as his back and legs and arms began to ache, Big Jim had hinted that it was time for Warren to take a shift. Just when he thought the Chief was moving over into position, he instead reached into his pocket and lit another cigarette. There was a metallic click of the lighter snapping shut, then, like a firefly, another dot of glowing light circling in the darkness; it appeared between the smoker's lips, burned to an incandescent red, and faintly illuminated his ghost-like, devilish cheeks and nose. Jim was perspiring so heavily, and had become so hot and uncomfortable, that he was about to cry.

"Say, Jim," the Chief said finally, as if his mind had all the while been on other things, "you don't suppose the missing parking lot funds have anything to do with a young woman named Sheila Waxman, do you?"

Now he *was* crying.

Well, there had been this convention of small-town mayors and town managers, and at the convention he had met Sheila Waxman, with whom he later fathered a child. Sheila had been pretty decent about it, all things considered, and never held him accountable, or asked for child support. But every so often she did have trouble making ends meet, so got in touch with him and asked him if he couldn't send her five hundred, even a thousand, she promised not to ask him again. He had his own kid in college and had grown accustomed to a certain standard of living, and hell, the town wasn't paying him anything near what he was worth.

So what the hell was he going to do? Caught up short—caught up in an execution chamber by this fierce, menacing representative of the law—how was he going to play it? Was he going to beat his breast and say he was ruined? Throw himself on the mercy of the court—throw himself on the mercy of a tiny dot of red light? Or was he going to try to bluff his way through it, talk to this dark, evil nose, these dark, evil cheeks, man to man? Should he get angry? Deny it outright? Threaten to have the matter out in court? Put his job, his reputation—everything—on the line?

"And that's when you started, uh, borrowing from the parking lot fund, is that correct?" Warren asked, calmly.

He was now a soggy, tearful mess.

"Yeah. For a while I was able to borrow the money from an outside lender—"

"Tony Angelucci?"

"Yeah, Tony Angelucci." *Where the hell was Warren getting his information?* "But the rates got exorbitant."

In the end, they decided that if Jim would replace the missing forty-six hundred dollars, a statement citing "accounting errors" would be issued, and the Chief would forget everything he ever knew about Sheila Waxman. They had had a good working relationship over the years, hadn't they? Jim had seen that his Chief got what he needed, and Warren in turn had run a discreet, self-effacing department. The Chief even volunteered to lend Big Jim money so he could take care of his obligations, but Jim said no, he'd come up with it somehow. Gradually their relationship had returned to being discreet, wary, and respectful.

*

"Of course that fool, Vodka Man, isn't going to be any more use to your purposes and the things you stand for than he is to mine," the Town Manager is saying to the now sickly-looking pharmacist at his side. "We'll be going into Town Meeting soon, and though it won't do irreparable damage if a member of the Board is missing then, if the voters think the spot is eventually going to be filled by Mr. Benedict, it'll have who-knows-what effect on every piece of business that gets transacted, every article on the Warrant, every discussion, every vote."

"Yes, his presence, even his *threatened* presence can't but have a deleterious effect," Duane replies, studiously picking a thread from his lab jacket. "This is indeed a quite unsavory turn of events."

"My reading of the situation, based on the names on the affidavit, is that a lot of people might vote for him as a lark, you know, a prank, without fully understanding the consequences of their actions."

Big Jim is relishing seeing his adversary squirming, sliding into the quicksand of expediency. Nor is the irony lost on him that in trying to save his own neck, he would be saving Duane's, too.

The time has come to play his high card.

"Uh, what about Bob Pettigill or John Savoy? I know Bob is sympathetic to your interests, and John made a good showing two years ago. Couldn't one of *them* be persuaded to run? I don't know why neither has come forward this time, but then it's not my business to be running around town encouraging people to run for the very board that appoints me."

But perhaps if Duane didn't want to chair a weekly selectmen's meeting in which one of the members was routinely absent, or incoherent, or passed out with his head on the table, it was his business? Didn't Duane have as much to gain from seeing this candidate derailed, trounced—laughed out of town—as he did?

"Well, perhaps I could talk to some people, especially, as you say, Bob Pettigill and John Savoy. Thanks for sharing the news. I *think*. I'll get back to you and let you know how I'm doing."

But there was more cynicism and self-destructiveness in the caper than even Big Jim and Duane Claggett realized, as was apparent two weeks later when Town Meeting began and no one except Vodka Man had come forward to run for the vacant selectman's position. The fans and supporters of Lamont Benedict, on the other hand, increased with every passing day, and they not only trooped into Town Meeting *en masse* like the royal court of a king, but sat together in a group surrounding him. Their candidate had upgraded his image considerably since the day he walked into the Town Clerk's office with his nomination papers. He was no longer seen loitering in the alley next to the Beach Variety Store, or taking his repose under the wrecked hulls in Fisher's Boat Yard, but shaved regularly and wore the presentable clothes his new supporters gave him. The shadow of his beard, however, like a glaze on crockery or something baked on, did not go away. Although he had somehow acquired the means to drink in the Whale's Tale and the Mermaid, he was rarely seen having more than a drink or two, and never—even when goaded by his followers—in a state of intoxication; his trademark, a wet brown bag in the side pocket of his coat, seemed to have disappeared forever. Propelled along on a zany groundswell and made to think some force he couldn't understand but would nevertheless submit to called him to a position of leadership in town, he spent his days on street corners, introducing himself to the voters, shaking hands, generally trying to undo in a matter of weeks the reputation of years. Although not everyone felt compelled to come up and speak to him, there were many who slapped him on the back as they passed, or cheered him from a distance, or otherwise egged him on. To the surprise of the Town Hall incumbents, campaign posters appeared here and there, and several ads were placed on his behalf in the Sun Town *Star*.

Now here he was, sitting in Town Meeting in a baggy suit and crumpled necktie, surrounded by a claque who seemed to take pleasure in trying to suppress their own laughter. As Mr. MacKinnon banged his gavel and called the first night's session to order, the audience fell into an unusually expectant hush. After it had been established that a quorum was present, the moderator offered a word of welcome, and called for a reading of the Warrant; Duane Claggett moved that this bit of protocol be dispensed with, and in a flush of unanimity it was so voted. Until the adjournment four nights later, it was the last uncontested vote of the entire Town Meeting. Even the motion that followed—Big Jim's—that certain people who were not residents of the town be allowed to speak met with resistance, for there were those who, cutting off their noses to spite their faces, wanted to deny the privilege to representatives of the company that had built the sewage treatment plant. After some discussion in which the traditional biases and resentments could already be heard bubbling, the motion carried. Then the voters settled down to consider the first of the forty-two articles on the Warrant.

In the week before the taxpayers arrived to use and scrutinize it, Town Hall had been given its annual facelift, an exercise designed less for the comfort of the voters than as an advertisement for the efficiency of those in power. The polished floors of the auditorium (which doubled as a gymnasium) suggested a fair degree of municipal well-being, and the fresh paint in the downstairs lobby proved that if the environment of government was inevitably more drab than glamorous, at least someone was trying. The defunct lightbulbs on the ceiling had been replaced, and the basketball hoops on the sides tied back. The banks of ancient wooden folding chairs, however, were a reminder of how long and tedious these meetings could be, and after the first hour made some voters feel like they had been sitting there since the previous year; the coats and wraps thrown over their backs and piled on the floor created a scene not unlike that of a crowded bus station during wartime.

Standing at the lectern at center stage was the moderator, Mr. MacKinnon; at a table on his right sat Betty Lacavalla, the recording secretary for as long as anyone could remember. Beneath them, on one side, were the Town Manager, the Board of Selectmen, the Chief of Police, and the Health Agent, and, on the other, the members of the Finance Committee, who periodically tempered the voters' whims and flights of fancy with reminders about what was—and was not—actually affordable. In the balcony at the rear of the auditorium, those who were not registered voters sat in quasi-exile, albeit with a view of the proceedings to rival that at Marineland. Outside in the hallway, constantly and without let-up, people huddled for private powwows, gossiping and deliberating on the business going on inside, and making just enough noise to keep the people in the back rows from being able to hear while not making enough to reach the moderator, who would certainly have banged his gavel over it.

Mr. MacKinnon was banging his gavel now, to encourage silence. The most important but least understood articles on the Warrant came first. These were the large institutional matters, operating budgets and debt financing, the disbursement and appropriation of sums of money so large that the average voter could not but be mystified. Although there were those well-informed enough to rise and make comments, the majority tried to understand the articles even as they were being debated, and noted whether the Town Manager or Board of Selectmen had requested them, and whether the Finance Committee had recommended them. Duane Claggett and Jim Kiernan, being impeccably civil with one another and directing their comments through the moderator to the voters, were the chief molders of opinion, and while the deeper implications of these articles were understood by few, the prospect of approving or withholding approval for such large sums of money was a source of satisfaction to all. This was bread-and-butter, nuts-and-bolts work, work that required concentration and patience, and it was not until the end of the first night that an article came up that wasn't a matter of abstract monetary issues and fiduciary inscrutabilities, but of MORALS in capital letters. For in the issue of public nudity on the beaches of Sun Town, the voters finally had an issue they could sink their teeth into.

The article was number thirty-six on the Warrant, but when the voters had begun to turn their attention to article twelve ("to see whether the Town will subsidize financing of certain improvements to the town pier, or take any other action relative thereto"), Mrs. Meldahl, from the Board of Selectmen, moved that the public nudity issue be taken out of sequence and considered instead. Her motion carried, and the audience came to life; those who were gossiping in the hall, or buying coffee and doughnuts at the Volunteer Fire Department booth downstairs, quickly returned to their seats. Electricity filled the air.

Mrs. Meldahl spoke first, and skillfully disguised her personal repugnance for nude bathing with arguments about the bad publicity the town was receiving on account of it; at the conclusion of her statement a sea of hands went up. As Mr. MacKinnon surveyed the now-impassioned audience and meted out his favor, Mrs. Meldahl was seconded, thirded, and fourthed by people who rose to denounce the effect nude bathing was having on the children of the town (and by implication the morals of the nation), and appealed to everything from law and order to the expressed wishes of the Divinity. This angry protest had begun to build up steam when the moderator made a tactical mistake, and chose from among the field of trembling flowers a blossom of a different kind.

The young woman in the floppy hat and brocaded denim jacket spoke with the earnestness of Patrick Henry:

"I think bodies are rilly, rilly *biewteeful.* "Y'*kniew?* Bodies are nothing to be ashamed of! If Sun Town isn't the place for us to get in touch with our bodies, where else are we going to do it? Dr. Straviniaskin, my therapist, says we have to learn to *accept* our bodies, that it's the first step in getting in touch with our creative unconscious. Y'*kniew?* Soo I rilly, rilly feel that there's *noo* reason for everyone here tonight to get *soo* uptight. Y'*kniew?*"

"Thank you very much, miss ahh. . . ," said the moderator when there was a lull in this fantasia, "miss, *ahh. . . .*" The young woman, apparently unaware that her speech had concluded, gave her name as if pleased to be registering it for all eternity, and Mr. MacKinnon repeated it to Betty Lacavalla—and no doubt filed it as One to Stay Away From.

The liberals and let-livers had their inning now, and rose in succession to pooh-pooh the narrow provincialism of the previous speakers, to appeal to civil liberties and the natural enlightenment of the well-to-do, to point out that nude bathing was being practiced by comparatively few people on sequestered parts of the town beaches, and finally to challenge the article on legal grounds. The debate was bogging down in legal technicalities, with Charles Swann bickering with the Town Counsel, when Mr. MacKinnon—perhaps assuaging his personal frustration—turned to his left, looked out over the crowded hall, and with his magic wand tapped:

"Mr. Benedict!"

There was a stunned silence.

Vodka Man rose up slowly, but in his crumpled and disheveled way, with dignity.

"I think we're makin' much too big a deal outta this!"

he said. He cleared his throat and wiped his face with a hand-kerchief. "This here bathin' in the raw ain't that big a deal, it just ain't that big a deal! You see what I'm sayin'?"

He waited until the effect of his statement had sunk in, and sat down. There were looks of horror mixed with looks of amusement, and then a burst of applause—an impish, cheerful outpouring—from those around him. The people closest to him reached over and patted him on the back, those at his side shook his hand; had it been any other issue or any other speaker, the contagion might have spread. But:

"Silence, please!" announced Mr. MacKinnon, banging his gavel. "Let us try to make constructive remarks, if you will, let us try to make coherent points. And especially, let us not have such outbursts."

The spirited defense of nude bathing by those on the right side of the aisle resumed, and after some further remarks on the issue by the Town Counsel, the question was put to a vote. It was decided "to take no action regarding nude bathing at the present time."

Many things were talked about, that night, by people wandering up Bay Street or conducting post-mortems at the Cannonball Cafe or the Sundowner, but none more than La-mont Benedict's debut as a public speaker. When he showed up at the second night's session—ushered in once again like a visiting dignitary—the anticipation over what he might say or do provided a tingle of excitement whose effect was to make the townspeople more attentive to the business at hand. But Vodka Man was apparently not one to squander his shot, and by the time he made a statement, many in the audience had lost hope for such diversion. The issue on which he spoke—and what he said—surprised everyone. On the surface it was a question of zoning, but what was really at stake in the article was permission for a fast-food company to open a franchise in town. It proved to be a classic case of development, redounding to the benefit of the locals on the left side of the aisle, versus preservation, appealing to the liberals and newcomers on the right. A number of restaurateurs, including Dutch Dugan, spoke against the article, then some folks who stood to profit from more relaxed zoning—including Dr. Burnham—spoke for it. The debate had bumped and stumbled along for forty-five minutes when Mr. MacKinnon, apparently trying to defuse passions, recognized Vodka Man.

There was a sudden relaxation of tension in the room; it was as though the question had been turned over to a wise and impartial judge who would now render a verdict. The veteran of beaches and alleys—despite his best efforts, looking sleepy and disheveled—got up slowly and turned to the crowd.

"I think we can do better than this!" he bellowed. "Can't this town do better than this? I been in this town a long time, and I think this town deserves better'n this!"

He stared significantly at the voters, and sat down.

Again there was a burst of applause from the people around him, this time accompanied by whistles and foot-stamping. It was as though the speaker had provided the definitive statement on the matter, settled the question once and for all.

Although it was not at all clear what he meant (as many observed later), his statement apparently contributed to the outcome of the vote. After twenty-five more minutes of heated debate, permission for a fast-food franchise was denied.

The next issue was the annual flooding on Creek Road. Did Vodka Man have an opinion on this, too?

He did.

"People got to have dry basements!" he boomed, from his stronghold on the right side of the aisle. "It ain't no fun bein' wet! Believe me, I been wet plenty a' times! And it ain't no fun! Besides, I think this town deserves better than this! Don't y'all agree? I think we deserve better'n this!"

This time, even the skeptical and disapproving responded. Across the room there was cheering, whistling, and applause. People smiled at one another as if to say, *hey, Vodka Man isn't so dumb!* and forgot their troubles, and Mr. MacKinnon abstained from banging his gavel and instead looked over at Betty Lacavalla, and winked. There could no longer be any doubt about it: Vodka Man was becoming a force in town.

In the final debate of the evening, however, the candidate was strangely silent. Although it was one of the few areas in which he might have considered himself an expert, a cloud descended over him the minute the discussion began. The article concerned Chief Hogue's request for a new police cruiser, and funding for two additional summer patrolmen. Although he was a persuasive advocate for his department's needs, Chief Hogue rose to speak at a time when the voters' attention was waning, and when, after an evening of spending and appropriating, they were having second thoughts about their own largesse. The first objection was raised by Barbara Troutman, an impassioned feminist who judged every issue by its effect on women, who rose to ask why the Chief always referred to his "men," and why the department couldn't "take more affirmative action in the hiring of women," specifically, why the officers he was requesting "couldn't be female." Without missing a beat, the Chief replied that while he was "personally in full agreement with the sentiments of the previous speaker," there were "certain physical realities of law enforcement" that made her recommendations "problematical," nevertheless he would "do everything" in his power to "accommodate" her. His reply did not come off with quite the spirit of conciliation he intended. Next, the chair recognized Bob Harlan, who stood up and in a brief, pointed statement planted seeds of doubt all around him. "When crime increases," he said, "police departments inevitably ask for more men and more money. But why shouldn't it be looked at the other way around, that an increase in crime means the police aren't doing their jobs? What are the criteria, here, for satisfactory performance? And how much money does this town think it can spend on its police department? Most importantly of all, why should a police department that isn't doing its job be rewarded with increased funding?"

As speaker after speaker echoed this sentiment, and the issue moved toward a vote, it looked for once as though Chief Hogue weren't going to get what he wanted. Then Mr. MacKinnon recognized the Town Manager.

Big Jim was positively eloquent on this one. He began with a personal testament to the Chief's character, and referred to the "great pleasure" it had been to work with him, over the years. He reviewed the situation of the town from the point of view of crime prevention, and suggested that there were certain "factors," certain "contingencies of a confidential nature" which only he as Town Manager could be aware of, that made it "absolutely imperative" that the Chief be given what he was asking for. Through his passion and pleading, his exhortations and veiled threats, Big Jim was at last able to rekindle the dampened fires of civic virtue, and when the question was put to a vote it carried handily.

ELEVEN

To the secret delight of the voters, he was there again on Wednesday night. This time the issue upon which he felt called to speak—and to which, in a curious way, he gave the definitive statement—was the town's leash laws, specifically an article prohibiting dogs from the town's beaches. Before he could rise and have his say, however, Mrs. Elizabeth Wilford Rainey, who turned up at Town Meeting every year with a lot on her mind, had, and had, and had, and had, hers.

"Mr. Moderator, I think it's time the people of Sun Town stood back and took a good hard look at what's happening to them in terms of their lives, as a consequence of big government infiltrating little communities like our own. I have here a document, Mr. Moderator, that shows that in a recent two-year period, Congress introduced fifteen thousand bills and passed five hundred, while states like our own, the states combined, introduced *two hundred and fifty thousand bills* of which *fifty thousand*, Mr. Moderator, became law. I submit that this body of law has crept up around us like the tentacles of an octopus while we, the public, slept, and that it now has us in a stranglehold. Do the people of this town know, I wonder, that anyone buying, selling, or transporting eggs must have permission to do so from the Department of Agriculture? Or that the states now require licenses for more than three hundred and fifty different occupations, everything from TV-antenna installation to cesspool cleaning? Well, these are just some of the ways that regulation—I should say, overregulation—has seeped into our lives, Mr. Moderator, and I think it's time we called a halt to these encroachments on our freedoms, it's time that we, the little people, stood up and said, *We're not going to take it anymore, we're not going to let the unknowing forces of history dictate to us what we can, and cannot do.* Now, another thing concerning this accumulation of government regulation—"

"Mrs. Rainey, are you saying that a leash law that would prohibit dogs from the town's beaches is a—"

"What?"

"Are you trying to say that a leash law prohibiting dogs from the beaches of Sun Town is a further example of government overregulation?"

"I'm coming to that, Mr. Moderator. I'm coming to that. But please, let me proceed. When the Founding Fathers met in Philadelphia during the terribly hot summer of 1787 to hammer out the principles by which this country would be governed—I don't need to tell you that their efforts culminated in the United States Constitution—they had an extremely arduous task before them. For it is not always easy to reconcile the demands of individual and group freedom, to determine the line where the I, or me, or individual ends, and the you, or yous collectively, begins. But they labored over these questions on days when the temperature reached as high as a hundred degrees, Mr. Moderator, and what they gave us was a charter of national organization which we now hold sacred, and which eventually came to include the Bill of Rights. Now, the Constitution guarantees many things, Mr. Moderator, but it does not—"

"Uh, Mrs. Rainey—"

"It does not, as so many people think, guarantee people the right to load up with every kind of weapon, the so-called 'right to bear arms.' Because if you read it closely, Mr. Moderator, the Second Amendment to the Constitution says, and I quote, 'A well-regulated militia, being necessary to the security of a free state, the right of the people to keep and bear arms shall not be abridged.' But you see? The 'right to bear arms' refers to a militia, and we don't even have militias, anymore!"

"Uh, Mrs. Rainey," said the moderator, shifting his weight and fiddling with a note pad on the lectern, "I think you're getting a bit far afield. Could I ask you, please, to come to your point?"

"I am, Mr. Moderator, I am. But don't you see? For two centuries, now, we've allowed every crook and hoodlum in the country to go out and buy a Saturday-night special and do god-only-knows-what with it—simply because of a confusion in the way we read the Constitution! And now we're about to let someone make yet another needless decision in our lives, I mean, where I can, and cannot walk my dog. And there isn't any precedent for it, clear or implied, Mr. Moderator, there isn't any precedent whatsoever! It's exactly the same thing with school desegregation!"

"Mrs. Rainey!"

"Yes, yes, Mr. Moderator, I know. I didn't mean to take up so much time, but I'm almost finished. I just want to say this. I just want to point to what's happening to this country as a result of our failure to stand up and be counted. Now, I know that dogs can creep up behind people on public beaches—

children especially—and from their own enthusiasm and exuberance, you might say, scare the *bejesus* out of them. But the consequence of our sitting back and letting those who make the laws do our thinking for us is that we now have a government that's spending two thirds—*two thirds,* I say—of its annual budget on defense and defense-related items, while it chisels away at school lunches and social welfare programs. Here we sit, with our nuclear bombs poised and ready to blow up the whole freekin' planet—excuse me, ladies and gentlemen—while the environment deteriorates with every passing day—"

"Mrs. Rainey! Now I'm telling you! That's about enough!"

"And totally apart from safety considerations, becomes hopelessly polluted. Take what's happening in the atmosphere, for example, and how it affects the rain that falls—"

"Mrs. Rainey, please! I really must ask you! I think you've made your point, and it's . . . perfectly clear! But there are other voters who would like to speak on the article, other folks who have opinions to express! And I think it would be polite if you left some time for them!"

"Okay, Mr. Moderator, okay. I didn't mean to go on so long. Really. I'll summarize, I'll just summarize. Me, the way I live—"

"Mrs. Rainey!"

"I'm just going to say this one thing, Mr. Moderator."

"Briefly, please!"

"The way I live, I get up about five-thirty in the morning, and take my dog, Fishbone, for a walk on the beach. Now I ask you: what's wrong with my being out on the beach with my

dog, at that hour? Who does it harm, who does it inconven-
ience? But if you're going to tell me that some gendarme who's
probably been up all night and has nothing better to do is going
to jump out of the bushes and start waving his badge—and
spoil the only minutes of peace I *get* in a day—well, I say to you
tonight, ladies and gentlemen: that's exactly what happened in
Nazi Germany, with the Gestapo banging on people's doors at
all hours. Ladies and gentlemen, let me ask you this evening, do
you know the word, fascism? If you don't, I suggest you famil-
iarize yourself with it, because it's what we are talking about in
this debate, tonight. *Fascist* leash laws. A town that has *fascist*
leash laws. We once fought a war against a man who would
impose such laws; his name was Adolf Hitler, and the policy he
instituted of—"

Mrs. Rainey, Mrs. Rainey! I cannot let you go on! No
no, that's it! I'm afraid I've allowed you all the time you're going
to get! You've had your say, now you *must* sit down!"

Nonplussed, Mrs. Rainey looked up at the stage.

"Mr. Moderator, I know I've gone on much too long,
and I apologize to the good people of this town. But I have my
dog with me. Can Fishbone say something?"

"No, that's it, Mrs. Rainey! Please take your seat! Don't
force me to resort to more extreme measures! Is the sergeant-
at-arms in the house? Where is the sergeant-at-arms!"

"I have *Fishbone* here, and he'd like to say something."

"Is there a goddamn policeman in the house? Christ,
where is the sergeant-at-arms? Someone call the sergeant-at-
arms!"

"Just a joke, Mr. Moderator. Just a joke. So I'll conclude.

In conclusion, I'd like to say thank-you to everyone. Thank you, ladies and gentlemen, for your attention this evening."

Mrs. Rainey gathered up her papers, and from the microphone in the aisle where she had been speaking, edged down the row to her seat and sat down. Her demeanor suggested that if she had considered her listeners to be on her own intellectual level, she could have said more.

But it was Vodka Man's oration that was recalled and savored after the four nights of Town Meeting were finally over. Rising up as if oblivious to all that had gone before—as if in the light of his own intense brooding little of it mattered—he wiped his cheeks with a handkerchief.

"Mr. Mard'rator?" he said. "There are dogs in this town that live better than people do. Why so much rantin' and ravin' about dogs? I know certain dogs that eat an' live better than certain people! Can't this town do better than this? I think this town deserves better'n this!"

Once again, it was not only his own crowd who cheered, but the entire auditorium, which erupted into a deafening chorus of clapping, stamping, and whistling. If it had been a presidential nominating convention, this would have been the moment when the delegates stood up and strutted around the hall, the band playing, placards waving, balloons pouring down out of the ceiling. *Whether he made sense or not, Vodka Man was fun.* Why *not* rock the foundations of town politics by getting him elected? The applause fed on itself, swelled to a tumultuous chorus; people traded handshakes and high fives, in the balcony several people began to dance. The voters tried to tease the performer out for an encore, or at least another bow, but Vodka

Man remained glued to his seat, stern and unsmiling. He looked like a man in need of a good stiff drink.

Whether or not it is what he intended, when the article concerning leash laws was put to a vote, dogs were *not* prohibited from the beaches of Sun Town.

Whether or not it was what he intended. . . . As they left Town Hall, that night, Big Jim and Duane Claggett and the members of the Board of Selectmen were not smiling. Most had been doing everything they could to ingratiate themselves with the voters and to defend the status quo, all the while spicing their remarks with lighthearted ridicule of the man who had nothing more to offer than that "the town deserves better than this." Some were buttonholing voters before, during, and after the sessions to express concern over what was happening, all were growing more nervous as the election—with its single candidate—neared. On the fourth and final night, he was there again, surrounded by his entourage and being treated like a celebrity, a silver-tongued orator, a modern-day Daniel Webster; his mere ability to sit through the entire four nights of Town Meeting was winning him unexpected sympathy. And once again, at the end of a long debate on a sensitive issue, the ball was dropped into his court. This time the question was whether the town "should construct a new residential care facility for the elderly," or "make state-mandated renovations to the existing structure." Everyone who spoke on the article was sympathetic to the problems of the elderly, but most knew that the tax rate could not support a new facility. There was Vodka Man, however, standing up like a gnarled tree among tangled underbrush:

"These are just old people!" he rasped, as if this were a

profound insight. "These are people that are just old! It ain't no fun bein' old! Hell, I known *plenty* a' old people! And I think this town deserves better than this! Frankly, if this'ere town can't do better'n this, I for one don't want to live here anymore! 'Cause I know in my heart that this town deserves better'n this!"

Now, pandemonium. The entire auditorium burst into clapping and foot-stamping; hats, gloves—even doughnuts—filled the air. Mr. MacKinnon banged his gavel, but a chant of "Vodka Man for Selectman, Vodka Man for Selectman!" started up, and in the midst of it the grizzled candidate stood up and led a great cheering crowd down the aisle. Half leading, half propelled along by those behind him, he spearheaded a march up Center Street to Crescent Street and the high school football field, where an impromptu celebration began; with his quorum dissolving, Mr. MacKinnon adjourned the meeting, and a large number of curious townspeople followed. A bonfire was constructed, and the event turned into a town-wide rally, one the police made little attempt to break up. Mock-somber speeches were given on Vodka Man's behalf, and tongue-in-cheek toasts offered; before the flickering pile of sticks and leaves—like a knight bowing to accept Holy Orders—Vodka Man was officially christened: Humanitarian, Conciliator, Spokesman for the People . . . Candidate for Selectman.

With the deadline for filing only two days away, the beleaguered representatives of the status quo mounted a last-ditch effort to restore sanity to the electoral process, to stop the foolishness and return to the selectman's race a semblance of normality. To the relief of Duane Claggett and Jim Kiernan, Town Meeting had been conducted with just enough decorum to restore confidence in the way the town was being run, and with Vodka Man no longer having a forum in which to amuse and titillate the voters, to appeal to their seemingly endless capacity for perversity, reality intervened and he became less of a threat. The factions that Duane and Big Jim dominated were each able to come up with candidates who, if their chief qualifications were that they were not too repugnant to the other side, were at least *alternatives*. There was no getting around the fact, however, that Vodka Man held out the promise of something neither of these candidates could match: the spontaneous, the perverse, the offbeat—the comic and unpredictable.

The police were never able to determine who was responsible for the mischief that took place four nights before the election, and after doing what they could—talking to parents and teachers, questioning the usual ringleaders—they gave up trying. There had been a gaggle of kids hanging around the cannon on the village green, that night, playing guitars and trading shadow punches, and having heard about Vodka Man's Town Hall antics, perhaps some of them had taken umbrage at what they felt was a mockery of their town. Some were probably confused over whether Vodka Man was now a respectable character or just the old street bum who, for as long as they could remember, had been part of their landscape, the butt of their humor. In a sense, Vodka Man had betrayed them. If, by the rules of the street they could ridicule him from afar, he also had his own sanctuaries in which they did not belong and into which they did not venture. It was an uneasy alliance, and he had violated it; he had made himself still another component in a chameleon-like world whose rules kept changing. The kids had learned to express outward regret over the gay-bashing that occasionally took place during the summer, but for one of the townspeople—one of their own, in a sense—to defect and join the world of the chameleons was just too much.

When the call came saying that Vodka Man was being roughed up by some bullies on Creek Road, Warren Hogue and another officer hurried out of the police station. On his way to the cruiser, the Chief stopped at his car and grabbed a satchel off the front seat; then, with siren screaming, they raced across town.

"Well, if it ain't the *blue taxi*," Vodka Man snarled from the bottom of the caved-in hedge where they found him. He stared up at the glare of flashlights: "This had better not mean a trip to the motel with no windows, 'cause I ain't done nuthin'. I ain't had a drop. Just some kids mad at me 'cause I'm *runnin'*."

He tried to extract himself from the mass of shrubbery but his arm gave way, and with a wrenching of twigs and branches he toppled back into the bushes.

"Keep your mitts off," he growled from the bottom of the heap. "I said. I ain't had a drop. An' I ain't done *nuthin'*."

"Okay, okay," said Chief Hogue. "Just tell us who did it, and we'll let you go."

This time the victim accepted the hand that was offered, but this time the officers—two more of whom arrived —saw that he was in real pain.

"What is it, Monty? Your shoulder?"

Gently, now, the four officers pried back the tangled bushes and helped the candidate to his feet. They had had enough experience with drinkers to know when they had an emergency on their hands and when, for reasons of his own, the victim was feigning, and this was a Vodka Man they had never seen before.

"Sam," said Chief Hogue, "call the dispatcher. Tell her to get hold of Dr. Burnham and ask him to come down to his office. There's no need to get the rescue squad out on this one; we can take him over there ourselves. Now you guys, look around and see what you can find. I don't think you're gonna find *much*—I think it was just some of the kids bein' vindictive —but look around anyway. Now, Mr. Benedict, if you'll come with me—no, we're not gonna take you to the station, I promise, we're *not* gonna lock you up. If you'll come with me, we'll take you to the doctor's. You're a, uh, pretty important person in this town, you know."

They led their twig-twinkled victim over to the cruiser and helped him into the back seat; then the Chief and his driver got in the front.

"No need to floor it, John," said Chief Hogue. "Let's just take it real nice 'n easy."

He rested his arm on the top of the seat and looked back at his passenger:

"That hurts, doesn't it."

"Yeah, it hurts. Damn *right*, it hurts. If you ask me, this town deserves better'n this."

The Chief opened the satchel at his side, and from

beneath some first-aid equipment and a blanket removed a
bottle with an ornate label. He turned to his passenger.

"Like some?"

Vodka Man stared at it, then at the Chief. Eventually he
braced himself and reached forward with his good arm. He
held the bottle up and took a prolonged swig, wiped his good
arm across his mouth, inspected the bottle again, and took another gulp. He rolled his tongue around his lips, smacked them.

"Go ahead, have some more. In fact, you can keep the
bottle."

On the Chief's whispered instructions, the driver took
the long way around to the doctor's.

"Well, Mr. Benedict, they must have given you quite a
shove!" said Doctor Burnham, as he palpated the neck and
shoulder of his subdued patient. "I could tell by the way you
moved that you hadn't *broken* your shoulder, but I think you
may have dislocated it. In any case, it's popped back into place
so there's not too much I can do for you. But I'm sorry to tell
you that it's going to hurt like hell. For all the pain you're going
to have, you might as *well* have broken it. I'm going to give you
a sling that you should wear for a couple of days; try not to
move your shoulder any more than you have to. And I'm going
to give you some pills that ought to ease the pain, some."

The doctor glanced at Warren Hogue as if it were necessary to give his instructions not to the patient himself, but to
a responsible guardian. As he reached for the pills, in fact, he
spoke directly to the Chief, looking at him with an insider's
smile and staring at him pointedly as he said:

"But these pills are pretty strong, so you don't want to

mix them with alcohol. Stay away from alcohol, will you? I'll give you enough to get you through the night, and a prescription that you can have filled tomorrow. But please. Stay away from alcohol."

Looking vulnerable and haggard in his sling and twig-dotted overcoat, Vodka Man was helped out of the doctor's office, down the front steps, and into the back seat of the police cruiser. The Chief knew that of the various places he slept on cold nights, the garage behind Mrs. Ganzi's rooming house on Water Street was his chosen preference. After a bit of persuading, his passenger agreed to be taken there.

"*Personalized surface*," Lamont Benedict muttered, as he got out of the car with the help of his chauffeurs.

"You need a coupla bucks?" said the Chief.

Vodka Man was swaying slightly. He extended his good arm from inside his coat and accepted the offer, then turned around, headed down the walk, and was gone. As the chief got back in the car, he glanced into the back seat.

So was the bottle of brandy.

Even before he confronted him, the next morning, Duane Claggett knew that Vodka Man had been drinking. He had seen him with a brown bag in his pocket on his way to work. Now, with Vodka Man standing beneath him, he could smell the alcohol on his breath. The pharmacist felt sorry for Vodka Man, sorry for the way he looked and sorry for the pain he was in. But Percodan, *1Q4H or PRN?* Percodan, one every four hours, or as needed? Percodan and alcohol? Alcohol and Percodan? He would as soon have mixed glycerol with nitric acid.

For reasons he did not understand, Duane's hands were moist. It was as though he were a priest preparing a sacrament, but there were some irregularity in the way he were going about it. He looked up to see if anyone were watching. The cashier below him was stocking the shelves, the people at the soda fountain were engrossed in their conversation; behind him there were only boxes and bottles, capsules and tubes. *Lamont Benedict probably wouldn't know better than to take two or three at a time, take them by the handful, swallow the entire bottle. Could the man even read?*

As he stood studying the prescription, Duane's fingers began to shake.

But this isn't my responsibility. I didn't write the prescription. I'm just a middleman, the executor of other people's orders. They're trained to do what they do, I'm trained to do what I do. Is this any more than the logical outcome of the way the man lives? Just one more disaster in a life full of disasters? No, no, it's not my responsibility.

For some reason, Duane thought of his father, and of his grandfather who had founded the store. He was perspiring now, and the store was beginning to twist and spin; he felt he was being sucked into a dark hole, a whirlpool. Surrounded as he was by medications, *there was not a single one of them, at this moment, that would solve his dilemma, salve his conscience, tell him what to do. For once, there was no prescription for the correct behavior.*

Now and for the next few minutes, Duane Claggett was not himself, but someone else, a trained professional, a functionary in a white lab jacket taking orders, filling orders. Someone else took control of his shaking hands, and someone else reached for the supply bottle and poured out, and counted, the pills. Someone else produced a label and peeled it off, and applied it to the amber vial; someone else dropped the vial in a paper bag, and stapled it. Someone else came down from the platform and around to the front, accepted the payment and placed it in the cash register. Hurriedly, someone else went on to other duties.

Whether Vodka Man could actually have won the election is talked about in Sun Town to this day. Although he made a strong enough showing to embarrass Jim Kiernan and Duane Claggett, he received fewer votes than the other two candidates. There was no doubt, however, that his behavior in the days immediately preceding the election seriously undermined his cause. Loud and belligerent where he had always been docile and self-effacing, he would provoke someone to call the police, then, by the time they got there, would have gone somewhere else, all the while waving his good arm and shouting obscenities. Because he had misplaced his overcoat, his sling got covered with dirt and grime, and in order to stay warm—so he later told the police—he had started drinking again.

Having had its laugh, however, the town now took pity on him. After discreet conversations between Jim Kiernan, Jack Burnham, Warren Hogue, and the Board of Health, it was decided that if he were placed in an environment where he would have no access to alcohol and where his medication could be carefully monitored, he would gradually settle down. Although technically not yet eligible for the town's nursing home, arrangements were made to have him admitted, and gradually his anger and hostility abated. While his behavior continued to be unpredictable for as long as he lived, a constant mild level of sedation was sufficient to keep him from being a problem either to the town or to himself.

Although it was Jack Pettigill, Duane Claggett's man, who won the election, Big Jim also got a taste of victory, and it was not long before the genial bear and the pious stickler were back at their tug of war, pushing and pulling at one another as they attempted to run the town according to their own philosophies. With Chief Hogue, Big Jim's relations returned to being civil and discreet; each gave the other his sphere of influence, and did his best to stay out of the other's hair. On the matter of a zoning variance for the house Dr. Burnham wanted to build on Kinriddy Point, pressures were put on the Zoning Board of Appeals, and eventually he got the permit he needed. For years afterward—for as long as the doctor, the Police Chief, and the Town Manager continued to work for, and do business in the town—their relations remained very cordial.

TWELVE

"Another cara*fay*," Felix says, smiling. "Another carafay of cha*blay* for Lee Castleton. How's the augustitis? Think you're gonna make it?"

Between its starting line—Memorial Day—and finish line—Labor Day—the season in Sun Town moves forward over a series of hurdles: Father's Day, the Blessing of the Fleet, July 4th, its weekend and parade, then the most important one of all, the one greeted with the greatest fear and trembling, the first day of August. It is locally thought that the start of August marks the end of rationality and clear-headedness. Workers in the shops and restaurants must be prepared to operate on automatic from here on, because the crush of people and cars, the daily toll of heat, noise, and confusion, will make forethought and patient planning impossible. Precisely because they have begun to see the light at the end of the tunnel (and even to talk about how fast the summer is going), when the disease they call *augustitis* strikes, the workers of the town will inevitably be caught with their defenses down. Say or do what they will, August will settle on them like a massive leaden weight, a flying machine so loaded with strange freight that it resists all efforts to get it airborne again. For the shop clerks and street vendors, the boat renters and taffy pullers, the taxi drivers and chambermaids, this is the time of stoicism and willed endurance. These are the dog days, and they go doggedly on.

"Barely," Lee replies. "I'd be doing better with it if Dutch would keep his hands off me."

For the owners of the restaurants and businesses, however, this is the boom time, the time when the gold rush starts in earnest. This is the month in which expenses have been re couped and the break-even point reached, the month in which a profit, if there is to be one, must be shown, the month on which, finally, the entire economy of the town depends. This is the month in which you find out *whether they love you or they don't*, and Dutch, standing behind the ficus tree observing the hustle and bustle of his restaurant, senses—indeed, knows from the top of his head to the soles of his feet—that he is home free. In the kitchen, plates are clattering, in the lounge people are waiting to be seated, at the front desk new names are going in the rezzy book; *why, they're even serving on the patio.* The scene strikes Dutch as a complicated wind-up toy of which he is the inventor, and of whose workings only he has a complete understanding; he contemplates it with immense satisfaction. It is a carnival, a county fair in which all the lights are swirling, all the rides are full, and all the people are having fun.

But he cannot just stand there doing nothing, no. He must make sure that things are under control in the kitchen, he must ask Felix if he needs anything brought down from the liquor closet, he must tell Kathy and Karen that he is available to help if they need him. He has become the coach of a great team, a plump little man surrounded by players who, despite their broad shoulders and bulging muscles, are dependent on him for strategy, require his guidance from the sidelines. He grabs a busboy and points to a table that needs clearing, and with a pat on the shoulder sends him back into the fray. He stops a waiter who, while being entrusted to carry a play out to the huddle (*23 jump, quick out*), is painfully aware that he is losing valuable time. He gives Kelly Furness some personal advice and exhorts her back onto the field. He heads to the bar to check on things, but finds it so crowded that getting within striking distance to do any good is out of the question. He returns to the ficus tree, and surveys the happy spectacle—

And sees Courtney Johnson standing over a paunchy diner who has his shirt unbuttoned. Courtney pulls his own shirt up to his chin, and the man opens his further. They're holding their shirts up, and smiling! Now Courtney rolls up his pant leg—are they going to undress right there in the middle of his restaurant?—and the man bends to his side and does the same. They point to one another's calves and inspect them; even the ladies are straining to see! What the hell is going on? What the hell are they doing, right there in the middle of his restaurant, their big fat stomachs hanging out?

"What the hell was *that* all about?" Dutch screams, when Courtney comes off the floor. "What the hell are you doing!"

He is up on his toes with excitement.

"Zipper Club," Courtney replies. "We've both had open-heart surgery, and it's interesting to compare scars." Dutch starts to say something, but: "They take some of the veins out of your calf, and we who've been through the operation like to compare that incision, too."

Courtney smiles with such innocent pride that Dutch, flabbergasted, hesitates. In that instant Courtney glances at his order book—*I'd like to tell you more about it*, his expression says, *but time is money*—flips the sheet over, and disappears into the kitchen.

The genial proprietor is not convinced he has seen what he has seen, and decides to take the issue to his court of last resort in such matters, Karen and Kathy. But Karen is calling to a group of patrons in the foyer, and Kathy is not impressed.

"Cross of the Bypass," she says, as if it were a military decoration, and definitely Old News.

He wants to have a few words with Karen, but Karen is dutifully leading the party to their table, and two customers who apparently didn't understand that their waiter would take their money—*are they getting behind out there?*—are waiting to pay. He thinks to check on the lobsters out front, then decides it would be better if he got downwind and away from the eager, milling crowd. He steps to the side so that he will not again have to confront Courtney, then—*primus inter pares*—bursts through the swinging doors into the kitchen.

"I got a veal parma-pajama!" Dave calls, over the din. Using the end of his apron as a pot holder, he places the platter in the pick-up area. "I got a bay and beef! I got a one-half spring! Two minutes on the haddock, two minutes on the sole!" He turns back to the stove before Dutch can get his attention. Dutch makes his way through the kitchen, sees one of the line cooks hunched over the Frialator—*don't tell me, you dropped your ring in it*—and gets sidetracked by the sight of the dishwasher standing in spilled food. Plates stacked everywhere he doesn't mind, even on the floor beneath the counter. But garbage in which a worker is standing—

"Hey, you gotta do better than this!" he says to the Sage

of Slop, who takes his eyes off the apparatus long enough to acknowledge him but not long enough to see where he's pointing. "You gotta keep this area cleaner than this!" He feels he's talking to someone through a shower door, in a steamy bathroom. The kid trains his attention on the control knobs, the temperature gauge, the tray of dishes he's sliding into the machine:

"'Cleanliness is next to impossible.'"

"What's that?"

Dutch feels his temperature rising.

"Hey, I'm not talkin' *possible*, I'm talkin' necessary! I run a clean restaurant, and in my restaurant the absence of food on the kitchen floor is a necessity!"

The machine starts to hiss and gurgle, and send steam shooting out the doors. The kid gazes at the contraption as if he were conducting a scientific test and some unwritten rule specified there should be no talking while it was in progress. Dutch feels assaulted by noise, feels steam gathering on his face and neck; the kid is showing him nothing, giving him nothing, he wants to slam his fist into the machine, crush the gauge, wreck the levers.

"Breeds contempt."

"What?"

"Necessity," the kid says, as if talking to himself and accustomed to a noisy wet world in which no one was listening anyway, "breeds contempt."

He wants to slam his fist into it, crush the gauges, send the whole contraption flying, he wants to grab the kid by the back of the neck, and pummel him.

"If this area isn't cleaned up by the time I return, you're fired!" he shouts. He storms out of the kitchen, wondering what in the world he would do without a dishwasher, this late in the season.

"Hey!" Dave calls to Lenny, when they're alone again. "You know that chili bean soup we've been serving? We ought to call it 'Last Gas Before Expressway'!" He turns to the kitchen's central aisle. "I got bouillabaisse goin' hungry! I got haddock! I got chicken bosom! I got sole Provençal! I got . . . deep-fried Doberman!"

These are the dog days, a time when only tempers are easily aroused, a time when ceaseless movement is required on the part of the few to produce satiety and lethargy on the part of the many. These are the days of sunburn and sand in suitcases, of stomach acids and stretched-out credit cards, of ripeness and excess, of the last-minute escape and the long-awaited fling. Still, it is odd the things that can happen at this time of year, thinks Sharon Lowd, as she picks up her haddock and sole Provençal. As she pulls the tray toward her, she adjusts her apron so that the checks in its pocket will not crush the little plastic tube at the bottom. The tip she had received earlier was decent—nothing special—but along with the money, there was a thin cigarette in a neatly labeled plastic tube. "THIS IS A NICE JOINT," it said. Were they teasing her, or going out of their way to show appreciation? Who knew? Who could tell, in this business? And last night it was that other guy. He'd come in with a lot of friends, acted very self-important, and proceeded to tear his shirtsleeve on the arm of his chair. His group racked up a big bill, and on the back of their check, in tortured scrawl, he had written: "Can't Dutch afford some better chairs? *The Phantom Diner.*"

Now as she makes her way through the kitchen, Becky Dent calls to her:

"I had a guy leave me some subway tokens, once! I think I still have 'em!"

Sharon smiles beneath her load, goes and makes her deliveries, and stops to check on one of her parties.

"I have a little seafood problem," says the man at the head of the table.

"A little . . . 'seafood problem'?"

"Yeah. I see food, and I have to *have* some."

The people at the table break into laughter.

"Oh, I've had sufficient, I've had s'fanciful, my shimmy, shirt, and pants're full!"

It's mathematics, thinks Felix. *Simple mathematical probability.* The refrain goes through his mind as he works, and in thoughts he has had so often they do not need thinking—the bar is jumping now—it stays with him for the rest of the night. *Take the probability that a person will exhibit stupid or obnoxious behavior in a public place. Now multiply that probability by the number of persons. The result is the* cumulative *probability that there will be some pretty weird and unpleasant things going on. Now expand your field of inquiry to the variety of life-mistakes people make, the probability that they will make the wrong choices, bog down in indecision, succumb to illusion. Multiply that number by the number of individuals: There you have it, the total number of wrong, stupid, and self-defeating things people do, there's the mathematical basis for understanding that the world will always be a crazy, and not very coherent place.* "Be right with you!" he calls, to a man who is waving money at him. *Thus it requires neither sociology, psychology, nor theology—only a simple mathematical calculation—to show that the world—through no fault of its own, in a sense—is fundamentally compromised, to show that the world will never be without a measure of stupidity and bad taste, that it will always be more or less—and here's the kicker—what it is.*

"Hey, quite the racing hull you got here," says his newest customer. "When's the last time you had her in the water?"

By his expression Felix encourages the man to state his order, then goes to prepare it.

Across from him, Doug Brindle is looking secretive, conspiratorial. Doug is studying the figures he has been compiling of the number of people having dinner at the Dockside. Dutch sweeps by, and Doug sets his beer down on the paper. He overhears the phrase "zipper club," wonders what it refers to. He steals a glance at Dutch.

"That creep says he has a friend in the commercial laundry that does our cloth napkins!" Dutch is telling someone. "This guy, Tony, thinks he can tell *me* how many dinners we do! Thinks he can shake *me* down! Can you believe that?"

Doug takes a rueful look at his numbers and, wondering how he could have been so naive, crumples up the paper and sticks it in his pocket.

"Can I, uh, get a draft?" he says, when Felix returns.

"Sure. Open the window."

Felix catches himself. He has seen enough people *in extremis* to know when to show clemency, mercy. "Hey man, just kidding," he says, as he sets the mug on the bar. "Here, this one's on me."

Does Felix know I'm a writer? Doug thinks.

Next to Doug, a conversation is under way between Mike Cavaliere and a young couple who are entwined in one another's arms.

"Hell, it's nothing but a bunch a' people wigglin' like orangutans!" Mike says, when the conversation turns to disco-dancing.

"But it isn't!" the young woman replies, freeing herself from her companion. "You're only looking at the appearances! When you get out on the floor and actually do it, it's a whole lot of fun! You shake a lot of bad energy out of yourself, shake out all the tension!"

"She's right," the young man agrees; "you can't believe in appearances. Disco's a lot more innocent than it looks, it's just fluff and foolishness, a game in which everybody wins and nobody loses. You see, everyone can think he's the best dancer, and the most beautiful person, on the floor. It's just that the old fogies—no offense—don't get it, and are therefore threatened by it. But it's a lot more innocent than it looks. *All* popular culture is more playful, more innocent, than it looks."

"What ever happened to the foxtrot?" Mike asks. "And the waltz? The jitterbug? Dances where you actually looked like you knew your partner, and *liked* them?"

"Ah, when you waltz or foxtrot, you do it for, and with, your partner," the young man announces, grandly. "But when you do disco, *you dance for the gods.*"

"I'll be sure to tell that to Father Mahady, my parish priest. Aw hell. Hey Felix, give these nice young people a drink!"

But it isn't more innocent, thinks Doug Brindle. *Somehow, the whole damn town is more innocent than it looks—and it isn't.* Eventually he pushes the memory of the Sand Bar restroom—and a man named Tony—out of his thoughts, and returns to more pressing worries. *Why is it that the people who have all the stories don't know how to write them, and the people who know how to write them don't have any stories? Like that jerk, Toby What's-his-name. Oh, he had plenty of stories, all right. But he probably couldn't put one word after another to save his soul. Damn it all, the life of adventure sure doesn't co-exist very well with the solitude required by the life of the writer. So when am I going to start on my novel? I've* got *to get started, and soon.*

Felix comes over and props his foot up on the cooler:

"Hey, didja hear what that guy was sayin', at the end of the bar? I don't know whether he's part of the jet set, or just some kinda international stud, but he was talkin' about all the women he's had in his life. And he says"—Felix tightens up his throat, makes his voice deep—" 'I've had *Vroossian.* I've had *Flench.* I've had *Eeetalyun.*' I felt like saying: 'creamy garlic, thousand islands, oil and vinegar'!"

Doug rocks with laughter, forgets his troubles for a moment, and is pleased that Felix is finally treating him like a Regular.

Statistics. Mathematical probability. Felix makes a drink, collects for another, tends to somebody at the service rail, stuffs some glasses in the glass scrubber. A woman is telling him how she went to a costume party dressed up as a bag lady, only to sit next to a woman who actually *was* a bag lady ("what was I supposed to say to her?"), and now a man is explaining how, when he was young and had no money, he took a single red rose to a girl he was courting, only to have a deliveryman arrive with a full dozen from a richer suitor.

"Write a story about it," Felix says. "Call it 'Baker's Dozen.'"

He moves to the next person, the next story, the next task. His sense of the world is not something he elaborates to himself, but is simply there in the background. His tendency, for example—owing to the *x* in his name—to think in mathematical terms. In a sense, the unknown quantity—*x*—was a component of his name, his name—the very sound of it—contained a mathematical variable. *X-ray. X-rated. The Double Felix.* He flashes on his high-school science teacher, who was always drawing graphs on the blackboard. There had been one about the life of stars, another that related the pressure of a gas to its volume—oh, and in economics—one that showed the marginal propensity to consume in relation to . . . something-or-other. Felix continues to go about his duties, smiles at a joke Doug Brindle tells, and hurries to the end of the bar.

And there it is. Larger than life.

The couple that have been downing tequila and effusing about disco are now well along on what Felix calls the *X Curve*. In Felix's scheme of things, the *X Curve* is a graph in which one line starts at the lower left and curves gracefully upward, and another starts at the upper left and slopes gracefully down. This flattened *X* defines the way communication takes place in the presence of alcohol; it says that *the moment at which a person will share his deepest secrets will always coincide with the moment when his listener is least capable of hearing them.*

And here it is. With the young man firmly gripping the

gunnels of the bar as he speaks, and his girl friend firmly gripping the gunnels as she listens, they perfectly exemplify the *X Curve*: His passion, sincerity, and intensity are intersecting—perfectly—with her incomprehensibility, sleepiness, and fatigue. *And is not that the way with all things?* Felix thinks, standing before the couple. *Is it not true that for every rising curve, every curve of progress and advancement, there is a falling curve of hidden cost or debit, a tendency toward backsliding? The up and down lines cross in the middle of the graph, but few people know why or where they cross, because few people understand the concept.*

"I'm de-pwethed."

Then there was always humanity in the flesh to spoil one's abstract schemes. Materializing like a genie out of a bottle —what angel looked after him that he should so often get his favorite seat?—is the brooding, morose, witty, ingrown figure of Grubby Eddy.

"You're what?"

"De-pwethed."

"*What?*"

"De-pwethed!"

It is as though Grubby Eddy had been waiting all day just to tell him that, as if anything so monumentally important could not be expressed in the normal language of adults. Knowing there is no point in asking why, Felix goes and gets him the usual.

"Augustitis?" he says cheerfully, placing the drink in front of the Buddha-like form.

There it is. And it's on. Grubby Eddy takes a sip of his drink, and leans forward for a better view of the television. A weather forecaster is standing before a map of the nation—*why don't they make it the entire world?*—and smiling earnestly, hopping about, pointing, gesticulating. *I know. Don't tell me. There's a front. There's* always *a front. You're going to tell me there's going to be a change in the weather because a front is coming through, and millions of people are going to feel enlightened by that fact. But when there's a significant change of weather, it's* always *because a front is coming through. So you haven't told us anything!* The forecaster becomes unctuous and ingratiating, he has apparently been entrusted to explain the entire history of the weather, the entire history of the world. He pulls a panel back—he is almost dancing with excitement—and without listening, Grubby Eddy hears the familiar litany. *A blast of cold air unusual for this time of year will be moving across the western states and I'm looking for it to be a little cooler than normal for the next few days, meanwhile a warming trend caused by a flow of air up out of the Gulf will intersect with this front lying just out to sea so it's going to get hot and muggy hopefully it'll pass on through by the weekend, I'll have my forecast in a minute now let's look at the weather on the radar map, as you can see the metro area received some showers during the night but nothing I would call significant and down on the coast the haze that settled in burned off by this morning so here at home I'm looking for it to be warm and sunny, now here are some highs and lows from around the country.*

Of course! You could have walked out your front door and deduced as much! The solitary watcher stares down into his drink, then up again at the television. *Now I suppose he's going to go over to the news desk, like a child who's just recited something very important to the adults, and they're going to laugh and kibitz, chitchat over the fact that temperatures three thousand miles away are a little cooler than usual, and they're going to say Thanks Jim, and Thanks Bob, and Thanks Paula, and. . . . I can't believe people are watching this.*

Felix has placed a fresh drink in front of him, and when he returns his attention to the screen, several world leaders are conversing earnestly with one another. It bores him, it irritates him, it defeats him, he would like to have a private word with any or all of them. As he glances down the bar, he imagines them standing there—all the newsmakers of the day, the statesmen, the criminals, the religious leaders, the accident victims—with drinks in their hands, comparing their treatment by the press. Now it is scenes of combat; Grubby Eddy averts his eyes. *Getting so depressed I have to have another drink. Spending fifteen, twenty bucks a night trying to get over the fact that half the world is starving, being tortured, or hounded out of its homes. There has to be something wrong in that, somewhere.* He chastises himself for letting himself be the passive recipient of idiotic programs, cheap cultural handouts. *The national pastime, talking back to the television. Is that what it's come to? Is that all that's left? Talking back to the television?*

His drink has been freshened up, *freshened up, as they say,* and he watches his hand reach out like the mechanical claw of a robot, and slowly encircle it. *Now where was I? Lost my drain of thought.* He glances at the television again (time is losing its precision now), and a talk-show host is regaling his audience with teleprompter jokes. *For chrissake, let's get this boat on the road.* When he looks up again, the talk-show host is sitting behind a desk and chatting with a buxom starlet. *Press Lever A, and then leave her be.* As though she had won him in a contest drawing, a young man now emerges from behind the curtain—*her knight in flaming armor*—and throws himself into the young woman's arms. *A conservation devoutly to be wished.* The sparkles in the ice of his drink, and the play of light among the bottles behind the bar, have become enough to distract and amuse him. *What mode is this? What mode are we in? Mode lawn. It's a question of the nation's military radiance. Loose hips sink lips. Hands up, motherstick, this is a fuckup! Let's go screwing, you skiball!*

He does not need the television now, but looks at it anyway, contemplating the patterns on the screen, studying the flicker of light, the shifting of colors. Felix is in front of him. *Ah, the auctioneer,* thinks Grubby Eddy. *The man who does nothing but let human nature take its course. Who lets people be exactly what they are. I hate you for that, Felix, you let people be exactly what they are. Aw, just kidding. Would I like a relaxative? Is that what you said? Sure, why not? Gimme a relaxative.* With a serene, all-encompassing feeling of wisdom, peacefulness, and kindness (he is impervious, now, full of beneficence, tolerance, and understanding), he nods. Still there is something wrong. *Spending fifteen, twenty bucks a night to get over the fact that half the world—* No. No. *For once, there is nothing wrong.* He is on the crest of an alcoholic high in which life is an ephemeral game and doesn't mean very much, it's just the epiphenomenon of some more important thing, if only he could remember what that thing was. He is superior to it, outside it, reconciled to it, he is no longer intimidated by it. It's just a passing game, a play of shadows, a manifestation of some much more important thing, if only he could remember what that thing was. He watches his hand reach out like a wily form of marine life, and curl itself slowly around its prey. He does not hear Denise Lefevre's husband get up and say, "See you when the bars burn down!" or see Jack Freund slip through the crowd and take the newly vacated stool. He does not hear what the two bag ladies said to one another at the costume party, or hear Doug Brindle quote the bogus advertising slogan, "Kiss Painful Hemorrhoids Goodbye." He does not hear Courtney Johnson bemoaning the fact that the credit-card machine failed to print and he is going to get stuck with an eighty-dollar tab; he does not see Ed Shakey come into the bar with his friends, and vie over who will buy.

Ed has been thinking, all evening, of Helen, her unhappiness and erratic behavior, her refusal to go to a therapist, and of Lee Castleton's apparent decision to distance herself from him. He had been playing "Alone Together" and wondering whether Lee was seeing someone else, when a man had come over to the stand and said: "We love to have your asset at the piano!"—and had stuck a generous tip in his jar.

"Play something we know the words to!" someone had called. Startled, Ed had turned to discover . . . Steve Dirso! And Troy Fredericks and Larry Buttrick! The three jazz musicians he had hired for the Dockside opening!

"Play some *music*!" Larry called, mimicking the directive that people often gave to musicians who were trying to do just that.

He had someone to play for, now! This was family! He had done "I'm Beginning to See the Light," and "Out of Nowhere," then pulled out the stops and played "It Don't Mean a Thing if it Ain't Got That Swing." At the conclusion of the set, his friends had begun clapping, and continued to clap until the entire room joined in.

Now as he stands at the bar trying to get Felix's attention, Steve explains:

"I got some time off from work, and you can imagine what it's like in the city, so I called Troy and Larry and said: 'Why don't we go down to Sun Town and see what the Shake is up to? Maybe we can get a gig, and do some playin'.' So we threw our sleeping bags and instruments into my van, and here we are."

And nothing could have made Ed Shakey happier.

"Sure, sure," Dutch mumbles. (For a person haunted by the fact that someone wants to siphon off thousands of dollars from his business, whether or not a band plays is not a matter of overriding importance.) "Why don't you play the next two weekends? We won't need a band on Labor Day Weekend, Labor Day Weekend pretty much takes care of itself. And I hate to give up the space."

Now here they are, standing around in the Lifeboat Lounge at the end of the night ("I got left a lottery ticket, once!" a waitress calls to Sharon Lowd, "and a friend got left a pair of eighteen-carat-gold cuff links!") and sharing their news, trading shoptalk and gossip, and getting so engrossed in their reunion that they hardly even hear it when Felix calls:

"Last call, everybody! Hotel-motel time! Last call . . . !"

THIRTEEN

"It's just as well you guys are here, 'cause the television's broken," Dutch comments a week later, as he watches the band set up.

In fact, it is not broken. A loose connection on Tim Mullen's ham antenna is causing his signal to bounce around town and, at the Dockside, to fill the television screen with zigzags and blurs. Having lost patience, Felix has disconnected it.

"Where do you want your p.s.o.?" Troy asks, after Dutch has wandered off. The reference to *piano-shaped object*—musicians' humor—draws a rueful smile from Ed. The group has helped Steve bring in his drums and, the bandstand having been moved closer to the lounge, the question is whether or not to place the piano right next to the wall.

"Oh, leave it out a little," Ed replies, "so I don't feel like I'm playing in the Black Hole of Calcutta. I'm sorry to report that it's not in very good tune. I couldn't get Dutch to spring for a tuning."

"Not to worry," Steve quips. "Nobody listens to the piano player. You know that."

"Everybody knows that," Larry mutters.

"Did I ever tell you," Troy interjects, "about the pianist I knew who arrived at a gig and heard strange sounds coming out of the piano? He lifted the lid and found an angry note from the previous combatant, complete with curses and complaints, and threats about what he was going to do to the instrument—and the owner too, I think. The last line of it was, 'Abandon hope all ye who enter here.' "

"I had a girl friend, once, who had that tattooed over her crotch!" Steve quips.

Ed is pleased to be playing in a group, for a change. Not only could his friends' gentle teasing be forgiven (Steve Dirso, a physically small drummer who nevertheless *listened* could be forgiven anything), but he could detect in their humor an underlying sympathy for his plight. Was it true, as Lee had commented, that he was becoming jaded and cynical? As the group sets up, he considers the possibility, and at the end of their preparation, offers to buy everyone a drink. Felix is even more cordial than usual, and doesn't charge him.

"I don't know quite what I expected out of this life," he says, after they have slumped into a quiet booth and the truth serum has had time to take effect. "More friends, I guess, more close friends. And definitely more applause." He chuckles plaintively. "I guess I should have seen the handwriting on the wall. Did I ever tell you about my first gig?" (Musicians' stories are like salted peanuts, and can be consumed in endless quantities.) "I was still wet behind the ears, and was playing at a sports bar in the city called The Locker Room; to this day I don't know why they wanted a piano player. Anyway, the piano was up front by the window, and before I knew it I had a drunk staring in at me, and trying to *conduct* me. But that wasn't the half of it. Turns out there was a television right over the piano, and it was the night of the Keady-Olson fight. So here are these two black dudes, right overhead, tryin' to kill, maim, and destroy one another, and when I glance down the bar I can see that everybody's lookin' about three feet over my head; they don't even know I'm *there*. But I just kept hammerin' out the tunes; what else was I gonna do? Somebody told me later that in the seventh round, when Keady sent Olson down for the final time, I was playing 'Isn't It Romantic.'"

"Maybe it should have been 'Star Eyes,'" Troy says.

"Or 'You Go to My Head,'" Larry mumbles.

"But what gets me," Ed resumes, "is that I still only hear my mistakes. I practice hard—we all practice hard—and I *think* I'm getting better. But the more I know, the more it feels like I'm slacking off, not giving my best. So I'm always competing with myself, and feeling like I'm not playing up to my potential."

"Hey man, music is endless!" Troy exclaims. "There's *always* more to learn! You're always on the way, you're never there, you're *never* going to be as good as you think you should be. Anyway, you sound good to me. Better'n ever."

"Yeah, you sound terrific," Larry adds.

"Maybe my problem is that I'm always listening to the monsters, and measuring myself against *them*. Maybe if I listened to more dubbers and plunkers, I'd feel better about myself. For example, there's this guy named Dicky St. Regis—I doubt that's his real name—who plays at—"

"The Gaslight Café? Oh, he's awful!" Steve interrupts. "I heard him the other night. He's the pits."

"Still, I know what you're sayin'," Larry opines. "I used to go listen to the best bass players; I'd sit in the clubs, night after night, with my jaw practically dropping. Everything they did, they did so instinctively, so effortlessly. They probably weren't aware of how much I admired them, at least they never *acknowledged* my admiration. Then one day—believe it or not—I think, I *think* I was beginning to approach the level of playing of these, my former heroes. I had reached the point where jazz was no longer something of which I was just a spectator, but my own expression, the outward record of the inner struggle it had cost me; it *was*, simply, all those years of practice and study, it *was*, in a sense, me. Then, one night, when I was performing at one of those same clubs, I looked up and saw a kid staring at me, fascinated, maybe even worshipful. You see, I had become a hero for this kid the way those other guys had been heroes for *me*. But there was nothing in it that *felt* heroic, just as—I eventually realized—there was nothing in it that felt heroic to those other players. They simply did what they did, I did what I did, they were *their* music, I was *mine*. And isn't that always the way it is? By the time we get where we want to be, it turns out to be something other than what we expected; the way we imagine the roles is never the way they actually feel. And what's scary, if you think about it, is that it's probably that way for everything and everybody. Nothing is what it seems."

Waiters and waitresses are drifting into the restaurant, now, and beginning to set up. Ed turns with the hope of seeing Lee Castleton, but is disappointed. Steve Dirso starts to make a wisecrack, but Larry cuts him off: "That's what I call 'the parable of the jazz player.' The more personally he plays, the more individual he is, the greater the difference between who he really is and who he appears to be. His individuality, the thing that makes him appeal to so many different people, is the very thing that makes him so private, so unknowable."

"I like that phrase," Troy comments. " 'Music as the outward record of an inner struggle.' I think—no matter how good you are—you have to resign yourself to not always being at the top of your form, resign yourself to the fact that performance is largely a record of progress you've already made, growth you've already achieved. It's just that you have to be so good that what's a cliché to you is *art* to them. I've had times when I've gone and listened to the monsters, and I can tell they're having a bad night, leaning on simple riffs, repeating things they've already explored. But *I'm* still mesmerized, it's still news to *me*. They're such great players that what's a cliché to them is art to me. And when we play for other people, though we may not like to admit it, our clichés are their art."

There is more talk about music and performance, then Steve asks: "Hey, you guys wanna eat? Showtime isn't until nine o'clock, and I'm hungry. Shake, is there anyplace left in this town that a lowly jazz musician can afford?"

Music is endless. Our clichés are their art. The outward record of an inner struggle. The phrases are still reverberating in Ed's thoughts when, just before nine, the group reconvenes. Apparently word has gotten around, because a crowd has filled the lounge, and the tables out on the floor have been arranged in a semicircle. At nine he slips behind the piano, Troy takes his reed out of his mouth and attaches it to his saxophone; Larry picks up his bass and strums quietly. Ed hits a B flat and an A so Troy and Larry can tune, then they wait while Steve makes some final adjustments to his drums.

"Ladies and gentlemen," Steve says under his breath, as

he bends over, "we've had a request. But we're going to play anyway."

"Not too intense, in the beginning," Ed advises. "We don't wanna blow 'em out of the room."

" 'A Train'?" Troy asks, turning to the group. "Introduction please, maestro."

Ed plays the little choo-choo riff that is standard for the tune—that mimics the sound of a train starting up, and seems to say *all aboard!*—and suddenly bright, bouncy music fills the room, clean, crisp, joyous music. It's a standard, in fact a warhorse, and easy for the group: four individuals, four separate identities, quickly become a single happiness-creating unit. Ed concentrates on the sound level, at first, and adjusts to hearing his instrument as one among several. (Troy, he thinks, is louder than he needs to be.) He glances at Larry and smiles. *It's so sweet,* he thinks, wondering why he has worried so long. *Just so sweet.* He crisply punches in the chords—Larry and Steve are setting up a tight, buoyant rhythm—and feels that he is on the inside, way back in, that he is in the center of a great bubble of happiness and joy. Troy fades after several choruses, and now it is his turn. He keeps it understated, at first, playing sparse little lines and lowering the dynamics, forcing piano, bass, and drums into a tight-knit unit; then he stretches out for a second chorus. There is a burst of applause as he makes his exit, and now Larry and Steve take their solos. They regroup and join forces for the finale, they are back in full swing, making their combined statement, hammering out the traditional last-chorus riff in unison; Troy states the melody a final time and, slickly and easily as water filling up a narrow-necked bottle, they do a seven-beater—and go out.

There is a sustained burst of appreciation, which Troy acknowledges on behalf of the group. Then he turns around: "Nice work, guys." He adjusts the mouthpiece of his tenor sax and comes over and plunks a few keys at the high end of the piano. " 'Sophisticated Lady'?" he says. He snaps his fingers to indicate the tempo. Ed plays a rubato fantasia on the chord structure, then slows down and clearly establishes the beat. The tune is lush and romantic, and allows them to relax, to invent, to daydream, to enjoy. Troy gets a big echoing sound out of his tenor, Steve lays down a silky mood with his brushes, Larry fills the spaces with pungent kicks and fillers. An air of harmony and contentment suffuses the room, a newly established sense of peacefulness. They round out the tune, Larry bowing the notes at the end, then Troy—suggesting a bossa nova—puts his sax down and picks up his flute. " 'Meditation'?" he says, flicking his wrist and singing "bee-b'deep, bee-b'deep, bee-b'deep." They are in a groove, now, listening to and supporting one another, rediscovering one another's musicianship, playing as much for themselves as for their audience. They do "Just Friends," "Joy Spring," and a funky blues, and Troy comes over to the piano while Ed is soloing and says, "yeah, Shake!" The tunes are easy, effortless, fun; people are coming up to Troy with requests, and Ed is in the bridge of "Body and Soul" when Troy, graciously removing himself from the limelight, comes over and sits down on the end of the piano bench. At first he is the unobtrusive spectator of what Ed is doing. Then:

"So how's Helen?" he says.

Ed has some big lush, two-handed block chords going. When he looks down the length of the piano, he sees Lee Castleton smiling at him. *Helen*, he thinks. *Who's Helen? Oh, Helen— my wife. Well, to tell the truth, we're having some difficulties, just at the moment.*

No. He has to concentrate!

"I mean, we talked about so many things," Troy says, "but I forgot to ask you about Helen. And your daughter. Sarah, isn't that her name?"

As Ed leans to his right to advance a melodic line to the high end of the keyboard, he realizes that Troy is cramping him and he can't go any farther.

"It *is* Sarah, isn't it? It's kind of embarrassing, but I've never been real good with names. They just sort of drop out of the old noodle."

Ed can't hear the bass line now—he can't control the nuances of the tune—he feels like he's been suspended over a vast height, with no safety net.

"Do you think Helen'll come to hear us? I hope so, I'd really like to see her again. Though I understand, you know, if she has to stay home and take care of the baby—until you correct me—I'm calling Sarah. I bet it's not easy finding babysitters in this town, especially during the summer. By the way, wasn't there some Greek thing about a girl named Helen and a guy named Troy?"

Ed is now an entire beat behind Larry. He can't remember where his line is going, or even what the chords are.

"Hey!" he explodes. "Get outta my face! Gimme some goddamn room, will you? Get off my fuckin' bench!"

All of a sudden, Troy is at the microphone saying, "Thank you very much, ladies and gentlemen! We're going to take a short break, then we'll be right back! Stick around, we've got lots more music! Stick around!" On this cue, the group does a chorus of their break tune, "Straight, No Chaser," and in no hurry to confront one another outside the ring and *au naturel*, extract themselves from their instruments and limp away in four different directions.

As she slides her hand up his back, Lee Castleton beams at Ed as if to say, I didn't know you could play like *that*! But Ed has other things on his mind ("Don't talk to me while I'm playing! We listen to you, so why don't you listen to us? And don't be thumping my keyboard, I don't thump your little tin horn! And back off the microphone, for chrissake! Larry's only got a bulldog and I ain't usin' a mike!"), and by the time he has expressed them, and everyone has apologized and rallied himself back into a spirit of accommodation, Lee has disappeared. He has just enough time to get a drink at the bar ("on the house," says Felix) and then it's time to go back and play some more music.

As he stares at Troy, standing at the microphone, Ed's first thought is that he would like to murder him. But Troy is so wound up in the music, and so happy to be playing, that after two or three tunes Ed forgives and forgets. Art and comfort are not necessarily related—he has known more than one instance in which great jazz was made by players who could hardly stand one another—and if anything, the undercurrent of tension in the group is now making them play better. They begin digging in, staying away from easy riffs, and making their harmonic and rhythmic interactions more subtle. The audience applauds after every solo, and in response, the band begins really to cook; when they next do a blues, it is more than funky, it is smoky, roguey, dangerous. The intimacy and electricity on the stand solidify; in rapid succession there are sparks and sparkles of love, hate, tenderness, humor, defiance, attraction, repulsion. What could be more important—what could be more foolish—after all, than grown men making structured noise? What could be at once more significant and more ephemeral? As the night wears on, the players get to know one another well—almost too well —and the intimacy on the stand becomes that of a locker room: cramped, hot, and intense, with everyone forgiving—or trying to forgive—everyone else his sweat socks, his intense, hot, sweaty physical presence.

The following night starts out to be a repeat of the first, but when the band does "Satin Doll," an older couple gets up to dance ("uh-oh, the businessman's bounce!" Larry protests), and with the floodgates opened, a great tide follows. Troy turns and shrugs his shoulders (*what're you gonna do?*), and the group, deflated, adjusts to a different mood. *They don't want you to grow up*, Ed thinks, feeling sour again. *They don't want you to have a life of your own. People like us are just something to be used by the world, used and discarded.* The feeling of cohesion the group has established is replaced by one of vulnerability, and if Troy responds by becoming vaguely irritable, Steve gets everyone over the hump with constant reminders that there is nothing to do but to laugh: to laugh, play, and have fun. A woman comes up to the stand with a request, and Troy, drawing himself up with great haughtiness, says: "No ma'am. We don't know that one. But we'll play one just *like* it."

Someone else comes up, and Troy turns to the group: "'You Do Something to Me.'"

"And I'll do something to you!" Steve quips. "And when are we gonna play 'Lover Back Into Me'?"

"Or 'Armageddon Sentimental Over You'?" Larry whispers.

They laugh. They are smiling again. They are there in order that people enjoy themselves, and as each knows in a secret, forever youthful part of his soul, it's only music. They stay away from complicated tunes, now, but manage to trade fours, keep the rhythm tight, and get in some licks. " 'Enemas From Heaven'?" Steve suggests, during a quiet moment between tunes. Then, with a drum roll and rim shot: " 'I'm in the Nude for Love.' " Eventually there is a request for the old chestnut, and as he has provided a crisp rhythmic underpinning all night long, Steve—to the end—keeps everyone's spirits up. "You must remember this," he sings. "A quiche is but a quiche. A pie is but a pie. The world will always welcome . . . pastry . . . 'As Time Goes By'!"

"Hey, we're packin' 'em out!" Ed exclaims, when Lee Castleton comes up to him at the end of the night, and gives him a big hug. She is beaming like a proud mother. People are paying up and drifting away, and as they do, some come over and compliment the group, or stare at them appreciatively.

"But I'm mad at you!" Lee says, smiling.

Ed senses that it is one time when even if he is wrong, he is right.

"Why?"

"You didn't play 'Summertime'!"

Ed starts to explain that the group was getting lots of requests, and how "Summertime" wasn't particularly danceable, and how they had had a few problems to work out. *Oh hell, how can you explain? How can you explain what it feels like to be wedged into a cramped space like that, and practically dancing with your instrument, concentrating so hard you almost forget who you are?* He sees the others helping Steve with his drums and, realizing he is fit only to talk to kindred spirits, tells Lee he will be right back; he picks up the high-hat stand and one of the tom-toms, and follows the others out. It is nothing of much importance the group has to say to one another, they just stand around next to Steve's van and have a cigarette, and savor the pleasures of being who they are, and doing what they do.

"Well, see you next Friday!" Troy calls, going around and getting in the van.

"Believe me," Larry mutters, rolling down his window. "It's been a pressure."

As the van pulls away, Ed feels like a child who's been deposited, for the first time, at summer camp. He grows panicky. Will she still be there?

"What a great weekend it's been!" Lee exclaims, after he has found her, with a drink for each of them, in the bar. "I can't tell you how much I've enjoyed it! Cheers!"

"Cheers to *you!*" Ed replies, clinking glasses.

Dutch wanders into the lounge looking like a man who has had a religious conversion. *Did you hear that music?* his expression says. *We've got to do this more often!* He is in a good mood, joking and bantering, buying people drinks, patting waitresses on the back. Spying Ed (and studiously ignoring the fact that Lee Castleton has her arm around him), he wanders over to their table. "Did I tell you Duane Claggett was in this evening? Said we need a special license for amplified instruments. I told him, 'Hey Duane, loosen up! We're just havin' a little fun!'"

"So is it okay for us to play next weekend?" Ed asks, fearful that the bubble is about to burst.

"Of course! You guys sounded great! And oh, uh, Ed" (Dutch bends forward over the table as if about to confide a deep, dark secret), "next summer we're gonna get that piano *tuned.*"

Lee asks him to walk her home, and invites him into her cottage. They put on some music, make drinks, remove their shoes, and settle on the couch with feet touching on the coffee table in front of them. To his dismay, however, Ed senses that she is still thinking about the night's performance, fantasizing herself as part of the band, perhaps, or standing at the microphone singing. Even as they kiss, she seems to be thinking about the music, contemplating him as though he were a stuffed animal, a great big teddy bear. Still, when she walks him to the door he feels young and vibrant again, and hungry for more. Their embrace is tender and affectionate; she must stand on tiptoe and he must stoop a little, but they manage a kiss, a nuzzle, a fond farewell.

"You're absolutely terrific," she says.

The following weekend, the Dockside feels more like a nightclub than a restaurant, and Ed feels like a new person. Not only has he basked in the attention of his favorite waitress and been treated with new respect by the entire staff, but he has become a frontline musician for whom the restaurant now constitutes an audience. He has spent three evenings with Lee, and if their relationship has continued to be more chaste than he would have wished it, still he has savored her increasingly warm and intimate company.

Dutch is scurrying about like an impresario, adjusting the lights, arranging assistance for Felix, talking about his plans for the future ("more music, more advertising, a late-night menu"). The crowd has come to listen, so the band does mostly original material. Troy leads the group with enthusiasm and authority, and were it not for one unsettling moment on Saturday night, Ed would consider the date an unqualified success. Felix is handing him a drink at the bar when a morose-looking man —a man from whom he has been careful to keep his distance— turns on his stool and scowls at him. Ed knows who Grubby Eddy is, but doubts whether Grubby Eddy even knows they share a name. *Well, you can't please everybody,* he thinks, taking refuge in the first rule of performance, and heading back to the stand.

Not only has Grubby Eddy had two weekends of cacophonous music in his ears, but to add insult to injury, the television is broken. Broken but still present. Not only does it give him none of the talk and imagery he's used to, but the dull monochrome eye—like a lens that's grown cloudy from age—continues to stare at him, in its contorted reflections giving him back nothing but . . . himself. *It's a spy, and it's looking into the room,* he thinks as he studies the blank, swollen screen. *It's a glassy, gray-green eye trading stares with two other eyes. But it never blinks.*

It waits, but never blinks. Grubby Eddy glances up again at the silent television, realizes that it is giving him nothing, showing him nothing; it is faceless, it wears an evil, iridescent sheen for a mask. *It stares at me. Stares, waits, and never blinks. Well, there really isn't much left for it to see, is there? Life has pretty much dried up. Dried up and gone sour. The only things wet that are left are drinks, well, and dreams. It's all inanities, perversions, illusions, a blizzard of lies. How does that poem go?*

Felix, standing before him, is surprised that Grubby Eddy doesn't want another drink. Confronting the sorry spectacle of his friend, he makes a new refinement to his X Curve. *Maybe the graph describes not only what goes on between people, but what goes on inside them as well. What they most need to tell themselves they can do so only at times when they're least able to hear it. Maybe all the important things—even as they are contemplated and confronted—are simultaneously denied and deferred.*

"You okay, pal?"

How does that poem go? Twilight and evening bell and after that the dark, d'dah, d'dah, d'dah, d'dah. For though from out our bourne of time and place the flood may bear me far, d'dah, d'dah, d'dah, d'dah, may there be no sadness of farewell when I embark.

Thanks, Felix.

Leaving a generous tip on the bar, the taciturn man in the shiny windbreaker slides off his stool and makes his way through the crowd. Soon his place is taken by Jack Freund, who contemplates the one-eyed pirate across the bar with his usual dazed, thousand-yard stare. Two seats beyond him, another person who has taken no interest in the night's music has finally gotten Flipper McDougal into a conversation about the difficulties he's having getting going on a novel. Riding high on the companionship of his mentor and the cheerful, ambient blur of voices, he has decided that he should not try to describe the world, but instead make up a myth of himself, *be* a myth. Why try to describe things he didn't know about when he had all the ingredients within him? Who—or what—was more interesting than himself, if handled properly? *I must be larger than life*, he thinks, hearing the band start up and wagging his foot in spite of himself. Flipper McDougal says something he can't hear over the din and, feeling happy with his discovery, he repeats the thought. *I must be my own story. I must create my own myth. I must start tonight, this very night.* A funky blues is coming off the bandstand, and then a song he knows the name of, "Someday My Prince Will Come." As he glances around the bar, the festive mood slowly sinks in, and suddenly it all seems very easy. *There is a lesson in all this, a lesson in the life I'm leading, a lesson in the life of the entire town. Get drunk and let rip. It doesn't have to be so difficult. I must find—or make—a myth of myself, then get drunk and let rip!*

By the end of the evening there is only one person in the lounge who is happier than Doug Brindle, and that is Ed Shakey, who sits holding hands with Lee and wonders about the propriety of her hopping—as she does from time to time— into his lap. As he tries to keep up with Steve and Larry's conversation, Ed rubs his hand up and down her back and whispers tender and intimate things in her ear. He doesn't have to ask whether he can walk her home, and when they reach her cottage he doesn't have to ask whether he can come in. He doesn't have to suggest that they put on some music, and prop their feet up. So much goes without saying, now. The night is young, they both have the next day off, and there's no need to rush. Slowly, tenderly, he unbuttons the top button of her blouse. . . .

At the Dockside, Dutch is prowling around in the darkness. It is one of those nights when he is both tired and keyed up, let down and full of nervous energy. The restaurant, which only an hour before had been full of talk and laughter, seems more than usually deserted, now. In the shadows he creeps from the front desk, where he fiddles with the rezzy book and some memos and reminders, up to his office, where he fusses with things that do not need fussing with. He comes downstairs again and wanders into the lounge, pours himself a brandy and, curious why the lights are still on in the kitchen, goes and peers in one of the portholes.

What the—?

The crazy cleanup man is dipping his mop in the bucket, now stops and shakes his fist at the ceiling. For some reason it infuriates Dutch, this man working all alone—burning all these lights—in his kitchen. With fiendish pleasure, he senses that this is someone he can spar with, someone on whom he can vent some of his pent-up energy. He will do a little dance with the man, if necessary—a *pas de deux*—until he commits the necessary infraction.

Standin' at the seven-six-twos. Standin' at the door of the choppers lookin' for 'em in the swamp grass. Christ, how many people did I kill? Can't remember. Too many pills. Then the White Mouse got me, put me to work sweepin'. Sweepin' one pebble up and back, all night long. Is that my little friend? Well, hello there. Let us break bread together.

Tommy sets his mop against the counter, goes over to

the plate rack and gets a butter dish and a knife, walks to the refrigerator and makes an inventory of what is available. *A feast for my little friend.* A solitary, a man who works best when he is alone, this is currently as much communion with another living creature as he has. He places the butter dish in its usual place, in the corner behind the bucket full of rags, and as he walks to the sink, runs the knife along his lips.

Red-handed! I've caught you red-handed! So it's you! You're the one! I might have guessed, I thought it was you all along! Do you know what these desserts cost me? Do you think, every time you come to work, that you can just help yourself to whatever's in the reach-in? Sit yourself down and have a regular meal? Does it ever occur to you that when you take a slice out of one of these desserts, an entire serving might be lost? People steal from this restaurant right and left! Well, I won't stand for it! What? Whattaya mean, it's not for you? Who the hell is it for? Your little friend? What little friend?

They stand there and scream at one another, or rather Dutch screams and Tommy stammers and fumbles, looks alternately crazed and crushed. Eventually Dutch senses that Tommy is telling him the truth, that the force is being drained out of his argument and there is no real crime to complain about— and that only makes him angrier. Still, even taking the man at his word, one thing rankles him. And because he has had to accept Tommy's explanation and has ended up with nothing, he yields to a final outburst:

"How do you know it's the same mouse!"

There is more stumbling and fumbling on Tommy's part, but in the end—much as it irritates him to do so—even Dutch believes it.

"I just know, Mr. Dugan, I just *know.*"

Taking Ed by the hand, Lee leads him into her bedroom. The turned-back sheet, the bright quilt folded on the end of the bed, seem to him deliciously inviting; it is a blissful moment, a windfall, the unexpected finale to a trying summer. He would like just to lie there with her and feast his eyes on her, but the light on the iron floor stand is so bright it assaults his eyes; he must choose. Pulling away from her, he hoists himself up ("oh, don't go," she murmurs), and as he reaches for the chain beneath the shade and gives it a deliberate tug, he smiles inwardly, and thinks:

Maybe there's some justice in this life, after all.

FOURTEEN

Labor Day. The day, the weekend, the deliverance everyone has looked forward to—or dreaded—for so long is here.

Standing at her door on the back of the Sunrise Apartments on High Street, Kathy Shively contemplates the drab, overcast afternoon. A subliminal intensity is in the air. Though she cannot actually hear the crowds surging and milling on Bay Street, their energy seems to permeate her apartment. On Tuesday, they, *they*, as she tells herself, will all be gone, swept away overnight in a frantic, mad exodus. Right now, however, the town is under siege, and there is probably not another room, bed, or parking place to be had. Nor would a prudent person take for granted a reservation at one of the better restaurants. As she dresses for work, Kathy feels apprehensive about the chaos and confusion that has prevailed for the previous three nights. But *the customer is always right*, she thinks. What else can you expect, when *the customer is always right*? For isn't that what a restaurant at the height of the season in Sun Town *is*? A vast sit-in? A place for people to go—and go limp—when all else fails? It's a court of last resort, food as the excuse for the momentary domination of paid servants. *I can't go on, I can't go on*, Debbie Fensen has been saying . . . before pulling herself together and going on. *It's theater. Food theater. It's a stage, with props and settings (the décor, the furniture), and characters (the service staff). And the plot? The plot is nothing more than the interactions between the staff and the patrons. But with all the planning, all the rehearsal, the performance could be magnificent, and generate displeasure, or pathetic, and generate applause. For the customer is always right.*

Thinking she perhaps has it wrong, that the *customers* are the actors, and the servers their captive audience, Kathy nudges the screen door open with her toe, and rests her shoulder against the jamb. *Pretty soon it will be all over.* They had waited all winter for summer, and summer had brought the tourists and the necessity of accommodating, and kowtowing to them. So they waited all summer for the return of winter. *But soon it will all be over.* In October, there will be the first whiffs of wood smoke, then, as sea mist envelops the town, the aromas of kerosene, propane, fuel oil. The storefronts will be boarded up, plastic sheeting will reappear on house windows, the fog horns and Town Hall clock will reemerge with their distinctive personalities. At the price of looking weather-beaten and forlorn— the site of a carnival that has packed up and left—the town will become small and intimate again. In a patch of blue between the clouds, Kathy notices the contrail of a jet; from its bearing she deduces that it is coming from overseas. *The jet, too,* she thinks, *is almost home.* And will jets one day land in Sun Town? Will the sound of jet engines blot out the sound of the fog horns, the Town Hall clock, the twelve o'clock fire siren?

Kathy finishes dressing, applies her make-up and, fearful of being late for work, hurries down High Street. When she arrives at the Dockside, she realizes—instantly—that something is wrong. Karen greets her with an ashen face, and the waiters and waitresses, looking chastened and subdued, are clustered at a table near the kitchen. Some are dabbing their eyes.

Presidential assassination, Kathy thinks.

"What *is* it?" she says.

"It's, it's Grubby Eddy," Becky Dent answers.

"What *about* him?"

"He killed himself. Went out to Kinriddy Point, took his jacket off, and just started swimming."

"How do they *know*?"

"They found his windbreaker."

"And his shoes."

"His body washed up this morning."

"He hasn't been in for a week," adds Courtney Johnson. "Felix says the last time he was in, he left twenty dollars on the bar, that he thought it was a mistake and was going to return it. Then he . . . never came back."

"Jesus. Poor guy."

"He was such a *nice* guy, you know what I mean? You had the feeling that underneath his prickly exterior, he was a quite decent person."

"Decent and gentle."

"He was always so quiet. He never seemed to say very much."

"Who knows what kind of pain he was in, or what was going through his mind, at the end?"

"This town ain't gonna be the same without him, that's for sure."

"It's almost as though he had become a fixture."

Even Dutch has let Grubby Eddy's death get to him, even Dutch—who stumbles through the kitchen door now, looking like a man in a state of shock—has let himself be affected by something outside his own narrow range of obsessions.

"What I want to know," he says, "is who served him? Please, would someone tell me that? Who *served* him?"

"You mean, at the bar?" Polly Schreiber volunteers. "Why, Felix, of course. Most of the time."

"No, no! I mean the man who wrote *this!*"

Dutch waves the paper he is holding.

"The so-called 'Phantom Diner'! Just look at this, will you? This is a tear sheet of the review I'm going to receive in tomorrow's newspaper! And just look at it! What I would *very* much like to know is who served him?"

Dutch hurls the paper on the table as incontrovertible proof of what he had been saying all along, that someone was out to get him. The milling, restless group, wondering what all this has to do with Grubby Eddy, stifle their grief and huddle forward over the page.

"You see what he says about the veal Florentine? You see what he says—look, right there at the beginning—about tearing his sleeve on his chair? You see what he says about the bouillabaisse? Well, people, there goes my reputation! There goes everything I've tried to build, for the last thirty years, everything I've slaved and sweated for!"

It was the first time any of them had seen Dutch actually on the verge of tears.

"Now, I've already talked to our glorious chefs about this. But what I would really like to know—just for the record —is *who served him.*"

A torn shirtsleeve. The Phantom Diner. Sharon Lowd studies the tear sheet, and feels like she, not Grubby Eddy died. Slumping down in her chair to try to make herself invisible, she debates whether or not to confess.

"But Dutch!" someone says, distracting him—and relieving her of the necessity—"he doesn't say the veal Florentine was bad! He just says it 'could have been a little less heavy on the spinach'!"

"And the fact is, the review isn't all that bad! In fact, it's pretty darn good! Look what it says—right here—about the sole Provençal. 'Done to perfection.' And the poached salmon hollandaise. 'Flavorful, delectable, practically melted in the mouth.'"

"And look here, in the third paragraph! He calls the Dockside a 'venerable institution,' a 'Sun Town tradition'! What's so bad about that?"

"Besides, the way he talks about his torn shirt—it's really kind of funny! It's almost as though he were making a little joke, you know, being careful not to be *too* complimentary!"

"Yeah, but the service was 'somewhat glacial,'" Dutch counters, " 'in fact, bordering on the epic.' What the hell do I pay you people for? What do I have to do to get the food from the kitchen to the table? I have to think about my reputation, you know. Someone, tell me: what more can I possibly do than I've done?"

A vague drying-of-tears, sunshine-through-the-clouds quality begins seeping into Dutch's tone, as if things were not *quite* so bad as he were making out. Still, he will not easily be tricked out of the fury into which he has worked himself.

"Anyway," Lee Castleton picks up, "these reviewers from the city show up for one night out of the entire season, and try to judge the restaurant's entire performance by it. You know that. And this so-called 'Phantom Diner' probably came in on one of those nights when the place was packed and jammed. And if the place was packed and jammed, you *know* the restaurant was—and is—doing well. You know as well as we do that by any reasonable standard, your restaurant is a huge success."

Making money hand over fist is what everyone hears who isn't busy, now, chiming in.

The troops have almost gotten the commander's spirits restored to their usual state of fretful paranoia—and therefore lifted their own—when Roy Oberholzer makes a contribution that he supposes will be the clincher.

"Look at it this way," he says, "a bad review is still good publicity. And if you think about it, Dutch, you've hit the jackpot. Just remember the old saying, 'abuse is the sister to advertisement.'"

There is a stunned silence.

"Shut up, Roy," someone says.

Dutch glowers at him. They *all* glower at him.

"Well, next summer there're going to be some changes made around here," Dutch fumes. "Both in the kitchen and out here on the floor. We're going to find some new ways of doing things, damn right we are. But any minute now"—he stares pointedly at his wristwatch—"any minute now, they'll be coming through the door. So do me a favor, will you? Treat each and every one of them as the Phantom Diner. Because you *never know.*"

The troops gather themselves up and go off to battle feeling confused and demoralized, feeling that no matter what they do, it's never good enough. But privately they are too tired to care. People die. Restaurant reviews get written. It's not their fault. They are just waiters and waitresses working hard for the summer, and hoping to qualify for unemployment during the winter. If they were going to go through life weeping bitter tears, they would kill themselves. Or open a restaurant. It is Labor Day, and soon it will all be over.

But not before Dutch's worst fears, like self-fulfilling prophecy, are realized. . . .

In their room at Herschel's Guest House on Puritan Street, Byrne and Marjorie Landon are dressing for dinner.

"Let's not forget to take the soap when we leave!" she calls to him.

"What do you mean, take the soap?" he answers, wrapping a towel around himself and going to the bathroom door.

"Well, we paid for it, didn't we?"

"Well, yes. I mean, I *guess* we paid for it. But if you think about it, the price of the room doesn't include extra soap. Suppose *everyone* took the soap. Wouldn't they just have to raise their rates to cover the extra cost of soap?"

"Oh *Byrne,*" she says, rifling through the dresses hanging in the closet, "sometimes you can be *so* foolish. At these prices, they aren't going to miss a bar or two of soap."

"But look at it this way. If everyone took the soap—"

"Byrne. You're so silly!"

Ah, you could slow it down. But you couldn't stop it.

Dr. Landon glances in the mirror as he prepares to shave, then goes to the door again, as if to make amends:

"Let's remember to call Susie."

"Of *course* we'll call Susie!"

As he returns to the sink, he catches himself. *Stop what?* Well, so many things. The sheer willfulness of the world, for example. The brute inertia that seemed always to impede progress and understanding, that teased up thoughts of congruence and coherence only to mock and undermine them. Like the intimations one had of a total pattern, the glimpse of the completed puzzle, then the discovery of all the pieces left lying around the edges. The feeling that illusions were growing at a faster rate than correct perceptions, that the mistakes and errors of one generation were being perpetrated on the next, which would be able to work them out only by handing them on to the following generation. Susie, for example. Already, he could see her bad patterns developing, and know that if she had children—*god, has she already done it?*—they would suffer the consequences, and would have to work out their difficulties on *their* children. Who would then have to work out. . . . So you could already see several generations down the road. Dr. Landon studies himself in the mirror, and massages his cheek with his hand. *Yes, you could slow it down, but you couldn't stop it.* He squeezes some shaving cream onto his hand and dabs his cheeks, and dips his razor under the faucet. It was the same with tourist towns, come to think of it. If the town were attractive, people flocked to it. But in order to get them there, you had to build new bridges and highways. But in order to do *that*, you had to increase the tax rate, which meant encouraging new business, which attracted more people—which required more bridges and highways—until the thing that proved attractive in the first place had been obliterated. *It's a tide you can perhaps channel, but which you can never stop.* He runs the razor down his face, wiggles it under the water. Then there's the mind's ability to invent realities other than the ones that exist. If you had good sense, you got stuck in *that* cruel logic, for the more refined your taste, the more things there were to offend it. Not, of course, that he was exempt. That was the whole point. His compulsion, for example, to use certain stock lines whenever others were used, or the way, when people were telling jokes, he invariably came up with one his *father* had told him, one he *knew* was old and tired. But a switch closed in his mind, and the words came out of his mouth despite himself. Something would take over which he could perhaps slow down, but never, or rarely, stop.

"Let's not forget to call Susie!" he repeats, going to the door. "I'm really worried about her. Oh, and honey, have you decided where you'd like to dine tonight?"

"Yes. I think I've found a place that we'll both enjoy. But really Byrne, they certainly aren't going to miss a bar or two of soap."

You could slow it down, but you couldn't stop it.

At the Dockside, meanwhile, things are spiraling out of

control. As happens every summer, at this time—Dutch has never found a way to prevent it—several of the busboys have quit, and although Kathy has been able to find replacements, their unfamiliarity with the routine is putting everyone else behind. The extra waitress who has been hired for the weekend though her other virtues are obvious—has a curious habit of commenting on people's orders. "Dynamite!" Kathy hears her say, in response to someone's request for a Scotch and soda. "Yummo!" she says, about a Brandy Alexander. Kathy must tell her that it is *not* necessary to comment on people's drink and food orders. Just at the moment, however, she has her own problems. A party of eight has arrived that had made a reservation for five, and she is trying to figure out where to put them.

If only he had identified himself, Dutch thinks. *I could have let him have a taste of the lobster bisque, the shrimp scampi, the grilled tuna.* As a new wave of irritation sweeps over him, he decides to reestablish his authority in the sphere where his word is law, the kitchen. The kitchen is humming along in its bright, clattering, reassuring way. Dirty dishes are piling up, but the new kid seems to be dealing with them. "Isn't it time we had a little heart-to-heart?" he had asked the previous pearl diver. The smart-ass had looked right through him: "No. Because the way to a man's heart is through his soul." And when he had finally lost patience, and booted the kid out the door: "You, sir, have proved it! The *animal* is father to the man!" Dutch flashes Dave Lindholm a V-for-victory sign and picks his way along the line, getting a sense of how things are going, giving real and verbal pats on the back. "You okay?" he says to Debbie Fensen, who looks completely unhinged. "Hey, everybody, it's gonna be a long night! Let's go, let's go, let's go!"

When he leaves the kitchen, the line cooks and the newest pearl diver resume their game of book titles.

"Dishwashing Made Simple."

"Dishwashing for Dummies."

"The Golden Book of Dishes."

"Grime and Punishment."

Lenny backs away from the stove and leans over beneath the plate rack: "How about 'Through the Refrigerator With Gun and Camera'?"

Dutch wanders into the lounge, and waves the tear sheet in front of Felix as if it were a parking ticket, or court summons.

"Didja see this review I'm gonna get?"

"No, but I heard about it," Felix replies. He stuffs some glasses in the bar washer and leans forward confidentially. "You heard about Grubby Eddy, didn't you?"

"Yeah, yeah," Dutch replies. "Terrible thing. I'm sure gonna miss him. But look here, look what this hot-shot *newspaper* reviewer, this so-called 'Phantom Diner,' says about my veal Florentine! Can you believe that?"

He flattens the page in front of Felix and points to it, but Felix is besieged. "Hold on just a minute," he says, strategically moving to a customer down the bar.

The atmosphere in the lounge is vaguely reminiscent of the last days of Pompeii. If it feels like a group of refugees seeking shelter in a time of crisis—sitting out an air raid, or riding out a hurricane—the reason is not only that tourists and locals have been thrown together in the same small boat, but that for the locals, this weekend *is* a crisis. The town is on a threshold, it is at a beginning as well as an ending, and while tourists and out-of-towners make the most of their final fling, those who will be around to pick up the pieces can do little but cling to their thwarts, clutch the gunnels, and ride out the storm. The manic quality of the laughter, Felix thinks, results from the fact that here at the end of summer, some people are still uncertain whether they are waiting for the party, or whether this *is* the party. Will some clown who has let himself be over-served crawl out of the men's room on his hands and knees, as he did last year?

Occupying the stool Grubby Eddy used to favor is a young man whom Felix thinks is a fisherman, but can't quite place. Having made himself scarce for as long as he could stand to, Jody McGuire has thrown caution to the wind and returned to Sun Town. Hiding his exhilaration behind a scrim of wariness, he has spent the afternoon reconnoitering the Alibi and Mermaid, and inquiring about his former crewmates on the *Windswept*. The first thing he learned was that Manny Carerra had sold his boat and retired. ("Did pretty well for himself," Jody was told.) The next thing he learned was that Grady and 'Houn had left town. This news had come as a relief, at first, then a disappointment: Grady and 'Houn were family, after all, the family with whom he had hoped to make amends. Only Mario was still fishing, but on a different boat now, the *Sea Pearl*.

As he strolled along the pier, he had made an inventory of which boats were in (hawkers tried to sell him day trips on charter boats, whale watches, moonlight excursions), and before he knew it, found himself standing above the *Windswept* and looking down on her just as he had that first day when he had sought out the captain, and asked for a site. He contemplated her whaleback, her rope bumper, the rigging that gave her her distinct personality. Some fishermen he didn't recognize were at work on her deck. What changes had they made to the boat— *his* boat—he wondered? How was the new cook faring on *his* stove? He lingered in the late-afternoon sun, watching the muted light refract around the spar and through the hanging net, then moved along to her wheelhouse and afterdeck; he tried to imagine how it must have looked, that night, when he abandoned her. Now several of the crew glanced up at him disinterestedly. *We live in two different worlds*, their expressions said. *You have yours, we have ours.*

But he was *not* a tourist. He would never *again* be a tourist, in Sun Town. He had seen too much, and he knew too much. He had paid his dues on a Sun Town dragger, and he had paid his dues at sea; he had proven himself skillful at the one activity that was most *of* the town. If a thousand people, for a thousand reasons, could claim a piece of the town, so could he—and with as good reason as anyone. If he had survived the challenge of fishing, what challenge *couldn't* he survive? Oh, he would meet up with Mario sooner or later—and 'Houn and Grady too, for that matter—because people always came back to Sun Town. Isn't that what Frieda Ganzi had said? "No one can stay away forever. People always come back to Sun Town."

With the sight of the *Windswept* vivid in his eyes, he retraced his steps to the Alibi, and suddenly it was as though he had never left. "Hey, Magoo!" people called to him, over the

sound of the jukebox. "Where you been? What are you feedin'
'em, these days! You got a trip comin' up? What boat you on?
You been over the top lately? Hey, while you're at it, why
'ontcha buy us all a beer!" Pleased by the welcome he received,
he had done so; he had gone to the bar and bought drinks for
four or five people he knew. Then he had wandered back to
where Thor the Invincible . . . was no more. In the spot where
the machine used to be, there was now a video game with a
steering wheel and trigger handles, an ungainly contraption
emitting eerie beeps and squeals. Next to it was a flashy new
pinball machine called *Galactic Intruders*. When the person who
was playing it had finished, he stepped up and inserted fifty
cents; three balls popped up instead of five. He glanced over
the machine, placed his fingers on the flippers—two buttons on
each side instead of one—and pulled the plunger. The action
was faster than anything he was used to, and before he realized
that one of the buttons controlled a magnet that could be used
to keep the ball from going down the fish hole, it had careened
down out of sight. On the next play he did something that
caused a *second* ball to appear on the board, and before he had
decided which of the two to concentrate on, they were ricocheting wildly and slipping into oblivion. He checked his score
and discovered that not one, but ten million points were necessary to go over the top; then he pulled the shooter on the
third ball. This time a canyon in the middle of the board
opened up, and the ball dropped into it; the second set of
buttons, he discovered, worked flippers inside the canyon. The
game fascinated him, and when the ball disappeared, he pulled
two more quarters out of his pocket . . . and put them back. *No.*

This was something else in which he had already proven his mastery. If he weren't going to go at it methodically, why get addicted again? Didn't he have more self-control than that?

"So you're a fisherman," says the good-looking woman next to him, as Felix comes over. "That's wonderful! I love the sea, I love the water, I love the beaches! I love just about everything about this town!"

"Oh, this is a great little place," Jody replies, finding in his chance encounter with a beautiful woman on his first day back a confirmation of the fact.

"I love the smell of sand in suitcases, and sand among books, clothes, and perfume; I think of it as sachet in an old steamer trunk. I'm staying in a funky little cottage that's full of Contact paper and rickety old furniture; even the books are full of sand and salt. And there's this gas stove that you have to light with a match, that makes everything smell, well, like gas!"

There is something in the woman's tone that suggests she would have no objection to his seeing it for himself.

"And the people here! I was in the post office, yesterday, and I heard the woman behind the window sneeze, and mumble: 'Gave that cold to everyone in town.' When I went in the library, there was a woman opening boxes of new books. Her assistant looked at her, and in exasperation said: 'Lois, there's more to life than cooking and the church!' I think I'm going to like it here."

"Oh, if you want characters, we've got plenty *of* 'em," Jody says, feeling himself, in a rather pleasant way, becoming one; "that's what's nice about Sun Town. You see all sorts of people, and from every angle; you see people in the round. And no town ever enjoyed watching itself more than this one. That's what makes it different from Hillerton and Bucks Bottom, and the other towns up the peninsula. That, I suppose, and the way everyone mixes: tourists and locals, gays and straights, fishermen . . . and beautiful women."

Jody waves to Felix, points to the woman's empty glass, and squeezes in closer to her.

"People in Sun Town are like players in an endlessly ongoing theater production. The players may change, but the play remains the same. I've been out of town for a while, but this afternoon when I went into the Alibi—which is a bar up the street—people said hello just as though I'd never left. People don't *like* it when you leave Sun Town, but when you return, they welcome you back just as though you'd never left."

"That's sweet."

"It is. Apparently there was a guy named Grubby Eddy who used to come in here, who died a coupla days ago. I didn't know him personally, but I guarantee you, if he walked in here a year from now, people would say, 'Hi, Eddy, you been away? You down for long? Where you livin', now?' It wouldn't surprise anybody in town to see him back. Nobody would blink an eye."

"You said you've been away?" the woman asks, drawing back a little. "You're *not* a fisherman?"

"Oh yeah, I'm a fisherman. It's just that I had to get out of town for a while. But we all come back; once you've lived in Sun Town, you can't stay away forever. In fact, you don't really belong here until you've sold everything you own and moved away twice. Because this place is like Brigadoon. It's the place where everyone thinks he can come back and start over, where he can pick up right where he left off. Kismet, I call it. Lotus-Land."

Jody is bumped from behind, and turns to hear someone shout:

"Did you hear about Father Mahady? Found himself a sweet young thing down in Port Kimball! Leavin' the church to get married!"

"Thank god! I thought you were going to say he had run off with one of the altar boys!"

"Well, here's a toast to Grubby Eddy, god bless his soul! When I die—you mark my words—when I die, I'm gonna leave enough money at the Alibi so everybody can have a big party! I don't want nobody cryin' over me, no sir! I just want everybody to have a big party, and get drunk!"

Jody turns back to his companion. "Maybe it's better that way," he says, quietly. "Maybe it's better for people to treat life like an endless Mardi Gras, and go out before they get too old, then have everybody throw a big party for 'em and not grieve."

"But tell me, why did *you* come back? Was it the sea? You just couldn't get the sea out of your system?"

"Well, it's not quite as romantic as that," Jody replies, savoring the word *romantic*. "Fishing isn't nearly as romantic as people think it is. It's honest, it's invigorating, it's full of surprises. It's also dangerous, messy, and backbreaking. Believe me, it's not the greatest way to improve your mind; people don't exactly sit around the fo'c'sle, all day, and talk about Shakespeare. I wouldn't trade what I learned fishin' for anything. But I'm not sure I wanna go back to it."

"Then what will you do for the winter?"

"Well, I can coast for a little while, then I hope to get a job cooking. I'm a pretty good cook, and I'm going to ask Dutch—the guy that owns this place—about a job for next summer. But that can wait. Believe me, that can wait. I'd much rather talk to *you*. By the way, my name's Jody McGuire. What's yours?"

"Sheila."

"Sheila what?"

"Sheila Waxman."

"So what brings you to Sun Town, Sheila? Some vacation?"

"That and the fact that I'm a friend of the Town Manager."

"Well, it's certainly a pleasure to meet you."

"And to meet *you*. If I decide to move here permanently, I hope we'll be friends."

"I hope so, too," Jody replies, moving even closer to his new friend, then reaching out gently and nudging a curl back over her ear. "No, that's not strong enough. I wouldn't have it any other way."

FIFTEEN

Having finished dressing for dinner (but still grumbling over the metaphysical implications of soap), Dr. and Mrs. Landon go out to the parking lot and get in their car.

"Now, be careful, honey," Mrs. Landon says. "This is one of the busiest nights of the season, and the town is just *crammed* with tourists. It would be too bad if we had an accident."

He reckons that if he can listen for heart murmurs, palpate kidneys, and set broken bones, he can drive a car safely through the streets of Sun Town, but doesn't say so. *I just hope Susie's all right,* he thinks.

It's about the twenty-first time he has had the thought. Having called home, the previous evening, Dr. and Mrs. Landon had learned that their daughter had been in a motorcycle accident. Nothing life-threatening, apparently, but she'd been shaken up: he could hear it in her voice. And if past experience were any guide, she was in more pain than she was admitting to. *Just one more screw-up with that boy friend of hers,* Byrne Landon thinks. *If she couldn't find a way to get into trouble, he was always right there to help her think of possibilities.* Maybe it was only a phase, but as far as he was concerned, the sooner they split up, the better. *You don't need to worry,* she had said. But of course, he did.

"That nice man in the book store said they have a wonderful bouillabaisse at the Dockside," Mrs. Landon reports. "But he said they might not be serving it on a busy weekend like this, so I don't have my hopes up. But didn't we have a terrific bouillabaisse at your sister's, that time? Now there's a wonderful cook! And you remember the *bar-le-duc* she made from the berries on her currant bush? My, that was delicious! It was your sister who gave me the recipe for those cookies you like. It's the nutmeg that makes them so delicious. Let's see, what else do I put in those cookies?"

As Mrs. Landon begins to call up the ingredients of her recipe—*worried about Susie*, he thinks—Dr. Landon's mind takes off on its own food fantasy. *Cornflicts*, he says to himself. *The world is full of cornflicts. Cornflicts on the cob, cornflicts in black and white, and Technicolor.* "Careful on the right, here," Mrs. Landon says; "you've got a car right behind you." *Peas in the Middle East. Why can't the Onion Nations create peas in the Middle East?* Mrs. Landon says something about fruitcake, and suddenly his mind is concocting a full-blown culinary symphony, running on without rhyme or reason. *Why can't they? Because of the recalcitrant plebney, that's why. Owing to its scarcity, the recalcitrant plebney presents a daunting challenge for the new or inexperienced chef. The recalcitrant plebney is notorious for hiding out beneath cars in restaurant parking lots, or behind the painted stones and railroad ties that are so often a feature of these lots. The inexperienced chef's greatest difficulty with this dish will be ferreting out the recalcitrant plebney, beating it with a stick or throwing a net over it, all the while not attracting attention.*

"Careful, honey. There's a large gully or ditch, or something, on the right. Do you remember the time we climbed Mount Abraham with Lucy and Jack?"

He grunts, and wonders why the car in front of him is having so much trouble executing a simple left turn.

Happy memories soup, he thinks, recalling their visit to his sister and brother-in-law's. *Start with the old swimming hole. Add a penny farthing bicycle, mix in a barbershop quartet, a banjo, some straw boaters, a handlebar moustache—* "Careful, here. Do you realize you have someone right on your tail?"

Now try to recall the reason for making this soup. How well do the ingredients go together? Is your soup as good as your neighbor's? What is the relation between your memories, and those of other people? Between the memories of youth and those of old age?

"Turn left here, honey. This is our turn."

He does as he is told, which is exactly what he was going to do anyway, and is soon in the line of traffic snaking down Bay Street. Mrs. Landon suggests that they park the car on the waterfront lot; he counters that he can probably find a parking place on one of the side streets. When there is a break in the traffic, he turns right to go in search of it. But he cannot find a place, and his wife's continued efforts to help with the driving do funny things to his internal temperature. He looks in the next block, and the next, then comes to a T. "One way here," she says. He makes the turn and eventually finds himself back on Bay Street, several blocks farther away from their destination than where they originally started. Though he reckons it a small defeat, she a small triumph, he tries not to let it get to him. When they finally reach the center of town and are about to enter the waterfront lot, Armand Lucette steps in front of them, gesticulates wildly, and drags a sawhorse across their path.

SORRY, LOT FULL, the sign on it says.

Sheep dip. Truffled guffins.

"Where do you suggest we park?" Doctor Landon shouts.

Waving at the cars behind them as he comes forward, Armand leans over Dr. Landon's window.

"Don't really know!" he says. "There's probably some room out on Oyster Shell Road, but that's a pretty good walk from here! Your best bet is to go back and look up some a' these side streets!"

"We already did that!" Dr. Landon answers, by a defiant show of cheerfulness trying to elicit further advice.

"Then you didn't go far enough!" Armand bellows. "Go farther up the hill!"

At the moment, they are no more than a hundred yards from their destination; the lights of the Dockside glow cheerfully in the car's rear window.

"Margie, why don't you get out here," Dr. Landon suggests, "and I'll meet you inside. There's no reason for you to have to walk."

But her loyalty is unassailable. "Oh honey, I wouldn't think of it."

Boogoose bordelaise. Fish stuffed with turkey. Pickled trimmings.

So they get back in the line of cars trying to accomplish exactly what they are trying to accomplish, and after forty minutes find a parking place that requires him to obstruct a gate and compress someone's hedge. He hopes he won't get a ticket.

Crepe sole. Varicose beans. Danderchits in aspic.

In the Dockside kitchen, things are totally out of control: *in the weeds.* Perhaps the kid working the raw bar got behind, or someone didn't keep an eye on the soup and chowder, maybe too many *hors d'oeuvres* backed up at the microwave: It's impossible to tell, now. But there is definitely a backup at the Frialator; everyone knows that. Worst of all, Debbie Fensen is standing with her back against the Out door, and this time she means it.

"I can't go *on*," she says. "I *can't*. I'm not going back *out* there. Please. Don't *make* me."

She stands there petrified, as though someone were trying to push her out a high-rise window. Courtney whispers, "Go get Dutch," and—just as quickly—"No, *don't* get Dutch. Someone find out where he is, and keep him distracted."

The kitchen is noisy and intense, but at least—Debbie's expression suggests—it is full of people like herself, sympathetic, like-minded human beings. *But just beyond the door, the energy is evil, malevolent, life-threatening.* While some of the waiters and waitresses step around her and go out the In door, others hold out emotional safety nets and reason with her quietly. Dave Lindholm emerges through the crowd. He is smiling, and holding his arms out in a wide embrace. Long experience has made him someone whose calmness and self-control increase in direct proportion to the potential for disaster around him; now he is at her side, smiling, holding out his arms. Smoothly as a minister getting set to perform a baptism, he puts his arm around Debbie, then, as if nothing more needed to be said, he walks her to the rear of the kitchen. "Can you pick up a few of her orders?" he whispers to Polly Schreiber. He winks at Lenny. "We're going outside for a few minutes, to get some air. You don't need me, do you? Nah, didn't think so. This is just a restaurant, after all."

At the center of the pressure tank, meanwhile, and doing as much to quell the forces of chaos and destruction as anyone, Ed Shakey is producing beautiful, soothing music. Steadiness over Labor Day Weekend, he has learned, requires great discipline, and he has spent the preceding week preparing for it. Now he is relaxed and in control. It is a mystery to him why these holiday weekends should make what he does so much more difficult than usual, but with so many people determined to be entertained and to have fun, a musician had to work doubly hard to please them. *But you can't please everybody all the time*, he thinks. *The important thing is to have rules, and to stick to them. Never apologize, never explain. Less is more. Don't try to ingratiate yourself with your audience. End your sets on an upbeat note. Don't try to carry the room, let the room carry you.* As he sees Lee threading her way between the tables, he deftly slips into "Summertime," and knows that she hears it, and is happy that she hears it. In Lee he finally has a friend, an ally, a *lover*; he smiles as he recalls what they were doing the previous weekend. Somewhere across the room a baby starts to cry. He states the theme of "Liebestraum"—there is a vague stir of recognition—and uses it as an introduction to "Speak Low." And he thinks of the rule Lee had come up with. *There is no problem that doesn't become more manageable after a person has had something to eat, including the person who is having something to eat.*

Dutch heaves into view; Ed is relieved that he is smiling. Although the genial proprietor is still fulminating over the review that is about to appear in the newspaper, the sight of a full house—with more people waiting out front—is a great consolation to him.

"I like the way you hit most of the notes!" he calls to Ed, as he sweeps by.

Ed smiles back—and wonders what, exactly, he meant. He concludes "Speak Low," and does "There's Nowhere to Go But Up." Eventually it dawns on him that Dutch probably wasn't being sarcastic, but meant the way he made use of the entire keyboard. But why should it have bothered him? In truth, it hadn't. The secret was discipline. Making your own rules, and sticking to them.

Sure, Grubby Eddy's death is a terrible thing, Dutch thinks, seeing Debbie Fensen looking racked with pain, *but they can do their crying on their own time. Oh-oh, that tray looks none too steady on her shoulder. That's twenty dollars worth of crockery. Hope it doesn't go over.* He sees a table crying out for the services of a busboy, gives the appropriate order, and is carried by his own momentum through the swinging doors and into the kitchen.

"Everything okay, Brenda? Kelly? Lee? Hey, there're orders piling up! Let's go, let's go, let's go!" Everyone cringes at the thought that Dutch will find out how bad things really are, but through a communal effort, the camouflage is maintained.

"A guy just told me the coffee tastes like 'hot water with a dark color in it,'" Brenda calls to Kelly.

"Well, give him some from the other pot! Tell him it's twelve years old, and aged in wood!"

In the lounge, Felix is stoically suffering through a joke he has heard many times:

"And that's how they got him for transporting *gulls* across sedate *lions* for immoral *porpoises.*"

"In the mouth, around the gums, watch out belly, here it comes!"

Why does it have to be this way? Felix thinks. *Why is The Public so different from a collection of individuals? If you take a number of people and put them together, you get something more than a group of people. You get The Public. People are fine, I like people. But The Public is awful. Through no fault of its own, in a sense, The Public is awful. Ah, statistics. Mathematical probability.* He makes a martini, a margarita, and a strawberry daiquiri, surveys the boisterous crowd from within his barnyard trough, and thinks: *Stool samples. Generic people, whining and dining.*

"So this bus pulls into town," says a man across from him, "and the last person to get off is a fastidious little Englishman. On his way out, he asks the driver: 'I *say*, old man. Do you know where I can get scrod?' The driver ponders the question for a moment, and says: 'Well, I never heard it referred to in the pluperfect subjunctive before, but I'm sure there's *somebody* in town who'll accommodate you!'"

"Uh, can I have some more ice for my drink?" Doug Brindle asks.

"*Ice suppose,*" Felix replies, wondering how long Doug is going to nurse his glass of seltzer.

It's not going to work. Getting drunk and letting rip is not going to work. Having tried it for the preceding week, Doug has discovered that his writing sounded fine as he was writing it, in fact positively inspired, but when he reread it the next morning it was total drivel. *Maybe if I had gotten drunk while I was rereading it, it would have made sense, but how many people are going to read my novel drunk? What, I'm going to hand out cases of beer with copies of my book? No, it isn't going to work. But life doesn't go on forever, damn it. I have to get started on something.* He looks around anxiously, wondering if Flipper McDougal will come in.

"No, I'm just a hostage—I mean hostess," Kathy Shively replies, as she leads Dr. and Mrs. Landon to their table. (*Where did* that *come from? It's another sign that things are spiraling out of control.*) It is now nine-fifteen, more than an hour since the couple left Herschel's Guest House to dine at the Dockside. Kathy had told them there would be a "twenty-minute wait," and Dr. Landon had suggested that they go elsewhere; Mrs. Landon insisted that they stay. The lounge being a madhouse, they had waited in the foyer while larger parties—six at one point—were seated. Hungry, therefore irritable, they had done their best to help one another through the aggravation, but secretly each had a desire to murder—if not the other—someone. On his part, it was a renewed irritation about the way she bought coffee table books she never read, and insisted on having a cuckoo clock on the mantelpiece, and was far too lenient with their daughter. On her part, it was an irritation over the fact that he was on call at the hospital far too often, and was making such a fuss over a couple of bars of soap, and why he wouldn't be more patient with their daughter's boy friend. Dr. Landon knows full well that the woman leading them to their table is a hostess, not an *owner* of the restaurant, but there was something so authoritative about her manner that the question just popped out of his mouth.

"Uh, don't you have a better table than *this?*" Mrs. Landon asks.

Kathy is attempting to seat them in the old part of the

restaurant, at a table fashioned from a shellacked wire drum, and on the way in Mrs. Landon has spotted the shiny brass and polished teak, the more elegant furnishings, of the Chart Room. "I mean, this is just such a *tiny* little table. And there's hardly room for us to squeeze in between this plant stand and the window."

"I'm sorry," Kathy replies, summoning up her professionalism, "but this is the only table I have, just at the moment. If you'd like to wait a few minutes, maybe something will open up in the Chart Room. But" (and here she appeals to the universal sense of, and willingness to acquiesce to, the inevitable) "this is just our busiest night of the season."

"Oh, I think this will be fine," Dr. Landon breaks in. "We don't want to wait any longer, do we, honey?"

Mrs. Landon looks at Kathy as if to say *heads will roll, there's going to be hell to pay,* but working together, husband and hostess get her seated. Dr. Landon is relieved to think the aggravation is finally over.

Hamdigger. Himbugger. Diddle pickles.

"Good evening," Debbie Fensen says, in a weak, fragile, and cracking voice, "can I get you something from the bar?"

Debbie is as skittish as a doe in deer season. Mrs. Landon squints at her suspiciously, and after a lengthy deliberation she orders a martini, he a Scotch and soda. Then they turn to the consoling task of perusing their menus.

"Oh, look, they have sautéed pork loin diable," she says, her spirits rising.

"And sole Provençal. We'll have to ask her about that."

"And here's something called a 'Captain's Platter.' Do you think you'd enjoy that?"

"Sure sounds good to me."

"Oh, and here're noisettes of lamb wrapped with vegetables and herbs. You *are* hungry, aren't you?"

"I could eat a bull walking."

"Are you in the mood for meat or seafood?"

"Well, I suppose that since we're in Sun Town, we ought to gravitate toward seafood."

"Well, they have bluefish Monterey. And sole almondine."

"Let's remember to ask her to bring a wine list. I'm surprised she didn't leave us one."

When Debbie returns with the couple's drinks, she does not look well. The first thing she does is to tell the Landons what she is out of, and in this, by coincidence, she hits a number of bull's-eyes.

"On page one, I'm out of the lamb dijonaise, in fact all the lamb. On page two"—there is an unceremonious turning of pages—"I don't have the bouillabaisse, or the bluefish Monterey."

"Well, there are plenty of other things to choose from," Dr. Landon avers, watching the waitress skip nervously back into the woods. "Oh, and miss!" he calls. "A wine list, please!" As she recedes, he gazes longingly after her. "Who does she remind you of?" he says, turning back to the table.

"Who does *who* remind me of?"

"The waitress. Doesn't she remind you of someone?"

"No one I can think of. Certainly no one I'd like to know."

"But look at her glasses! And the way she carries herself! Her hair! Doesn't she remind you of Susie?"

"Oh *Byrne*, now I know you're worried, but there's no point in imagining things. Believe me, those two will be all right, they'll work this thing out. And we can call again tomorrow. But tonight we're on vacation. Please. Don't *worry*."

"It's not exactly that I'm *worried*," he answers. "And you're right, they can probably work this thing out by themselves. It's just that"—he turns and looks across a clearing which until moments before might have contained the most beautiful woodland creature—"it's just that she reminds me so much of our Susie."

Happy in the thought, connected to the world again, grateful for the drink in front of him and pleased to be dining out in Sun Town, the husband and father raises his glass.

"To you," he says.

On the other side of the wall, in motions as dark, secret, and furtive as the restaurant is noisy and bright, two men, one carrying a five-gallon can, scuttle toward the trash shed. Although they have done this kind of work for Tony Angelucci before, neither of them takes much pleasure in it; on the other hand, each is settling accounts with the organization that Tony represents. From earlier reconnaissance, they know that the propane tanks that fuel the restaurant's ovens and grills are close to the trash area, and while headlights from the parking lot pose a threat, if they stay behind the low brick wall they will have enough privacy in which to do their work. From inside his jacket, the shorter man pulls out a crescent wrench and applies it to the coupling on one of the tanks.

The last thing Kathy needs, right now, is to have to take another reservation, but she has instinctively picked up the phone and has no choice but to complete the process.

"Good evening, Dockside!" she says, holding the receiver to her neck as she staples a credit-card receipt. "Tomorrow night? Yes, I can do that. How many, please?" A very strange, very unpleasant apparition moves across her line of sight. She cups her hand over the mouthpiece, and leans forward over the desk to look for Karen. But Karen is apparently in the lounge. "Uh, could you hold on a moment?" she says. "I know, I know! But hold *just* one moment!"

The woman in pink hair curlers and immense, bulbous, mirrored sunglasses—pushing a baby stroller and leading a dog on a leash—has already rounded the desk. With grim purposefulness—as though on wheels herself—she walks with steely determination toward the center of the room. Kathy hastens after her, but has to wait while two waitresses and a busboy pass; in ghostlike silence, the woman moves on. Most of the diners are too absorbed in their food and conversation to notice her; those who do subtly recoil. Ed has just finished "Bess, You Is My Woman Now," and is beginning an up-tempo "I Got Rhythm"—Kathy, frozen in her tracks, sees it all—when he looks up from the piano. *He has committed himself to at least one chorus, the first four measures of "I Got Rhythm" are no place he can stop.*

She seems very busy beneath the piano, his wife does, and doesn't even bother to look up at him. *Ed leans to his right in an attempt to see what she's doing, bobbles the melody, and returns his attention to the keyboard.* She isn't even looking at me. *It's as if she's making subtle adjustments to a complicated piece of ma chinery.* People are turning and staring. "I got daisies—In green pastures—I got my man—Who could ask for anything more?" Helen slips the leash off her wrist, and wraps it around the front leg of the piano, and ties it; Ed, straining to see, tries to peer between his legs. "I got starlight—I got sweet dreams—I got my man. . . !" Taking great care as to its placement, Helen wheels the baby stroller to the exact center of the stand, and parks it facing him. Finally satisfied that she has done these things correctly and according to plan, she wheels around and, ramrod stiff, walks off across the room; the song seems never to end. "Old Man Trouble—I don't mind him—You won't find him—Round my door!" Ed's dog, Duke, walks himself to the end of his leash and, jerked suddenly to a halt, sits down and looks up at him in bewilderment. His daughter, orphaned under the bright lights with a crowd of faces behind her and cacophonous noise in front—"Who could ask for anything more?"— fidgets, kicks, looks around inquisitively, then, realizing something is terribly wrong, in a long agonized wail adds her voice to the chorus. "Who could ask for anything more?"

In the foyer, someone is stealing the lobsters. After two hours in which people have been milling around in it, the entryway is now deserted. A man in a light summer suit, carrying a satchel, approaches the display of culinary delights, casually studies the photographs beneath the leaping marlin, snaps open the satchel, and sweeps the dozy lobsters in. Then, with the air of a person ruminating on an enjoyable meal, he ambles back out. It will be Karen who discovers the theft; going to the foyer for a pack of cigarettes, she will spot the loss immediately. She will sweep clams and oysters into the now-denuded patch, rearrange the ice, fish, and parsley, then hurry to the cigarette machine. On the glass—to her horror—in garish pink lipstick, someone will have scrawled, OUT OF ORDURE. With a cloth napkin, she will rub the words out and, returning to the desk for a key to the machine, find Kathy standing with her mouth open. Now Dutch will come up and, sensing that something's out of kilter, demand to know everything.

"So how is it?" asks Dr. Landon inquires, pouring a glass of wine for his wife.

"Needs salt."

In the Lifeboat Lounge, Roy Oberholzer is violating one of Felix's cardinal rules. To save himself time, he has raised the lid of the ice machine and shoved a drink glass into it—in the process shattering the glass. What Felix sees, when he comes over, is *the need to remove every last cube of ice, and clean the entire chamber by hand.*

"I'm sorry," Roy says, staring at the disaster, "really I am. I didn't mean to do it. Look, I can just take out the biggest pieces of glass, and push the bad ice toward the back. I'll go get a flashlight."

I can bring ice from the machine in the kitchen, I still have ice in the well. But the kitchen machine is old, and slow, it'll never be able to keep up with the demand. Long night ahead. Busy night, busiest night of the season.

"Do me a favor, Roy" Felix says, struggling to control both his voice and his curling fists. "Get the hell. Out. Of my. Bar. And don't even. *Think*. Of ever. Doing. That. Again."

For the next hour, Felix will spend time on his hands and knees in front of the ice machine. Sometimes a busboy will help, and when they can, Karen and Kathy will take a turn. But he will never know whether the work will proceed fast enough to keep up with the demand, and besides, it makes him nervous having people underfoot. So he will do most of the work himself. Meanwhile, so as not to seem invisible to those he serves—*rule number one: no one likes a bartender he can't relate to*—he will do it as discreetly as possible.

"So I win this so-called 'Cruise to Nowhere,'" Ellen Kastner is telling him now. "Heck, I've never been anywhere in my life. But I have two kids, a dog, a cat, and a parakeet. So I hire a babysitter. But she isn't too comfortable with the dog, so I put the dog in the kennel. I leave food for the cat, and instructions for dealing with the parakeet. I drive up to the city and put the car on a lot, take a cab to the waterfront, and manage to get to the boat just as it's leaving. The minute the boat pulls away from the dock, all these lonely guys start hitting on me, and the band is terrible, and the food's not great. I decide to go to bed early. But before I drop off to sleep, I peer out a porthole. And you know where we are? We're right out there in the harbor! It's a 'Cruise to Nowhere'—and the damn boat's come down the coast and dropped anchor, and I can actually see my own house! And do you think they'd let me off that thing? Hell no! I could have swum to shore—but no! After a lousy night's sleep, we cruise back. I take a cab to the parking lot, retrieve my car, drive all the way home, bail out the dog, pay the babysitter, and—"

"Don't tell me. Your parakeet died," Felix says, smiling and moving on.

"So how's yours?" Mrs. Landon asks.

In fact, he thinks it's quite good, better than that, delicious. It's the sole almondine, and the almonds are nicely toasted and the butter has picked up their flavor. "It's so good," he says, "that I wish the breeze from this window weren't cooling it off."

"You mean it's not hot?" Mrs. Landon replies, with alarm. "Well, if it's not hot, ask her to take it back! They can stick it under the flame. They do it all the time."

"Well, it came *out* hot enough, it's just that the breeze has cooled it off some."

"But Byrne! No one likes cold fish! Ask the girl to take it back, and have it heated up!"

He demurs. She grows adamant. She argues that there's no reason for their experience at the Dockside to be marred by such a little thing as this.

"All right," she says, finally. "If you won't ask her, *I* will."

At the moment their "girl" is standing with her back against the kitchen door, and being consoled by Brenda, Becky, Sharon, Polly, and Lee. "I'm *okay*. I'm *all right*," she protests. "I can go *back*, I can go back *out* there."

The fact is, however, that she cannot remember what she's supposed to be picking up. She makes her way out of the group and to the steam table; *it must have been vegetables,* she thinks. A line has formed, and while she is trying to decide whether to remain in it or go around to the pickup counter, Roy Oberholzer steps in front of her, as he does so, mashing her toe. She is standing in a hot, steamy kitchen and doesn't know why, she is waiting for something and can't remember what. Now someone she detests has butted in. She stares at Roy's hateful back and shoulders, and suddenly she's *beating* on them, beating on the walls of a cage that's hot and stuffy, beating on doors that are keeping her out—or in—*beating, beating, beating.*

Felix is on his feet again. The towel he has been kneeling on has left damp spots on his knees, and he imagines that everyone can see them. As he clears away some glasses, he discovers two handwritten notes. He dries his hands and reads the first. "Honey, I know you're having a good time, and I want you to stay. But I can't take any more of this. Too many people! I'll be back at the motel. XXOO." Ignoring a call for his services, Felix picks up the second note. "Darling, this whole weekend has been crazy, wild, and wonderful. But I'm not sure how much more of this I can take! Just to show you I'm not possessive, I'm going back to the motel! Come when you're ready! Love." Wondering how the two lovers managed to miss one another—overlapping trips to the restrooms?—Felix returns his attention to the second note. "I don't have any small bills, so please take care of the bartender." He turns the first one over. "P.S. Don't forget to leave a tip."

"Of course you should," says Mrs. Landon.

"But honey, there's hardly enough of it left to worry about!"

"I don't care. It's the principle of the thing."

"But really, honey, I can't see what the point would be, now, in making a fuss over it."

When Debbie finally returns, she looks wounded, traumatized, looks like she wants absolutely nothing to do with these people—or anyone else. But Mrs. Landon will not be denied. She inquires whether it would be possible to have her husband's dinner put under the broiler, and he laughs uneasily and tries to win the waitress' sympathy by saying it really isn't necessary, and Mrs. Landon says of course it is, the girl doesn't mind, and finally it's only the conversation that gets heated, and Dr. Landon thinks how silly it all is, they have had an enjoyable meal and a lovely vacation, what is the point of making a scene now?

The piano player is returning the terrified stares of his daughter and dog, lobsters are disappearing out the front door in someone's briefcase, Felix is on his hands and knees in front of the ice machine, two men in the shadows are fiddling with the propane and sloshing the trash area with gasoline as they get set to torch the place, Dave Lindholm, cranky because his ranges and ovens are acting strangely, has bounded over the steam table to teach Roy Oberholzer a lesson—fists, mops, plates go down, waiters and waitresses are screaming and falling over one another—in the parking lot two Dobermans, sensing something is amiss, are rocking a van nearly off its hinges, tired of listening to their barking Armand Lucette is calling the police. Tim Mullen is sending high-frequency radio energy through the entire scene as he calls for contacts in the farthest reaches of the world, a million energies are radiating, pulsing, through the establishment—radar, radio, television, shortwaves, x-rays, cosmic rays, the light of million-year-

old stars, the entire place is invisibly lit up like a microwave, a time bomb,
a pressure-cooker full of imploding and exploding energies—
And now Dr. Byrne Landon, realizing how distraught
the waitress is, this waitress who looks so much like his daughter, feels his heart going out to her and, misjudging the distance
to the small of her back, reaches up and pats her affectionately
on the behind.

"Oh, sweetheart," he says.

SIXTEEN

People said later it started with hysterical shrieking near the wire-drum table in the back, but others said, no, they saw the flames first, then heard the screams. The exact sequence was something which, despite interviews that went on for weeks, police, fire marshals, and insurance adjusters had difficulty pinning down. It was typical of everything that happened that night: It was clear *what* happened, but the *why* eluded even the officials. The mad exodus from the parking lot, for example, the stampede that led so many people to try to exit the parking lot at once, and thus created the logjam that kept the fire trucks from reaching the scene. Together with the sight of flames shooting up from the rear of the restaurant, it was this scene of panic and confusion that led the announcer at the local radio station to interrupt his programming (Beethoven's *Ninth*), and report the disaster to the entire town. Among his listeners was Tim Mullen who, in keeping with ham radio's time-honored tradition of service to the community, got on 2 Meters and the Town Hall repeater, and spread news of the crisis far and wide.

It was the memory of the Great Fire of the previous winter, that other conflagration that could have leveled the entire waterfront, that galvanized the authorities into quick action, and brought out the fire apparatus of the neighboring communities. For a while, vacationers the length and breadth of Land's End were aware that a major catastrophe was under way, as fire and rescue equipment raced down the highway to Sun Town. It was the collision of one of these trucks with a utility pole (and not the fire itself, as was thought at the time) that led to the many power outages along the peninsula, and temporarily reduced the entire land mass to blackness. With a doomsday scenario taking shape at the tip of the peninsula, and up-to-date news cut off by the power outage, many vacationers decided to return home a day early. It was this evacuation that not only caused the fourteen-mile backup at Scavenger Bridge but propelled the matter into the national news, for among the reports on Labor Day traffic, few images on television were as vivid as the line of headlights coiling away from the bridge like a glistening snake, toward the horizon. It was a scene of congestion so intense as to prompt thoughts of calling out the National Guard.

What transpired inside the restaurant also received a great deal of media coverage. Many patrons complained of being confused, at first, because the Exit sign was not illuminated, but all spoke with admiration about how the Dockside staff took control of the situation and guided them through the darkened door, or maneuvered them through the fallen mops and brooms in the kitchen. It was this composure during a time of crisis that made the event especially newsworthy, and gave it its importance as a revealing glimpse into the "better side" of human nature. There were many cameos to which the news media could refer: for example, how the person playing the piano was able to rescue not only a child, but a dog that was on the scene; how one waiter, his eye already blackened from his efforts to fight the fire, had the presence of mind to confront his customers on the street and present them with their checks; how a vacationing doctor had applied the Heimlich maneuver to a waitress who was so hysterical she was choking to death; how a fire that threatened to destroy one of Sun Town's most famous landmarks had occurred not only on the busiest day of the season, but the night before a review of the establishment was to appear in area newspapers; how, when all was said and done, the only real damage to the interior of the restaurant was a loss of ice. The newspaper review, together with these reports that threw favorable light on the restaurant, catapulted Dutch Dugan into the national limelight, and briefly made him a celebrity.

But the real heroism that night went largely unnoticed. Furious that when the electricity went off, those drinking in the lounge raised a great cheer, lit candles, and went on with their party, Dutch grabbed a fire extinguisher off the wall and hurried out of the restaurant, absentmindedly disconnecting the propane tanks as he went. To his surprise, Karen Willis and Kathy Shively were already on the scene. While Dutch cursed and fumed and complained about "cigarettes" and "the damn kids," Kathy and Karen, using another fire extinguisher, went to work on the trash area. The three got covered with soot and grime, but were much too intent on their work to do anything but treat it as one more problem of the restaurant business; by the time the fire department arrived, there wasn't any fire left to put out. Bill Packard was there with his men, and John Savoy and Pat LeRoche from the Rescue Squad, and a huge contingent of firefighters eventually arrived from up the peninsula. But all they confronted were the *remnants* of a fire, a damp,

smoky mess of trash and garbage. Dutch trudged back into
the restaurant followed by his faithful assistants and, too
tired or cowed or distraught to do anything else, ordered a bottle of champagne and three glasses.

The following winter, he decided to run for selectman.
Although it was at the soda fountain of Claggett's Drug Store
and in the gossip and scuttlebutt of the town that his candidacy
was debated, and a myth of what happened that night created
—insurance took care of the minor damage, and when the re-
modeling was done, Dutch was able to add a service bar and six
new tables—there were many in town who were convinced
he could win. After testing the waters and letting himself be
wooed and courted, however, Dutch at the last minute decided
not to return his nomination papers to the Town Clerk; as he
explained to the Sun Town *Star*, he simply had "too many irons
in the fire." It was obvious to everyone, however, that he was
now a force in town. A brief appearance on the national news,
the following spring, as the town was coming to life again and
the restaurant was preparing to reopen, was only icing on the
cake. When, in a televised interview on tourism and summer
resorts, he was asked whether he didn't get tired of the hectic
pace of the restaurant business, he said no, it was a life he
loved, the only life he knew, that "people" were his life and he
"wouldn't have it any other way." It is estimated that forty million viewers then saw him smile the smile of a man who was at
ease with himself and with his future, and announce that he
was in negotiation with "a newfound friend, and business partner" to open "another Dockside," the "first of several"—"a
pilot, really"—in the city. Although he apparently did not con-

sider himself free to say so at the time, it was clear what he had in mind was a chain.